Thy Brothers'
Reaper

[handwritten signature and inscription]

About this Version

This is a pre-publication copy or preview edition, containing all the errata prior to the final edit. Because it is a preliminary *"First Edition"* version, many consider this edition a collector's item. The final first edition will reflect the corrections and lack of errata.
June 25, 2000

Thy Brothers' Reaper

Devin Centis

Silver Dragon Books
a Division of
RENAISSANCE ALLIANCE PUBLISHING, INC.
Austin, Texas

ISBN 0-9674196-9-7

First Printing 2000

9 8 7 6 5 4 3 2 1

Cover art by B. L. Magill
Cover design by Mary Draganis

Published by:

Renaissance Alliance Publishing, Inc.
PMB 167, 3421 W. William Cannon Dr. # 131
Austin, Texas 78745

Find us on the World Wide Web at
http://www.rapbooks.com

Printed in the United States of America

Dedication

To my family for their patience in the years it took to write this book and to my agent, Ivy, as well as my editors, publisher, and staff at Renaissance Alliance Publishing, Inc. who care enough about me and my art to present only the best.

Chapter
1

November 25, 2010;
Wilmington, Delaware

Gillian Montague caught part of the news on her car radio: ". . . entire family in El Paso, Texas, reportedly have been slain by massive sized humans with glowing red eyes. No confirmation has—"

She clicked off the radio. "Probably some crank report," she said checking her car clock: Nine-thirty p.m.; again she was late leaving the office. With her boss, Cyril, throwing the Grand Opening into her lap, she never seemed to get back home at a decent hour. She hated returning to an empty apartment late at night, in the cold of winter in downtown Wilmington, Delaware, with no one to cuddle up to. More and more she regretted having divorced Mitch, the only person she ever truly loved. Maybe she should invite him over for Thanksgiving.

"Darn," she cursed when no hot air came out of her car heater. She needed to change careers; this working as a private investigator was earning little money.

She'd have to talk to Cy about a raise but she knew he'd say, "Look, I just opened my shop at this new location; give me time."

What was that ahead? Rotating lights on a police cruiser? She slowed as she neared the scene on the dark back road where a police car had pulled over a black Lincoln with a gray-haired woman sitting inside, looking surprised.

"Must have been speeding," Gilly said aloud as she passed the car. Her eyes watched a tall, bulky police officer get out of his car, wearing a black helmet, high-top black boots, and the usual matching uniform. Just as she passed him, she saw his head turn in her direction, and his eyes connect with hers.

Her foot slammed the brake. His eyes! They flashed red . . . or did they? No, no, can't be. *Must have just imagined it after hearing that radio report.*

She looked back over her shoulder, checked her rearview mirror, saw the officer approach the old woman's car.

She drove off, perplexed.

Washington, D.C

Harry Gamblin watched the broad-shouldered, three-piece-suited man lean back in his chair and clasped his hands behind his head full of silver-graying hair. He seemed to work at listening to the ongoing briefing, but Harry knew he was more interested in the activity outside the huge Oval Office window where barricades blocked Pennsylvania Avenue. Beams of sun burst through white, puffy clouds, and yellow mums popped out of sleepy-eyed leaves. Harry saw the man's glance fall on his date book, and quickly pull himself to attention and sit erect at his desk. He interrupted: "So what you're telling me is that the experiment is out of control?" President Jackson Williams punctuated the last three words by tapping his index finger against the desk.

The dark-haired Secretary-of-Defense shifted his stance, grimacing while trying to appear collected. "Well, it's not quite 'out of control' but—"

"Either it is or it isn't, Harry. Don't play word games."

"Yessir." The chief cleared his throat, stared at the floor as if searching for the right words. "It's more like 'they' have minds of their own. They're dangerous." The chief rubbed his chin as if in thought. "Some of our people have suggested that we abort the entire operation, though how we could be sure that we got them 'all,' I don't know."

The president jumped to his feet. "Abort! After all that we've done to train them to be mammoth, dauntless, fighting soldiers who we can rely on for the upcoming battle? Think of all that money we've invested in them. We are not going to abort the operation."

"But, Mr. President, they are menacing—"

"Which is exactly what we want." Williams looked out the window, his hands crossed behind his back. "The rest of the labs, and the clinics, too . . . are they experiencing the same thing as Enolc 1?"

"Not yet, since Enolc 1 was our first project, but I imagine that as time passes and the products become more sophisticated, as they have at 1, then these other labs will experience the same problems. Innocent citizens are being threatened, maimed, even murdered."

The president looked at the chief over his shoulder. "No experiment is guaranteed, Mr. Secretary. I'm very pleased they're aggressive. We'll win that battle."

Harry sighed; there was no sense arguing with the man because when he had his mind made up, that was it. What did Williams care if there were trained, murderous, mad soldiers willing to die just to kill? It was a government's dream. Next year, the president would be on his way out of office before the battle erupted, free of accusing, pointing fingers . . . and protected—he and his family—for the rest of their lives.

Walking across the office to the cart with tea and coffee, the Secretary of Defense said, "The battle, sir, when is it scheduled to begin?" He poured freshly brewed decaf from the silver pitcher into the cup made of fine bone china.

The president turned around, reached for the cup. "It's uncertain when Russia will invade Israel—setting it all off—but we suspect it'll be within the year. Then Egypt and the Middle East will become involved, as well as China, and us, but with our specially trained military, we'll beat all of them and emerge as **the** leaders."

"Which will set up the global government, the one-world economy, and the universal religion."

"The plan's been in place for decades. Our country will take its rightful, front and center, position in this new government."

Secretary Gamblin sipped his coffee, patted his lips with a linen napkin. "I've never felt comfortable with the Enolc project."

"You don't get paid megabucks to feel 'comfortable.'" An old familiar look of exasperation came over the president's face, as if threatened by the questions. "Just do what you're supposed to, Mr. Secretary."

"Yessir." Harry Gamblin set the cup down on the cart. "Under your directive, then, I will commission the Enolc Project at Lab 1 ES Easton to proceed."

"That's all I wanted to hear from the moment you stepped into my office." Williams turned his back on his colleague and went for his desk chair, waving the secretary off.

Easton, Maryland

Dr. Leonard Hammond drove his car across the Chesapeake Bay Bridge, down Route 50, and onto Gwen Road, past the location of the once oldest oak tree in Gwen Estates. At the edge of the thicket, he hid his car, got out, and started walking. He hated checking secret emergency entrances and exits, but as director, it was one of his many tasks.

The silence of the dark night magnified Hammond's footfall as he picked his way through the leaf-ridden dirt path in the shadowy woods of Easton, Maryland, on the Eastern Shore of the Delmarva (**Del**aware, **Mary**land, **Virginia**) Peninsula. He entered the small, domed passage hidden among towering oaks, firs, and maples. Recently built, the emergency structure's dome was camouflaged by dirt, leaves, and twigs. The dome itself was no wider, higher, or deeper than seven feet, covering a sewer-like lid five-feet in diameter.

Dr. Hammond stole a quick look around him, and then furtively pulled out a specialized pick and jabbed it into the lid while using a wrench as a lever to help lift it, although not more than a few feet away rested an electric device that hydraulically elevated the trap door. But Hammond's job was to check not only the automation but also the emergency measures. Besides, he distrusted mechanized gadgets anyway, fearful that, in this case, the lid might close on him when he was only halfway in. The thing weighed a couple-hundred pounds and could easily crush a human.

Grunting, he managed to get into the hole, close the lid, and secure himself on the vertical ladder leading down to an earthen floor passageway to a back elevator in one direction, and the underground parking garage, in the opposite direction. He disliked using the elevator more than he hated opening the lid. In fact, he abhorred the whole blasted set up . . . a lab ten feet underground and ten stories deep. *Leave it up to the United States*

Government. Why couldn't they just have built the dang thing on street level the way they did the camouflaged main entrance of the lab? The newer labs didn't even have the emergency manhole exits. He heard yesterday that one of the new Enolcs—number eleven, wasn't it?—collapsed, with falling dirt having started out as a spray of dust, then picking up speed and quantity, and finally crumbling, tumbling, cascading like Niagara Falls, earth rushing out from every crevice, killing everyone inside, and ruining the entire project. Well, that was fine by him; there were now too many Enolc labs to begin with—maybe a dozen or so, when he had been initially told that there would be no more than two or three. This was how projects went astray.

At the bottom of the vertical stairs, he saw the lighted elevator button glow in the dim, small, squared off area. Waiting for the doors to open, he decided to confront the Secretary of Defense about the need for another emergency exit to the lab. Having just the main gate underground, and only this outside exit, gave Hammond the creeps, no matter how well constructed the facility was, or how many generators it had, or how well rigged it was for communication. He wanted a third way out . . . just in case.

As always, the elevator met him, opened with a WSSSSH, and dropped him three stories. When the doors reopened, his eyes were greeted by banks of bright lights leading to a set of steel double doors. He passed his palm over a monitor that read its line patterns, and the doors automatically parted to reveal a spacious chamber with other glassed-in rooms filled with lab tables and medical and scientific paraphernalia. At the far end of the huge room were doors that led to yet another large room. Hammond walked towards it.

"G'morning, Doctor," called out a technician near a scintillation counter.

Hammond noticed the two doors at the end of the

spacious room opening into the specimen room. He nodded to a colleague as he entered his 18 X 15 office and removed his suit jacket and replaced it with a white lab coat.

His secretary, widowed Althea Azar, entered, pausing at the threshold. "Here's the report. It won't please you. Then again, maybe it will."

"It's out of control, isn't it?" he said rhetorically.

"Makes you happy, doesn't it." She handed him the report. "Even I get scared and I know what they are. When is it going to stop?"

"It's just begun. Lock your doors . . . always." He stepped out of the lab and into the specimen room. "It's out of my hands now."

His secretary followed. "But you're the creator—"

"I do what I'm told, Miz Azar, and you would be wise to do the same."

"Always passing the buck."

He saw her sneer and reverse her footsteps back to her desk.

Suddenly she stomped back to him, pointed a short, chunky finger. "Don't you have any morals?"

"If what we do here bothers you so much, quit. Or don't you want to give up your sixty-grand a year job? That's the problem with our government: Overpays the unskilled."

"I put thirty-five years in, Dr. Hammond. I paid my dues. Where I was at the Library of Congress before coming here gave me a lot of responsibility. I went through endless training and—contrary to what you think—I acquired a lot of skills."

"And your being my executive secretary is worthy of your salary?" He jammed his hands into his suit pants pockets.

"You're no cream puff, sir."

"If I'm difficult it's only because I have an even more difficult boss: Secretary of Defense Gamblin. You know that." He strode away from her, yelling over his shoulder, "Go back to work, Miz Azar." He recalled how she had come to work for him three years ago after losing her cushy job in D.C. She had cried age discrimination, having been sixty then, and the government shipped her over to Hammond's operation—one that she bitterly hated because she disliked being underground and disliked Hammond as much, as well as what he was doing. "Too bad," he muttered to the air.

Chapter 2

Wilmington, Delaware

She was late getting out of the store. It was only weeks before Christmas and everyone was shopping, especially in gift boutiques like hers. She went to the wide doorway, looked up and down the mall corridor but didn't see any merchants, customers, or guards. She shrugged, turned the key in the wall lock, and watched as the steel bars rolled down, clanking as they slowly lowered. The noise echoed in the mall's hollowed halls, sending a shiver through her. How could she be running so late?

She peeked at her watch. Nine-thirty. Where had all the time gone? If it hadn't been for that last customer—the football-sized guy wearing an ear-flap hat, round framed glasses, and a p-coat—she would have been out and home forty-five minutes ago. He had acted strangely; said nothing; just walked around the store fondling jewelry, posters, art work, wicker baskets, novelty items. And that smell about him!

"It's nine-o'clock," she had reminded him. He had

nodded but kept on browsing. Now, fifteen minutes later, having closed the cash register and locked the entrance gate, she worked her way to the back door, flipped off the last light switch, her eyes adjusting to the dimness from the lighted "exit" signs and the few low-watt lamps she left on. Then she punched in the numbers of the store's alarm system at the keypad, and stepped outside into the darkness from the rear door. Her car was only forty-feet away, the sole vehicle in the small employee parking lot. She breathed in, tightened the collar around her neck to ward off the icy wind, and hustled to her 1995 Sprint.

Suddenly, the hairs at her neck rose and her fingers quivered. Hastily she looked around. 'Calm down, Sarah; you've done this hundreds of times.' She let a nervous giggle escape between her lips.

At last she was in the driver's seat. A sigh of relief gushed from her lips, and she turned the key in the engine and locked her door. *Ohmigod! My car door was unlocked!* Uneasily, she studied the back seat through the rearview mirror to make sure no one was crouched behind her.

Nothing.

Through the mirror, she could see the plastic flower arrangement her goofy sister-in-law, Dixie, had given her for the store's grand opening that she never took into the house afterward, as well as the jumper cables setting on the rear window shelf, but other than that, nothing looked amiss. She steered down the road.

"Aruba, Jamaica, oooh I wanna take ya," blared from the radio, and she turned up the volume, singing along, loving the oldies. As cold as it was, she cracked her window a little as she entered 95 West to Wilmington. She liked the feel of the breeze hitting her face, keeping her alert. Grabbing her cell phone, she hit the automatic button and her husband came on the line. "I'm running late, hon. Just got on the ramp and whizzing your way."

His voice sounded broken up: "Hey, babe."
(Crackle) ". . . won't you driv . . ." (crackle) . . . "late.
Be careful. Lock yo . . . " (crackle) ". . .iss you."

She blew him a kiss, knowing he was unaware of it,
and shut off the phone. Hearing "The Rose" playing
over the radio, she turned the volume back up, and
began belting out the words. She tried remembering the
song verse by verse, her mind periodically wandering
to the shop's inventory, what to get the kids for Christmas, if they should put up a real tree, and —

She jumped. What was that she saw in her rearview
mirror? She tried studying it while yet not wanting to.
Quickly she took her eyes off the road and looked again
in the mirror.

Nothing there.

Maybe it had just been car lights reflecting off
something.

But fire orange lights?

Calm down. She reached for her cell phone to call
the police; then she'd zip off the nearest ramp and into a
populated place. Just hold on, she told herself.

Fleetingly she peeped into the rearview mirror as
she drove down a ramp. *Nothing there. Stop! this!* At
the end of the ramp, blackness loomed.

Her shoulders shuddered. Was that air on her neck?
Was someone behind her? My God! They could have
been lying on the floor and she would have never
known!

Slowly she lifted herself in the driver's seat and
shifted her vision to the mirror.

Her gasp rang out so loud that it made her jerk.
There they were again—the glowing lights . . . no eyes!
My God, they're blazing red eyes!

She screamed.

Arms jerked the steering wheel, maneuvering the
car to the side of the road. A huge dark form with the

glowing eyes draped over her. Before complete blackness engulfed her, she saw deep into its eyes, and realized nothing was behind them. Then she felt a puncture
at the base of her neck, something sucked out in a gurgling sound, and excruciating pain that exploded within
her brain.

****

The line to the funeral home wound through the hall
and out the home's entrance. Gillian pulled her 1998
yellow Volkswagen Beetle into the parking lot, locked
all the doors, and straightened her skirt. She disliked
funeral homes and all the services attached to them,
like this one, which tonight was some long Catholic
rite.

When she got into the front door of the funeral
home, her vision took in the dozens of people standing
in line, others in pairs and groups whispering, and still
others at the closed coffin or hugging the deceased's
husband who looked so distraught that Gillian thought
he was going to collapse. Then she spotted him, slipped
out of the line, and walked past ten, twelve people
ahead of her, and over to him.

"Excuse me. I know you don't mind," and she
stepped in front of him.

"Honestly, Gilly," he muttered. "Wait in line like
the rest of us."

She turned and flashed him a smile. "I love you,
too." She watched him roll his eyes. "How ya doing,
Mitch? Miss me?"

He shrugged as if to toss her off. "How can anyone
miss a wasp in their hat?"

She chuckled. "Mixed metaphor."

"How would you know, Miss Detective-Secretary-
and-not an-English-teacher. This is the very reason why
we got divorced."

"We got divorced because you never had direction

in your—our—lives."

"I can smell the lemon scent in your freshly washed hair. I like how your auburn highlights reflect the room's glow." Seductively, he whispered, "Let me wrap my fingers in your tresses like I did those seven years we were married."

"You're full of crap," Gillian laughed . . . those seven years, she thought, before we tired of each other, before the "itch" came, before he learned he was incapable of having kids. She turned and looked at him behind her. "Really, Mitch, how are you?"

He hunched his shoulders. "I miss you, Gill." She saw his hazel eyes plead with her. "I keep telling you this."

"We've been divorced for over a year and still you persist with this . . . this reunion. It's not going to happen, Mitchell Bentley Frey. How can you worry about our remarrying when my dearest friend has just lost her sister-in-law?"

"Dixie's sister-in-law isn't lost; spell the word: m-u-r-d-e-r-e-d."

"Humph!" She spun back around, taking a few paces forward until she reached the large viewing room where she held the hands of the children and hugged the deceased's husband, muttering, "I'm so sorry, Rick." She shuffled over to a woman in her early forties. "Oh, Dix, I'm so so sorry. I know you were close to Sarah."

Dixie burst into tears; they embraced, swiped at eyes with white hankies.

"He mauled her," Dixie bawled. "Waited for her in the back of her car after she left the mall. What did she ever do to deserve this? She was a good woman, sweet. Now my brother's a widower." She sobbed louder. "That monster brutalized her . . ." here she lowered her voice, "punctured her skull. . . . They haven't caught him. What a Christmas this will be." Dixie wept into Gilly's arms.

Minutes later, Gillian headed outside with Mitch at her side. She stood in the vigorous crisp air, letting it jolt her. With him standing next to her, she sniffled, "How could there be such vicious people out there?"

She felt his hand rub the back of her neck. "I'm here for you."

Chapter
3

In the small, downtown Wilmington office of the recently relocated Collier Investigative Agency, Gillian sat at the decrepit, splintered wooden desk, making phone calls. The puffy black sky did little to illuminate the dark office with its stained ginger-colored hardwood that buckled in some spots and sank in others. For as cold as it was outside, it was just as torrid inside, with the old, clanking radiator hissing and blowing steam.

"Gosh, Annie, it's hot in here," moaned Gillian, mopping her head with a tissue. "How can you sit there in this heat and not sweat?" She got up from her desk and leaned over the window's latch, hoping that on this second try the window would budge. "Darnit! Nothing in this place works. We operate in a dump," she whined to the secretary sitting across from her at a desk as equally rickety as hers. "There you sit with a skirt up to your rear, a top down to your navel, and it's no wonder you're not over-heated." Gilly sat back down, her chair squeaking loudly, the cushion replying with a "whoosh."

Annie snapped her gum, dabbed more red lipstick on her full lips in reflection of the blank computer monitor screen, and with a ring in her voice, said, "Maybe you're like suffern' from them hot flashes . . . I mean, at your age and all."

Gillian glared. "My age is mid-thirties."

"**Late** thirties. I do the paychecks . . . as small as they are." She smacked her lips to even out her lipstick. "When ya gonna decide what you wanna be when you grow up?"

Gillian stood again, paced the twelve-by-twelve room, continually trying to open the window, only to return to her desk, then walk back to the window.

"What is your problem?" the secretary asked, enunciating each word.

Throwing her hands up in the air, Gilly said, "Great. Cy goes out on an investigation and leaves me here to organize the opening reception. I should be the one to go with him. I'm the junior detective, not that goofy Wally!"

"Goofy Wally is Cy's nephew." Annie took out her nail file.

Back at the window, Gilly gripped the frame tightly and, with an "ugh," tried again to open it. Not succeeding, she stood looking out, exhaling loudly for effect, and blowing the hair at her forehead. She watched through the glass the activity below, seeing a man, without a coat, standing on the corner selling newspapers; women walking in pairs across streets, carrying shopping bags; bikers pedaling in traffic carrying envelopes; people leaning into streets flagging taxis; customers entering and exiting revolving doors carrying gaily wrapped holiday packages. "What a life."

"What?"

"I never wanted to be a detective."

"Umph." Annie slammed shut a desk drawer. "I know what you mean." She cracked her gum. "I had applied to cosmetology school to be a hair dresser but my grades weren't good enough to get in."

Gilly turned and looked at her, rolling her eyes, then glanced back out the window. "I had wanted to be a doctor but then my parents died in that plane crash when I was a pre-schooler, and down the drain went all my plans. I was sent to live in an orphanage because neither of my parents had living relatives. That was the end of my college dreams. I was lucky enough to get out of that institution by the time I was eighteen and work my way through a community college. And all for what? To hook up with Cy who's training me to be a detective? Then what will I do with that? Become President of the United States?"

"Lock up, will ya, Gilly? And don't forget to finish getting a count on who's coming to our re-opening reception on Saturday." Annie yawned, set the nail file down and yanked her coat off the wooden tree.

"Sure." 'Get a count,' she repeated in her head. Now there was a tough assignment . . . probably required at least a fifth grade education. She heard the secretary walk towards the door and click it open. "Annie, wait! Your guest list didn't include Mitch, did it?"

The secretary looked quizzically at her. "As in Mitch, your ex? Now what'a you think, Gilly? He's the real estate agent who rented this building to us, and Cy said to include everyone who helped us get up and running. Besides, I think he's handsome. What a fool you are to give him up." Annie closed the door behind her.

Gillian went back to studying the downtown area through the window. With elbows propped on the windowsill ledge, Gilly scanned the outside, watching a Vette run a light, the sky gild over with puffy golden-gray clouds, promising snow, and holiday carolers form on a corner to belt their lungs out in the freezing weather.

Through her window, her eyes suddenly caught sight of a figure moving stealthily in a shadowed alley. She turned her head to focus on it, gawking at the size of the man who took two steps forward and, with brute strength, tore open a driver's door, yanked him out with one hand, and flung him against the concrete street.

Her hands fumbled as she tried throwing up the stuck window. She shouted through the glass, "Hey! Hey! Stop stop!"

In horror, she watched the huge figure kick the man between his eyes as he lay in the streets. The victim thumped backwards, his head hitting the sidewalk. Gilly could see blood squirt from his face, nose, mouth, and she could almost hear his skull squash like a melon flung against cement. Quickly, the attacker leaned over the man, did something to him, snapped out bills from his wallet, and pulled keys from the man's suit jacket. Striding over to the car, he turned once to survey the area, making sure no one saw him. Immediately, his eyes met Gillian's.

She stared back. Hadn't she seen those eyes before? *Yes, of course! The police officer who pulled over the little ol' lady!* She didn't know whether she should leave the window and run out of the building, or hot-foot it down to where the colossus stood, eyeing her. A chill coursed through her, raising the hairs on her arms when she saw an eerie incandescence seemingly emanating from his eyes. The figure jumped into the car and started it, running over the victim he had thrown into the street, and peeling out of the alley.

Easton

From outside a large glassed-in partition at Enolc 1, Dr. Hammond watched the two monkeys nuzzle each other, pick at one another's coat, grunt and coo. He sighed. This was how he had wanted the experiment to turn out but the government had insisted on the implants. He looked around the spacious lab with two identical sheep in one, two dogs in another, and raccoons in a third corner. Walking over to the other end of the room where the apes huddled against the wall, he lightly tapped the windowed cage just to assure himself the outer protective pane was secure.

He watched them, wondering why they had withdrawn. He should go in and check but the thought of walking back to his office, unlocking the special key box to get the key card to open the cage, and returning to this very spot to unlock the enclosure and enter it, seemed all too tiring.

Squinting, he almost pressed his nose against the twenty-by-twenty-foot pane to get a better look at the simians. The one ape—Abigail—was drooling—or was she foaming at the mouth? Its orangish pellet-like eyes seemed to be slanting—almost sagging—to one side. For some reason, her stump of an arm looked raw, festering.

His vision lowered to the cement floor. What was that red stuff by Simon? Vomit? Hammond cupped his hands around his eyes to block out reflections from the glass and tried making out what was going on. It was blood! He ran over to the wall near him and hit the emergency button. Instantly other technicians and lab experts appeared. His eyes sought out one of the caretakers authorized to have key cards to the locked cages. He pointed to the gate. "Open it. Now!"

When it electronically unlocked—with the automated voice announcing, "Security to entrance is breached"—Hammond glanced around, hoping maybe one of the techs would willingly enter. No one budged, so he stepped inside, not realizing he was holding his breath. Abigail took a step forward, whimpering in pain, as if trying to rush into his arms for comfort. But the second she moved her body, Simon yanked her back, chomping into the stump.

"My God! He's eating her alive!" Hammond screamed. "Get Security! Get the vets!" He instinctively took a step backwards. "I need a gun!"

Abigail sank to her feet. In seconds, Simon was on top of her, gnawing away. The gate clanked open and a tech dressed in the standard white lab coat appeared with a powerful dart gun.

Hammond watched him sneak up behind Simon to the pathetic, ear-piercing screams of the gnawed Abigail. "Be careful," Hammond warned the technician. "Aim for Simon's chest." He could hear the quick, shallow breathing of the tech, and knew the man was as nervous as himself. "Don't kill him; he's vital to our existence here."

The tech tip-toed toward the mad primate, his hand outstretched with the loaded gun. He moved in, five feet away from the ape.

"Careful," Hammond whispered.

The tech took a few more steps. He stood only three feet away.

"Easy now." Hammond backed up toward the gate. Behind him, the couple dozen of personnel remained stark silent.

A few more paces and the tech was a foot away from Simon. He aimed, cocked the trigger.

The hush in the large cage grew as thick as gravy.

"Shoot, shoot, now!" Hammond tried yelling under his breath.

Abruptly Simon turned, faced the tech, his mouth slavering with blood, meat hanging from its teeth.

"Get out, run!" screamed Hammond, shaking the iron gates. "Let me out!"

Personnel glanced from one face to the next, with no one moving. Their grim expressions turned twisted, and their eyes lowered to the floor.

"Get me out of here!" Hammond squealed.

Behind him, Simon charged the tech who barely got off a dart. Down he went with the big ape on top of him. The tech squealed, pummeled his fists against the furry monster but still Simon wouldn't budge. When the ape bit into the tech's ribs, everyone heard the bones crunch followed by more screams, then a gurgling sound.

Hammond banged harder on the iron door, his shrieks sounding much like a banshee on the loose. Just as the ape looked up from his prey and started quickly undulating his feet and arms toward Hammond, a technician stepped up and opened the gate, and then just as quickly jumped back away from it.

The ape—only feet away from Hammond—rushed forward, its mouth open, its reddish-orange eyes flickering. Hammond raced out the gate, chastising himself for having gained weight. His lab coat snagged on the gate latch as his foot smacked the wrought iron staves.

Simon swiped at Hammond's back, its unnaturally long nails ripping the white cotton lab coat to shreds, but no matter how hard Hammond tried unsnagging his jacket and slamming the gate shut—even with the help of several large male techs—the ape pushed from the other direction.

"It's getting out!" screeched one worker, as the others instantly stepped backward.

Sweating, Hammond, his shirt and lab jacket ripped, stood fumbling with the door, trying to get out, and just when he sensed Simon gaining power and about ready to burst through the opening, the ape collapsed to the cement floor, moaning. Hammond shot out of the cage. Simon writhed until the drug slowed his movements to a complete halt. Its eyes fluttered, then closed.

Workers flew into the cage, several placing Simon

on a wheeled gurney; others doing the same with the mauled Abigail. With his heel bloodied and sore, Hammond limped to his office, his tie undone and barely hanging from his shoulder, his lab coat a mangled mess of threads, and his Christian Dior starched white shirt, shredded.

Ms. Azar and one of Hammond's assistants met him in his office.

"Are you all right, Professor?" asked the assistant who still called him that from her days at the university where he had worked before joining President Williams' administration. Hammond knew, to his assistant, he was the best geneticist, not only at the University of Arkansas, but also throughout the midwest.

"The situation could be worse," began Azar, "Simon could be dead."

"That will be enough, Ms. Azar. Call the supervisors together for a meeting within the hour."

Chapter
4

December 14, 2010;
3:00 p.m.; Washington, D.C

Harry Gamblin looked over at President Williams sitting next to him, and then glanced around the room at all the faces waiting in anticipation. Williams had called this meeting to make an announcement, and Harry wondered how many of those present anticipated what he was going to say. The president cleared his throat, waiting for the shuffling of papers to stop and the servants to quit serving. Gamblin couldn't help wonder how at fifty-seven, a two-term president could have made such a mess of the presidency and the country, and soon the world. His vice president—Bert Greenman—the likely incumbent—promised to be even worse. At least with Williams, one knew he was crooked, but Greenman, younger and more handsome, was a true deceiver.

The meeting started.

Harry Gamblin eyed Greenman sitting across from him—the man who claimed nature as *prima facie*, and yet littered from his car window; the man who had a bill passed that fifty-percent of all national reserves would be off limits to the public. And just who did he think owned those reserves, anyway? It seemed to Gamblin that the veep and Williams were doing what they could to limit the rights of citizens in order to make government Big Brother.

Harry worried how he was going to get out of his position. The president had chosen him for defense secretary because years ago, during their college days, he and Williams had roomed together their last two semesters, and Gamblin had helped him get answers to exams. Then, a few years later, Harry also aided him in getting elected to West Virginia's governorship where he gained fame, power, and money. Even during Williams' tenure as Lieutenant Governor, Gamblin never saw the incredibly sinister acts Williams did, or perhaps if he had seen them, he had attempted to rationalize them. But in the last seven years of Williams' presidency, Harry had seen so much that he attempted to resign twice. On both occasions, Harry's attempts had been thwarted by the president via threats, blackmail. Now with Greenman coming up for election, Harry wanted even less to do with the White House.

"Would you not agree, Mr. Secretary?" The president glared at Gamblin.

"I'm sorry, sir. I guess I didn't hear what you said." The pencil in his hand twittered with nervousness.

"I said," and here Williams leaned toward Harry for emphasis, "our troops are ready to be deployed at a minute's notice . . . aren't they?"

Harry swallowed hard, trying to wash down the dryness filling his mouth. "Er, yes, we'll, uh, be ready . . . if it ever comes to—"

"Not if, Mr. Secretary . . . 'when,'" clarified Greenman. "You do have our fighting 'machines' prepared?"

Machines was the right word, thought Harry. But

should he go into the problems Enolc 1 was having? He
glanced at Williams who seemed to transmit the answer
"no" to his private thoughts. *The creep even acts like he
knows what I'm thinking.* "Per your request, Mr. President, our, uh, 'machines'—our augmented military—are
already stationed in our ally territories. Several have
been integrated into American units." He corrected
himself, "I mean, our United Nation units . . . to assimilate with those troops."

"Any report on how well this augmented military is
doing?"

"No sir; it's too early to tell. Only a week has
passed since we started the assimilation project. We've
only deployed about five-thousand into the ranks, so we
may have too small a sample to make a determination."

The president looked uneasy. "How many more can
safely combine with U.N. Forces without our country
running short of manpower for foreign combat?"

The Secretary of Defense shrugged. "It depends on
how soon the female models will be ready. Enolc 1 con-
tends that will be within the next five months."

"Make it two months," ordered the president. "We
need those recruits pronto."

"But, sir, they have to be tested and trained."

"Make it one month, Mr. Secretary." Williams then
centered discussion around the United Nation's military
prowess, battle strategies, the state of the economy during the anticipated war time, and how the citizenry
would fare if the ground war turned into a nuclear hell.
Gamblin gave all the necessary and much expected
reports.

Then, not more than a half-hour later, President
Williams, who began slipping his papers and reports
into a briefcase, casually mentioned, "By the way, since
my 'Open Trading' bill has passed, we are going to commence commerce with China, as well as open trade with
Cuba, Iraq, Iran, and soon, other Third World countries,

including those considered to be enemies."

Murmuring reverberated among them.

"Perhaps you can enlighten this group on these plans, Madam Secretary." The president nodded to Julianne LaHabla, the Secretary of Commerce, who went into her spiel about the great accomplishments this policy would promote for the world via a one-world economy. "A common currency for a common economic market is the goal—"

"Surely, Mr. President," interrupted one of the officers, "you know our corporate partners will resent and resist this new plan, as this kind of policy puts American businesses and corporations at a great disadvantage; furthermore, America as a whole will not like this since China has committed unfair commerce with the United States, especially after it has squashed, over the last ten, twelve, years, any attempt at a push for a democratic government. I know you must remember Tinnamen Square. And—"

"That was over twenty-five years ago," Greenman snapped. "This will be good for the world, not just America. Start thinking 'globally.'"

'The world government,' thought Harry who knew what was coming by allowing trade to open up with enemy countries. The can of worms just had its lid unscrewed.

Wilmington

Shook up by what she had seen from her office window, Gilly quickly locked up shop and hurriedly but cautiously jumped into her car and stormed off. On the highway, she turned off a ramp and headed for her best friend's place in a towering apartment complex.

Gillian saw Dixie peak between the blinds, then heard the door unlock.

"You look white as a ghost, Gil. What's wrong?"

"I saw something that absolutely scared me." From beginning to end, sitting in Dixie's small living room near the roaring fireplace, Gillian disclosed what she had seen from her office window. "The eyes. I'll never forget what they looked like . . . demonic, possessed." She shook her head. "You know I saw those same kind of eyes on a policeman just a few weeks ago."

"Eyes like a druggie's?"

"More like flashing reddish pin-point pupils. I can't explain it! It was weird. Gives me the heebee-jeebees just thinking about it." Gilly stared into the fire. "Red hot eyes like this fire."

"Sounds like something out of 'Puppet Master.'"

"This isn't funny, Dix."

"How about some wine to calm you?" Dixie was on her way into the kitchen before Gillian could answer. "Maybe your mind tricked you into thinking you saw flashing red eyes."

Over and over, Gillian ran the scene through her head, as if her brain stalled on 'replay.' She could see the innocent driver being yanked out of the car and flung across the street, how he tried to raise his head for help, only to flop back down like an injured deer; how the huge brute had taken a step forward and kicked him, then ran over him with a car.

Dixie returned to the living room and handed Gillian a short glass of claret.

"It was monstrous." Gillian took a sip, rose, and leaned against the fireplace mantle, her free hand tasseling her shoulder-length reddish-brown hair. "I saw it all from my office window."

"How tall?"

"I don't know; maybe seven feet."

"Yeah sure. I think you've already had too much to drink, kiddo." Dixie walked over to her best friend, saying, "But if it's any reassurance, the pathologist who did the autopsy on my sister-in-law said that whoever

had killed her had to have been pretty big, too. Just stay
away from them, Gil."

Gilly looked at her. "Stay away from whom?"

"Whatever they are."

Gillian ran her hand through her hair. "I have to go;
I work tonight. Detectives don't work nine-to-five jobs.
Cy wants to go over cases, and since Wally can't be
there until six-thirty, we couldn't meet any earlier."

"Just be careful, Gil."

4:00 p.m.; Easton

His foot and other minor injuries having been
attended to by a staff physician, and his torn clothes
replaced by spare ones in his office closet, Dr. Hammond seemed more presentable, although his stomach
still jiggled from nerves. He took the chair at the head
of the conference table. "I have a lot of material to
cover but under the circumstances, for now we'll just
concentrate on what happened today. Catastrophe, that's
what it was. We need to reexamine our policies and perhaps reinstate new ones. Things never should have gotten as far as they did." He paused. "I'm disappointed
that none of you came forward to help Johnson and me
in the cage. You let us fend for ourselves. Johnson
died and I was nearly trounced and eaten to death
myself! The least you could have done was gotten
another dart gun and entered the cage to help us."

Hammond saw his chiefs of staff look at each other
but say nothing.

"First off, have any of you observed prior to today
the aberrant behavior by Simon?" Hammond wrote
something on a paper.

"Speaking of which," piped up Dr. Glazier, "Just
how are Simon and Abigail?"

"Abigail's still in surgery. Simon remains drugged
and under examination." He rubbed his stubbled chin.

"What happened out there?

One by one, he had his key staffers relate their observation of the primates over the last several days. Nothing turned up to help pin-point the problem. One staffer said he had seen Simon turn aggressive in the past but it had been so infrequently and so fleetingly that he never thought anything of it.

Dr. Glazier offered, "Could it be that Simon suddenly realized that Abbie had an abnormality that—"

"Of course not!" Hammond glowered at her, patted down his few remaining strands of hair. "That fat Simon has known Abbie and her limb defect since her birth, so it suddenly wouldn't have bothered him. That mammoth ape just went berserk."

The room remained quiet.

Finally Glazier said, "It's what we've been afraid of all along—the chip went bad."

"I don't believe it, and hopefully none of you in this room does either." Hammond looked around the elongated conference table at each of their faces. "There must have been signs of something being wrong with Simon." His tone sounded almost pleading. "Simon will have to be destroyed."

Dr. Glazier pressed, "Does that mean the other . . . specimens in the public will also begin to display signs of insanity?"

Hammond stared at her. "How would we know? You—my own people—here won't admit to seeing anything abnormal in our specimens, so how would we know about a field specimen out there?" He rose. "Maybe Simon's violence today is just a single isolated case."

Glazier chirped in, "If not, we have one mighty ominous situation."

6:30 p.m.; Wilmington

Gillian flipped through her notebook, reciting aloud for Cy's benefit. "So far, out of sixty invitations personally sent—or about 120 invited—forty-five have r.s.v.p.ed favorably. Tomorrow's the deadline; I imagine a few more will still trickle in. I don't have a count for the earlier part of the grand opening—the open house."

Cy propped his feet on his wooden desk, stuck a cigar in his mouth. "You know, Gillian, that we have to hold this at your apartment?"

"That wasn't part of the deal."

"Where else can we have it?" interceded Wally, Cy's twenty-year-old nephew, as he sat on the edge of a stool on the other side of the inner office, downing a large glass of ice water. He chomped down on an ice cube. "There's no room in this office." He looked around as if searching for space.

"I don't have the space either," she protested.

Cy and Wally exchanged glances.

"Okay," she conceded, "but only if you two clean up. Planning and hosting a party isn't part of my job description as a detective." She looked up from her tablet. "Why won't you let me in on a case, Cy? That's why you pay me, but all I've been doing since you hired me is administrative work."

"Too skinny."

"What?"

"I said," he unpropped his legs from the desk, puffed on his cigar, "You're too skinny to do dangerous work."

Wally chuckled.

"And you're a too plump, black and white plaid-suited penguin," she hymphed, crossing her arms at her chest, "and you're smelly . . . from all those old stoagies."

Wally howled, and Cy threw back his head and laughed. "Okay, Gilly, when another case comes in."

"When will that be?"

He shrugged. "Go out and get one." He looked past Gilly and winked at his nephew.

She rolled her eyes, plopped down in an old chair next to Cy's desk, and rifled through her tablet, checking off things on her list. Cy was hopeless. He was never going to see her for what she could be: A sure-footed P.I. who could spot irregularities miles away, see quick hands before the shoplifter left a store, sense a mugger's intent before he moved, feel the anger in a murderer's eyes . . . .EYES!!! "Cy," she blurted out. "Have you ever seen or heard about people—behemoth-sized men—with electric red eyes?"

He looked up from papers on his desk, stared at her, moving the cigar back and forth in his mouth. "Like what?" He tipped up the rim of his hat with his index finger, and leaned forward.

"Like . . . like radioactive eyes . . . reddish colored. I don't know how to describe them. It sounds crazy, but I saw two guys just like that." She gave him the details of what she had seen through her office window and that one night she had been driving home and spotted a cop pulling an old lady off the road.

"Hmmm." Cy looked at Wally, then back to Gillian.

She added, "I'll never forget how these guys looked: Giants with cement pilaster arms, steel beamed legs, and a face that made me cringe."

"Sounds like Uncle Cy when he gets out of bed in the morning." Wally giggled.

Cy made a clucking sound, then looking back at Gillian, said, "So these, uh, big men are ugly, huh?"

"No, not at all, just rugged looking faces, with tight lips, and those on-off piercing, glowing red eyes."

"Glowing red eyes," Cy repeated.

"Laugh if you want, but I know what I saw."

"I'm not laughing, kiddo. Your report is the third one I've heard in the last month. Maybe it's time we did look into it."

"My own case?" Her voice held enthusiasm.

"Not a case—there's no client—just an in-house study." He puffed harder on his cigar. "Go for it." He slipped the cigar out of his mouth, and pointing it at his nephew, said, "Make use of Wally as protection."

"Right," she mumbled, sizing up the puny kid.

Chapter 5

Zakowicz panted, stopped in his tracks. He looked at the man next to him. "You're a better soldier than I am, Girard. You haven't needed to rest once, and, here, all along, I've considered myself to be in excellent shape." Leaning on his rifle, he removed his cap and wiped the perspiration off his forehead with the sleeve of his camouflage uniform, in spite of how cold it was this winter in the hills of northern West Virginia.

The soldier next to him looked on, expressionless. "Get fit, Zak."

"Yeah, right." Zakowicz eyed the man who easily managed his reconnaissance pack, rifle and other gear, while yet not breaking a sweat. He was a strange fellow: Talked in short, simple sentences and phrases, bigger than many pro football players, and had magnificent gray eyes that looked almost translucent. Most impressive to Zakowicz was the man's strength—one that could lift a half-dozen fifteen-inch steel pipes at one time without a snag in his breath. Yet, Zak knew, the soldier's strength could be used to advantage. He couldn't think of anyone else he'd rather have with him in a battle. Still, there was that mark on the back of his neck. Oh, sure, it wasn't real noticeable but conspicuous enough for Zak to have seen it on one or two occasions—a mark like an identification symbol branded by a hot iron, some government I.D..

"Hey, Girard," Zak began, his breath coming in gasps as they climbed a steep butte, "Where you from? Have any family?"

Girard seemed to be hoisting himself up the high mound as if he were tip-toeing while Zak could barely get his footing. "No."

"No what?" Zak huffed. "No, you don't have any family?" Jeesh, the man was incredible, the way he was scaling the mountain. "Everyone has a family, Girard." Zak looked down; it was a long way to the bottom. Just one mis-step would send him plummeting, his body hitting jagged rocks on the way before crashing to the ground, fragmenting every single bone. But he figured in Girard's little pinky alone was enough power to hold him, if necessary. Amazingly, Zak recalled, he had seen other soldiers built like Girard; maybe they were a test group on some kind of steroid. Zak yelled louder to Girard who was near the top of the mound, his breath coming out like popcorn balls in the cold, "Slow down!"

"Come, we must make our time."

Zakowicz looked up the hill at Girard who always had to be the model soldier. "Almost there," he called up when he saw Girard's boot hit the crest. Besides wanting to complete this bivouac exercise, Zak couldn't wait to get back to the base so he could call his pregnant wife and three-year-old son. He was hoping to fulfill his term before war started. Tomorrow would mark the beginning of the two months he owed Uncle Sam before he was discharged.

As he neared the top, Girard leaned over, thrust his hand out, saying, "You're slow. Come. Now." He opened his hand to expose his palm and help Zak up.

Zak took it, smiled his thanks, and within seconds was standing atop the mound, adjusting his gear.

They trekked toward their target, the frigid air frosting their faces, turning Zakowicz's cheeks rosy. "Dang, it's cold," he offered as a way to make conversation until they engaged in their recon activities.

Girard said nothing.

"We should be meeting up with the others so—" He stopped when Girard suddenly came to a halt. "What's wrong?" He looked around; saw nothing out of place, then studied Girard whose hand pressed against his forehead as if suffering from a severe headache. "You okay, man?" Then he saw Girard remove his hand from his eyes, his pupils widening and changing to a dark rose color, then brightening to a pink that interchanged with his normal steel-colored eyes, and then to red. Zak backed away, a shiver overcoming him.

With his index finger, Girard poked Zak's chest, making him lose his footing.

"Hey!" Zakowicz cried out as he struggled to regain his equilibrium. Another inch and he would have gone sailing over the cliff. "Stop it, Girard. I could've fallen off the ridge."

Girard stood stoic, his finger still posed in a poking position.

Dusting off his BDU pants, Zak took a step forward but instantly felt his body jerked backward. "I said, stop it!" he yelled at the big lox.

Girard spun Zak around to face him, his eyes looking eerily aflame. "Play, like cat."

What the hell is he talking about? "Knock it off, Girard. We've got work to do."

The slap came hard across his face, so fast and

crushing that Zakowicz thought his head had been whacked off. Rattled, he never saw the undercut plowing into his stomach, soaring him into the air. When he hit the ground, he heard something snap in his body.

The toe of Girard's boot gingerly touched Zak's side, massaging it.

"Help me, please," Zak sobbed. He tried turning his head to see the mammoth form, but nothing in him moved.

Girard's kick skyrocketed Zak like a rag doll hurtled across a room. Girard walked over to Zak, picked him up with one hand and dangled him in the air, with Zak's howls and sobs reverberating off the cliff.

Zak's body swung like a clapper in a bell.

Holding Zak out with one hand, Girard punted him like a drop kick. Zak's body—limp and torn—fell only inches from the crag's rim. Girard lifted Zak and plunged his knife into his skull, placing his lips over the puncture wound. He sucked fluid.

When finished, Girard gathered all his strength and heaved Zak's lifeless form over the cliff, watching it buffet air currents on its nosedive to the bottom.

7:00 p.m.; Wilmington

Gillian pushed her auburn-highlighted hair off her face as she dashed from one room to the next, greeting guests, offering trays of wine and punch, hoer d'oervues, and sweets. Occasionally, her glance would catch Dixie and Annie who were helping her, looking as frazzled as she. The number of people who showed up for the grand re-opening at Gilly's apartment astounded even Cy who expected not more than a handful. But Gilly had reminded him that, "When you promise free food and drinks, you get everyone in the White Pages."

Hustling back into the kitchen, Gillian rifled through her refrigerator for more cheese. "Shoot! I thought I had bought enough," she mumbled to herself.

"Don't answer yourself; it's a sign of mental ill-ness," came the voice behind the opened refrigerator door.

"Mitch." She was surprised to see him. "I didn't think you were coming; you didn't RSVP, which is another reason for our divorcing—your lack of drive and etiquette."

"In addition to my not doing what I promise? And my inability to confront people, make waves?"

"We went though all this before."

"Not counting my lack of enthusiasm for your inter-ests: Symphonies, arts—"

"I have a houseful of people, Mitchell, and you're rehashing all this now. You're nuts." She looked absently around the kitchen.

"My being nuts—another reason. Then there's your complaint that I didn't like you working this P.I. job, which is true. I think it's too dangerous. Yet you have this big-to-do of a grand re-opening for an old dick who looks like Lou Costello with a cigar burning from his mouth."

"Something brought **you** here tonight." She sliced off more pepperoni from the long, seasoned stick.

"An invitation." He took the knife out of her hands and assumed the slicing job. "And the fact that I rented the downtown office to him, the super real estate agent that I am." He winked at her.

She felt his hands go around her waist and heard him whisper into her ear, "Divorce or not, I never stopped loving you. Let's try again."

She looked over her shoulder at him. "How many martinis did you have tonight?" She liked his tight fit-ting slacks, starched white shirt with a chic tie. The smell of Aramis on him made her want to inhale all of him while consuming his deep blue eyes, and touching his short, wavy, blondish-yellow hair. How could he be

such a good looking guy and yet so remiss as a husband? "Come on, Mitch; I have guests to serve. If I
don't get out there soon with trays of food, Cy's gonna
come in here and ring my neck. You know he's no
socialite."

"More like a Socialist." Mitch released his hold on
her and returned to slicing the pepperoni. "Got a new
project I'm working on." He tossed a slice into his
mouth. "Remember a few years back when that scientist
guy—a Doctor Hammond—from a lab down by Easton
bought twenty-nine acres of land but never put up a
structure?"

"You deal with a lot of strange people."

"Anyway, his secretary—a Ms. Azar—called me
yesterday, saying he wants to buy more acreage. I'm
going down there tomorrow, but why he doesn't use an
Easton real estate agent is beyond me."

"Maybe because you lived there all those years
before moving here, and know the land really well.
What does he want to do with all that land if he's not
putting buildings or labs on it?"

"The mad scientist syndrome." Mitch helped her
load crackers with pepperoni and cheese.

They went into the living room.

Gillian made her rounds, meeting guests, telling
others about Cy's agency.

"World's crazy," she heard a client say to Wally. "I
mean, they're talking about a possible world war
involving Russia, Israel, and God only knows who else,
as well as a major market crash that will dwarf the
Great Depression, along with hysterical rumors about
food and water shortages, and an evil ruler rising—
Gosh! What else is going to happen?"

Wally nodded. "Now there's reports about attacks
and deaths by giants with red eyes." He chuckled.
"Must be the Incredible Hulk."

Gilly swept past them, hoping to sight a spot where

she could privately sit and catch her breath. Her eyes glanced around the apartment; instead of discovering her goal, she came across a small cluster of faces, two of whom she never saw before.

She went toward the new faces, her hands extended, her words out before skin met with skin. "Hi, I'm Gillian Montague, employee of Collier Investigative Agency and owner of this tiny apartment.

The first figure reached for her hand. "I'm Chase Chandler." A partial smile seemed to turn up the corners of his mouth, and his hazel eyes lit up the room, touching something deep inside her, titillating her. He had to be the most handsome man she'd ever met, with his straight, black, fluffy hair, and such cleft dimples that his eye color seemed even more heightened. He definitely was model material.

To Gillian, he seemed to forever hold onto her hand, warming it and her insides.

"And," he added in his sonorous voice, "this is my twin, Leslie." He pointed to the woman next to him.

Leslie looked at Gilly with soulful eyes. "Hi," she said in a raspy voice.

Gillian's first thought was that compared to her brother, the woman was homely, with her large features and rough texture; something about the woman bothered Gillian. Maybe she was everything Gillian was afraid she would someday become. For the sake of conversation, Gillian asked, "What brings you two here?"

Chase lifted his glass toward Dixie. "We were her ride."

"Dixie?" Gillian had invited her best friend but she didn't recall telling her to bring guests along. "What's wrong with her car?"

Chase and Leslie looked at each other. "Well," began Chase, smiling so his dimples would disarm Gillian. "We know her through a mutual friend at the fertility clinic where she works, and since we had to take

the friend back to the clinic, we offered Dixie a ride."
He smiled again, fiddled with the swizzle stick in his
glass.

Gillian's brows creased. Something seemed off
about his story but it was too hot in her apartment to
matter, and she was too busy and too tired to care, and
the Chase guy was too cute to contradict.

The three made small talk, with Gillian telling them
a little about the area since they said they were from up
the peninsula. Chase made her giggle even though he
kept a straight face with every word he spoke.

At some point during the night, Chase asked, "May
I call you sometime?"

She looked at him. "Okay."

When eleven o'clock rolled around, most of the
guests had left.

"It's late, gotta go," Dixie said, hugging Gillian and
waving to Leslie and Chase who quickly fell into step
with her.

Gilly thanked her best friend, finished cleaning up
with Mitch, Cy, and Wally's help, and then walked Cy
to his car in the frigid air.

"You oughta put a coat on," Cy scolded. "Remember, work, Monday. You have lots to catch up on."

"I keep telling you, Cy, that I'm a detective—a professional—not a party planner." She held open his car
door for him. "Besides, Monday's Christmas Eve day."

"People still work that day."

"But I have Christmas shopping to do, and I want to
do research on my own case—you know, those goons?"

"Goons?" He looked thoughtful as he inserted his
car key into the ignition. "Oh, the flashing eyes guys.
What's your first step?"

"I thought I'd start at the library. Dixie said she'd
go with me to research the glowing eyes . . . see if it
was genetic."

"Hmmm," he said. "Then what?"

"I want to look into Leslie Chandler's background. She comes across really strange."

"Manly."

"You felt it, too."

Cy shrugged. "It might be hormonal." He turned the key and the engine coughed before starting. "Just be sure you're at work on Monday."

"We'll see." She gave him a little smile. "Tell me something, Cy, what would I do to get info on someone . . . I mean, besides the usual pyramiding and looking into vital records, military service files, talking to the subjects' neighbors and business associates, the organizations they belong to, motor vehicle records—"

"Check the databases on them. See if they're listed in the various biographical and marquis directories and references, as well as genealogical and court files, microfiches, credit reports, tax and medical records. Oh, and talk to their parents, church leaders."

She wrapped her arms around her shoulders to warm herself. "Somehow I get the feeling that things won't be so cut and dry with Leslie. She seems secretive."

"Based on what?"

"Woman's intuition."

Cy laughed. "Oh, that's real scientific." He pulled out of her driveway to the sounds of Christmas music on the car radio.

Chapter
6

Gillian pored over genetics books, then turned to the microfiche.

"Hey," said Dixie. "Let's go home. It's Christmas Eve day and I have better things to do than research flashing eyes."

"Wait." Gillian finished reading the fiches and went to the stacks. Checking the numbers she had written on scrap paper, she began pulling texts, and setting them down with a thud on top of a wide table. "Let's try the angle that some chemical causes flashing eyes, and all we have to do is determine what that chemical is."

"There are literally thousands of different chemicals, Gil." She shook her head. "Why don't you just quit this project?"

"I'm not a quitter. As my best friend, you're obligated to help me."

"Oh I can see what kind of choice I'm being given here."

The two dove into searching the books.

A half-hour later, Dixie pointed to a picture in an anatomy book.

Gilly looked at it, hid a giggle. "Stop this," she whispered. "You're supposed to be helping me gather info on genetics and here you're looking at all the nudes in medical books." Gilly closed the tome, walked over to a stack in the library, removed another book, and returned to the table where Dixie sat.

"We're not going to find anything on electric eyes; you know that. If we continue to pursue this, we'll become the subjects in these psychiatry books."

"Cy gave me this case—my very own—and I don't want to blow it. With this assignment, I can prove to Cy what I can do."

"You're also proving just how loony you are." Dixie went back to looking at the anatomy books, saying to the words on the page, "You don't want to become a Sam Spade, do you?"

"I feel directionless in life. Getting an associate's degree didn't go far to employ me."

"You can always change jobs. Snooping around doesn't fit your personality."

Gillian returned to reading the text in front of her. "It says here that eye color is determined by the dominant gene so that if a male is blue-eyed and a female brown-eyed, the progeny would be brown-eyed because that's dominant over hazel or blue."

"Like I don't know that from working in a fertility lab."

Gilly rubbed her eyes. "But this says nothing about glowing electric, red eyes."

Dixie yawned. "The flashing eyes could be an artificial trait like a crystalline substance put into the eyes via drops. Or maybe it's some kind of contact lens."

"For what purpose?"

"To give the monsters you talk about extra visual

power?" Dixie slammed the book closed. "Maybe it's a result of artificial insemination, cloning, grafting." She looked disturbed. "Look, let it go. You're getting too carried away with this."

"Wouldn't you, if you saw one of those big goons kill a man, and another go after an old woman? What's the matter with you? Why don't you even care?"

Dixie looked as if Gillian had hurt her feelings.

To take the sting out of her words Gillian kidded, "Electric eyes are horrendous but the guy I met at the company opening had a mixture of normal and sparkling eyes. Tell me what you know about him. You came with him and his sister. Where's he from? What does he do?"

Dixie yanked her purse off the chair and slipped it up on her shoulder. "Are you going to see him? Look, just be careful. You don't even know him."

"I realize that, but he was very sweet to me that night. He's so nice looking, Dix, that he takes my breath away."

"Watch your step; that's all I have to say." Dixie waited for Gillian to gather her papers and notes. "I don't really know much about Chase and his sister. Do you remember Gordon Byers at my clinic? Well, through someone he knows who knows this Chase, he got Chase to drop off my briefcase to my condo, since I had left it at work. Knowing that you were waiting for me, I asked Chase when he came if he could give me a lift to your place because my car wouldn't start. He was a gentleman about it and agreed, though I think he took it as an invitation for him and his sister to come to the party, which worked out anyway, since they ended up being my ride home; otherwise, I would have asked you to take me home that late at night."

Something's wrong with her story. "Aren't you the very one who told me, not more than seconds ago, to be careful because I didn't even know this guy?"

They headed for their cars in the library parking lot.

"Oh, I get it," began Gillian. "You and Chase have something going that you don't want anyone to know about. How could you, Dix, when we're best friends?"

"Really, Gillian." She looked at her friend. "It's between Gordon and me."

Gillian gasped.

"Yep," teased Dixie. "All six-hundred pounds of him.

"Tell me, Dix, if these goons are created through some artificial means, they wouldn't have souls then, would they?"

Dixie stared at her. "Only God puts souls into people."

In a D.C. Park

President Williams waved to spectators lining streets who watched him and the vice president jog through the park, with security all around. Williams knew that placing himself and Greenman together, in the same spot, was a bodyguard's nightmare but it was the only way he could talk to the vice president without fear of being overheard, bugged, or photographed close up. Besides, moving targets were harder to hit than stationary ones.

"How's Project Depop going?" The president's gray hair blew in the cold wind which didn't bother him; he relished running in his wool sweats in the dead of winter.

Huffing and puffing, the vice president said, "It's tough to feed the public acceptable reasons for liquidating society's aged, infirmed, and mentally ill. But the sooner we skim off that layer, the healthier the rest of the strata—"

"'Liquidating'?"

"I need to find a more euphemistic term, I know."

"Project NAR?"

Greenman stopped, put his hands on his knees, inhaled deeply.

"You're out of shape, boy," laughed Williams. He turned and again waved to spectators and flashing cameras.

Having caught his breath, Greenman said, "NAR's coming along fine. Since the pope's finally agreed to publicly accept evolution and down-play the Holy Bible while promoting Jerusalem as the intended world capitol, we're more easily transitioning the world from Christianity to 'Spiritualism' or NAR—our 'New Age Religion'—which, by the way, is now among the teachings of Baptist churches. We aren't far off track from our blueprint to close all Christian churches."

"Nice work, Bert." The president got his sneakers moving again, with his sidekick following. "And our EPA plan of taking over private ownership of lands, and imposing heavy fines on citizens for breaking even minor environmental laws?"

"That, Mr. President, is meeting with protest. I'm continuing my work on it since the environment and our slated water shortage will be pivotal in our New Age transition."

"And the 'smart card' viz a viz the global common economy?"

"We're still working on eliminating U.S. currency and implementing the smart card which will easily slide us to the mark on the back of the hand to buy and sell all goods."

The president nodded, looked around to make sure no one was near, and then turned back to Greenman, satisfied that FBI men were too many feet away to hear, and that the spectators, photographers and reporters remained a ways off the park's path. "What about the BCI combined with Project Enolc 1?" This he whispered so low that the vice president had to lean toward him to hear. "Keep moving when you answer."

"Yessir." Greenman gulped as much oxygen as possible as he took up a trot. "From what Dr. Hammond has told me, it seems that the BCI—the Brain Chip Implantation—project should be put on hold since one simian with an implanted chip went mad for no reason. A very gruesome sight, sir, from what I'm told."

"A gorilla's one thing; a human, another." The president waved to a photographer/reporter while ignoring a spectator who screamed, "Down with satanism, down with Williams." Another bystander hissed, "Down with Williams' Cabinet." Williams widely grinned his mouthful of white teeth, waved harder, than turned back to Greenman, saying, "I thought the irregularities were caused by a chemical deficiency in the brains, and not from the chips."

"I couldn't say for sure, but I'll look in to it."

"That's it, unless you have something else to add?"

"A little more detail on the date of the proposed, uh, war?"

"Same as previously scheduled. The exact date hasn't yet been decided. I'm waiting to hear from the Premiere."

"One more thing . . . can we walk from here?"

The president turned his head to look at his assistant. "You pansy."

Greenman panted.

The president slowed to a stop, then resumed in a leisurely gait. He grinned, pointed to Greenman, saying loudly to the small crowd, "Our young vice president said he'd like a nice stroll from here to the White House."

Everyone laughed.

Greenman curtsied and bowed for effect.

Gwen Estates; Easton

Dr. Hammond and Mitch stood outside the electric gate of the government lab grounds, talking. Mitch could see Hammond's secretary, Ms. Azar, in the government car, disinterestedly watching them, and seemingly perturbed that she had to work on the day before Christmas. Maybe she was just an unhappy woman . . . or unhappy with her job and Hammond.

"Come on." Mitch heard Azar mumble from the car.

"So, that's where we stand?" Hammond said to Mitch who returned to concentrating on Hammond.

"I can go back to my clients and present your offer, Dr. Hammond, but they're adamant about their asking price. There are a lot of grounds here, as you know." Mitch's hand swept over the lands. "By the way, I don't see any buildings here. Having previously sold you most of this land for what you said was to be used for research labs, I wonder where the structures are. Didn't you go through with your plans?"

Mitch saw that Dr. Hammond was hesitant to say anything. He watched him shift his stance, heard him say, "Top secret, Mr. Frey. Trust me, though, our plans haven't changed. If anything, we want to expand our operations, which is why I'm talking to you."

"Top secret, huh? What're you people doing? Building bombs?"

Through the open car windows, Ms. Azar remarked, "Top secret in our government is usually top manure."

Mitch laughed.

Hammond glowered at her, lit a cigarette, asking Mitchell, "Aren't your clients the same ones you represented in our last negotiations?" He puffed on the Marlboro. "What were their names? Crawford, Dietz and Pepperdine—accountants?"

"Yes, though how you'd remember, I don't know since their attorneys had handled everything. You must have done your homework."

"What else would you expect from the United States government?" He took a long drag on his cigarette. "We know and remember everything." He cleared his throat. "Like I said, call me; the sooner the better. I have a boss to report to, too."

Mitch watched him walk to the car, head held high.

Abruptly, out of nowhere, a tremendous hulk pounced from behind bushes, rushed towards Hammond holding a knife in the air.

Azar screamed so loudly that Mitch jumped and Hammond dropped his cigarette.

Mitch's legs turned in motion.

Hammond threw one arm up in a natural motion of defense while his other blocked his face in protection.

Mitch arrived just as the form brought the knife down on Hammond's arm, piercing a bicep by at least two inches, the knife remaining impaled in the skin. Hammond stumbled to the ground.

The figure bolted at cheetah-like speed.

Hammond groaned, struggled to get to his feet.

Azar got out from the car and ran over to her boss.

Mitch stood shocked, mumbling, "What was that anyway? It looked like a giant version of a man but yet it was different."

Hearing Hammond moan and pitch forward as he grappled to stand, Mitch grabbed him. "Can you walk? Miss Azar and I will help you to my car and I'll call and ambulance from my cell phone."

"As long as we don't remove this knife, I'll make it to my lab where physicians are present. Ms. Azar can drive me."

Mitch figured that as soon as Azar and Hammond left, they would drive down the road a piece leading to some hidden structure. Mitch also figured that Hammond's refusal to go to the hospital had something to do with his government confidentiality.

Azar suggested, "Maybe we should take you to the

ER. You're hurt badly."

"We can't, Ms. Azar. You know that." Hammond gave her a dirty look.

Mitch asked, "Why would anyone want to hurt you, Dr. Hammond? What was that 'thing' anyway?"

Hammond grunted, and inhaled loudly to catch much-needed oxygen for his rapidly weakening body. "Look, Frey, don't go blowing things out of proportion just because some hoodlum mugged me—"

"Hoodlum! That thing was a—"

"Get a hold of yourself." Brushing Mitch off, he said feebly, "Let's go, Ms. Azar."

Azar looked at Mitch, shrugged, and drove off, with Hammond sitting next to her, looking pale and sweaty.

Mitch hung back, then got into his car, and keeping his distance, followed them down the dirt road.

Christmas Eve, Early Evening; Delaware Coast

Gillian slid into Chase's new car when he opened the door. She watched him lumber around to the other side and get in, seemingly too large for the sports vehicle and yet making it putty in his hands.

"Nice car," she said. "What is it?"

"It's called the Animator; hand-made in Switzerland; fully computerized and climatically controlled. Has six gears, too. Here, where we sit, is called the cockpit; I mean, just look at all these buttons and dials."

"Looks like something out of the future."

He grinned, the last rays of the winter sun reflecting in his mirrored sunglasses. "It is nearly 2011; we are the future."

"You maneuver those gears like a piece of cake."

"I've been programmed that way." He looked over at her and grinned. "Leslie hasn't a clue on how to shift, or run the dashboard controls."

"Must have cost a pretty penny."

"My, uh, boss bought it for me."

She thought about that. It was time to pump him for info. "Who's that?"

"I told you I worked for a stockbroker."

"How long?"

His eyes shifted in her direction. "A couple of years."

"The name of the company?"

"This sounds like an interrogation."

"I'm trying to get to know you better." She gulped. "Please slow down. We're not in the Indy 500." She forced a smile. "Tell me about yourself."

He let up his foot from the accelerator pedal. "Nothing to tell. My sibling and I lost our parents when young and—"

"Me too. I was raised in an orphanage."

"I knew we had something in common." He beamed at her. "But Leslie and I were raised by an organization, and—"

"What kind of organization?" *This is odd.*

He frowned. "Not an 'organization' organization. I mean, like a convent. Yeah, a convent. The organization of the Sisters of Good Heart raised us."

She looked quizzically at him. "Your sister Leslie seems unusual; kind of, well, manly. I don't mean to be insulting—"

"I know, but don't let her hear that; she's very sensitive. It's hormonal. The nuns, of course, didn't do anything about it, and when Leslie and I were finally able to go out on our own, doctors said it was too late to correct the problem. Since we're twins, the doctors said it had something to do with the genetics."

She wondered if she had read that anywhere in her study of genetics.

"That orphanage where you and Leslie were raised,

where was it? Since I was raised in one, too—"

"You can be sure mine wasn't located anywhere near yours." He accelerated.

She could tell he was angry, so she let the matter drop.

Minutes later, he said, "Look, how about a drive to Bethany Beach where we'll dine at a chic restaurant, take in a movie, and walk the sand along the ocean?" Chase brought a smile to his face.

"What 'chic' restaurant? Besides, it's too cold. Let's skip the movie tonight and just go to dinner. I'm pretty tired." Why did she suddenly feel so uncomfortable with him? After all, the few times she had met him at a coffee shop in Wilmington, he seemed perfectly fine. Now, alone with him in the car, heading at night to the beach several miles away, with his penetrating eyes, his tall, muscular form, she was beginning to have second thoughts. She groped for the pepper spray in her slacks pocket—something she always carried as a female and as a detective.

He looked at her, making her feel uneasy for a second. "Okay . . . this time." He sped up again.

A thought came to her: "For twins, you and Leslie have different eye color."

"It happens." He drummed his fingers on the steering wheel. "So, what are your plans for tomorrow?"

"Not having a family, I'll probably spend Christmas alone unless Dixie or Mitch stop in, but Dixie usually goes to her brother's for the holidays."

"And this Mitch?"

"He's my ex but we've remained good friends."

"Do you still love him?"

She cocked her head. "That's a personal question . . . coming from a stranger."

"That's how I felt when you asked me all those questions."

"Mitch doesn't like my being a detective."

"Just what are you 'detecting' these days?"

"Not much of anything, unfortunately. I suspect this line of work isn't my forte either." She sighed. "Please slow down, Chase."

He again released the gas pedal. "What kind of a case are you working on?"

"I'm looking into goons with flashing red eyes."

He glanced at her. "I've never heard of such a thing." Turning up the volume on his car's CD, he added, "You sure I can't interest you in that walk on the beach? It'll give us some time to be alone."

"Next time." She would be glad when the night was over.

7:30 p.m.; Washington, D.C.

Harry Gamblin, Secretary of Defense, hung up the phone and looked at his assistant. "Well, it's done."

The deputy nodded. "Won't be long now before the war is in full swing."

"And to think Israel's supposed to sign a peace treaty with the PLO at the same time."

"Now there's irony. The president has us shipping arms to Russia to commence war between it and Israel, and yet he has Israel making peace with Palestine. What a genius he is."

The Secretary lit a cigarette.

"You're not supposed to smoke inside the building."

"What difference does it make? All hell's about to break lose anyway." Just as impulsively as he had lit a cigarette, Gamblin quickly stomped it out, rose from his chair, and announced, "I'm going home to be with my wife and kids. It is Christmas Eve. To hell with all of you."

Chapter
7

Harry rubbed his eyes and tried focusing on his four-year-old son who was jumping on the bed, yelling, "Mommy! Daddy! Wake up. Santy was here!"

Joan Gamblin groaned, pulled herself out of bed and stepped toward the shower, telling her son to stop jumping on the bed.

"Come on, Mom; let's open presents first. You can shower later," whined their thirteen-year-old daughter. "I hope there's a new computer under the tree."

Harry coughed up his usual morning phlegm, reached for a cigarette but changed his mind when his wife shot him a look. "I said I'd give them up as part of my New Year's resolutions; that's a week away."

The four-year-old yanked on his arm to get him moving.

"Hey, Dad, I'm expectin' car keys for a shiny red, 2K X7 Turbo Souzati, loaded," called his sixteen-year-old son from the bedroom doorway.

"He can't afford to buy me a computer and you a new car, too. Don't be so selfish, Junior." The daughter rolled her eyes.

"Pop's a big shot in this country and makes big bucks," teased Junior.

"Stop it, both of you." Joan wrapped herself in a terry cloth bathrobe, saying to Harry, "Let's open presents. The coffee's on automatic, so it's ready."

Harry slipped on pants over his white Jockey briefs. He looked at his three children and wife, and felt a sense of elation that was instantly replaced by doom the second he thought about his job at the White House.

11:00 a.m.; Wilmington

In the living room, Chase slipped the needle into the vein on the inside of the crook of his elbow. He slowly breathed in as the solution filled his vein, flushed through his system.

Leslie walked through the room carrying a mug and the morning newspaper. "Getting your daily fix, huh?"

"Merry Christmas to you, too."

"Like you care."

"You're right; I don't." He unsnapped the tourniquet, slid the needle out of his vein, and held a cotton ball over the injection site. "Going to Mother's for the holiday?" He threw his head back and laughed. "Why don't you take that wig off? No one's going to see you here, even though you're one ugly es-oh-bee without it."

"If I'm ugly, so are you." Leslie stomped off to her bedroom.

Chase gathered his syringe, tourniquet, and vial together, thinking he should call Gillian and visit her for the day. Just as quickly as the thought entered his mind, he instantly rejected it. *Naw, she'll be with friends and that Mitch guy, no doubt.* There was tomorrow. He'd call her then . . . felt a need to be around her to know what she was doing.

2:00 p.m.

In between her scanning books and making Christmas dinner for Dixie, Wally, Cy, and Mitch, Gillian leafed through her old college texts trying to glean information on twins and eye color. Maybe there was a connection between glowing eyes and genetics. "That's really far-fetched," she chided herself. She liked having people around on the holidays, especially Mitch. She was sorry they had broken up but she would never tell him that simply because he might feel pressured to go back with her. She wanted him to do it on his own volition, with the intent to change his bad habits, just as she would work on changing hers, of which the primary one was not focusing on anything permanent and constructive in life. The detective job never should have been an issue in their marriage because she wasn't even sure she wanted to be a gumshoe, but as long as he griped about it, the longer she kept at it. When she first started with Cy she was doing basic tracking chores—insurance frauds, adulterous spouses, missing children—and Mitch complained about the danger then, but now that she was working on her own case, he seemed really put out by it.

"Sugar!" she said, lowering the oven door to check the turkey. "I forgot to baste the bird!" Cooking had never been her forte; she was glad everyone was bringing a dish. Dixie made the best pumpkin and mince meat pies. She had told Gillian she would leave right after desert because she had other plans but she hadn't explained what those plans were. "Maybe fat ol' Gordon," laughed Gillian, though most likely Dixie was going to her brother's house and Mitch was going to visit his mother later in the evening. Gilly had always liked his mother who was sarcastic and witty. As far as Cy went, Gillian figured he and Wally would make the two-and-a-half hour drive to his sister's house in Baltimore and stay overnight. Wally's mother was Cy's sister, and the two were close.

Gillian crossed over to her apartment window. She liked Cy a lot, and the more she got to know him, the more she respected him. This coming summer would be two years she had worked for him, but it seemed that novice Wally had the makings of being a better detective than Gillian. "So what am I supposed to do for a living?" she asked herself, standing in front of the window, watching snow tumble lazily from the sky. She clicked the remote control button to her high-tech stereo and "The First Noel" sounded.

Her thoughts drifted to Chase. What was it about him that endeared her as much as it scared her? Everything she had researched on him turned up a blank. It was as though he didn't even exist. The same was true for Leslie. Once, Gilly got excited about a lead that promised a link to Leslie. The librarian had directed her to a 2009 reference book titled, *The Marquis of Promising Americans.* Chase wasn't listed in it but there was an entry for: *Chandler, Leslie*, but the entry was limited to the name and the phrase, "See *Who's Who of Future Leaders 1998.* When Gillian pulled that work, it, too, only had a name listed with no information and no picture. It was as if someone had dictated that the background information be deleted at press time. Or maybe it wasn't even the same Leslie Chandler. After all, "Chandler" wasn't an uncommon name, and neither was "Leslie."

The year 1998 would have made Leslie about twenty-nine, thirty years old back then, so why would someone delete her background info. Was she a fugitive from the law? Surely Leslie must have worked throughout her life; yet, no work records existed on her.

Something just didn't seem right. *Those kind of reference books don't delete entire biographical information at the last minute, unless ordered to do so by very powerful entities.*

Gillian thought about that. Was Chase—or perhaps both he and Leslie—involved in governmental work? Well, she resolved, she would just have to do more research. This part of her job she liked; the pursuit of cops and robbers, she didn't. Now Cy was bugging her about getting a gun which she would be allowed to do since she was in law enforcement. Cy had told her, "Do it, Gil, before politicians pass a law prohibiting even detectives and police from owning weapons. Every year we lose more of our rights."

She returned to the kitchen to check on the bird. Her thoughts flitted to upcoming New Year, and she wondered what 2011 would bring. Maybe she ought to have a New Year's Eve party—invite her friends over, as well as Chase and Leslie, and maybe even Gordon. She laughed aloud at that.

She knew one thing for sure: She would spend the entire next week researching Chase and Leslie, as well as the goons, and whatever other case Cy wanted to throw her way. Somewhere along the way in the year 2011, she would find her niche, and if that was to be P.I. work, then she would become a darn good one!

5:00 p.m.; D.C.

President Jackson Williams buried his head inside his furred London Fog, and in the escort of two Secret Service men, he slinked out of the hotel and into the car awaiting him. He never looked back at the swank inn where he had his usual rendevousz with one of his many mistresses. This one had breasts the size of helium balloons, and he enjoyed her the most when he felt down and stressed out, like now, with the converging of events to formalize the one-world government. His worry wasn't over America's role in it, but rather **his** place in it. Her enlarged, voluptuous boobs gave comfort to him, allowing him to bury his head in her cleavage and lose himself long enough to let the world go to seed and he not be controlled by it.

He checked his watch. "Let's get back to the White House. My wife and kids expect me home for Christmas dinner."

"Your wife, sir," began a bodyguard, "is out . . . uh . . . taking care of her worries."

Williams snickered. "Whatever she catches, she better keep it to herself and her bedmates." Leaning toward the security man to his left, the president half-whispered, "Do you think anyone saw me go in?"

"We checked it out first, and vacated the entrance and elevators for the short time you were there. Besides, sir, you could have been at that hotel for a special meeting, for all anyone knows."

"Except those who do know me well, know that I put my whores in that same hotel on the nights we're to meet."

"Well, it hasn't been reported in any tabloid yet, and I doubt it will be, with all the penalties you impose on any publication that reports unfavorably on you."

"My 'seditious libel' law does seem to be working, doesn't it?" He laughed. "And to think Cosby lost against Zenger when that first went to court."

"I don't think it's the law so much the publications fear, sir; I think it's more your retaliation. They know you'll make their existence insufferable by your sic'ing the IRS and other forbidding government agencies on them."

The president reclined in the back seat, sipping on a manhattan that a bodyguard fixed him from the limo's bar. "The power is in my hands. And I love it."

Monday, December 31, 2010;
9:00 p.m.; Wilmington

Mitch stood at the kitchen table examining the label on the champagne bottle. He turned the green bottle over and over in his hands before saying to Gillian who was cooking a ham in the oven, "This isn't a good sparkling; in fact, I think the most aging it has done is twenty-four hours. You never were savvy about such things."

"I didn't go to Choate or Columbia. I was lucky to get out of that orphanage and attend a community college." She licked her finger with the pineapple juice on it. "How's your mom doing? You saw her after you left here last week?"

"The roads got bad so I had to wait until the next day, after the salt trucks were out. She sends her love, Gil; worries a lot about you, too, especially since you've become a P.I. She just doesn't seem to understand that."

"Well, at seventy, I can see why she doesn't. She's from a whole 'nother generation. But I love her all the same."

"You can still go back to her."

Gillian looked at him. What did he mean? Was he asking her to re-marry him? She would in a second if he were really serious, and could accept her wanting a career, even if it was being a gumshoe.

The silence made Mitch say, "I know, I know . . . I'd have to do all the changing to be acceptable to you."

"I need to change, too." She thought a second. "In my orphanage, acceptance was the path to 'love' which was always conditional."

He checked the refrigerator for other bottles of champagne. "I know there was no love in your growing up years. But I loved you."

"Past tense?"

"Do you need to ask?"

"You know, Chase told me that he and Leslie were also raised in an orphanage—actually, by an organization."

"An organization?"

"I know little about it except that it was run by the Sisters of Good Heart or something like that."

"Back thirty years ago or so—when Chase and Leslie would have been youngsters—the population of Sisters had greatly decreased, and orphanages, let alone 'organizations', were hardly in existence. It seems to me, Gil, that this Chase fellow is feeding you a line of bull. I don't trust him; I don't like him."

"Like you, I'm wary of the orphanage-organization story. I did attempt to research their backgrounds but amazingly nothing turned up on either."

"What's amazing about it? People change identities all the time without leaving a trace. I know," Mitch put his hand up in a halting position, "you're going to say as a detective you should be able to find leads as to whom they are, but let me tell you something, if someone wants to abandon a former identity and take on a new one, it can be done, and without a trace." He paused. "This is especially true for people who are in government witness cases. To protect them, the government erases all their records so that only the new identity is in existence."

"I thought they faked the person's death."

"That, too. Hey, maybe you ought to be checking death records."

"I did do that, Mitch, and there's nothing. Since I don't know if there was a pre-existing identity before the Chase-Leslie personalities, I wouldn't know what names to check in death—or any—records. No, I think you might be right that whatever records they had, someone, somehow, got them erased."

The doorbell rang.

Mitch quickly said, "They're here. I have no problem with Dixie, Wally, and Cy coming to New Year's dinner, but Chase and Leslie are another thing. Why did you invite them?" He left to answer the door.

11:30 p.m.; D.C.

President Williams pulled on his tux's tie to loosen it. Then turning to the Premier, he said, "Soon we'll mark a new year here, and a new beginning."

"Yes, **my** beginning. Your job is to make sure everything's in place."

Williams watched the White House servants pour champagne in the glasses of guests who filled the ballroom—celebrities of all types, from movie stars to literary giants to political bigwigs, all dressed formally and eating richly.

Vice President Bert Greenman walked across the ballroom floor towards them, his wife on his arm.

"Here comes your sidekick, Jackson," said Cinzan. "It's pitiful that such a good looking woman as she, is connected with such a power-hungry monger as he."

"Mister Premier," said Greenman's wife, bussing Cinzan on the cheek.

He graciously nodded at her. "Madam. May I have this dance?"

Elegantly they stepped out onto the dance floor to the sounds of big band tunes.

Left standing with Williams, Greenman said, "So how's our future dictator extraordinaire?" He sipped his martini. "Think he'll have a spot for you in his Cabinet?"

Williams smiled at a guest passing by. "What about you?"

"He's already promised me a position." Greenman stirred his drink with his swizzle stick. "I'm not sure I trust him."

"Funny thing, Bert. He feels the same way about you."

Greenman's eyebrows raised and he left to retrieve his wife.

Seconds later, Cinzan returned to Williams' side, this time escorting the First Lady, while saying as he unhooked her hand around his arm, "I wouldn't mind being married just for the companionship . . . like you." A sneer crossed his face as he turned to talk to Harry Gamblin.

The President and the First Lady exchanged glances. He scoffed, "I told you to keep your sexual preferences secret. You're an embarrassment."

"Well, Jack, I'm sure it won't be long before the press gets word of your AIDS. With that, you won't have to worry about being snubbed by Cinzan in the future; you won't even be here." She picked up the hem of her gown and pranced away, calling over her shoulder, "Happy new year, darling."

Midnight; Wilmington

On television, they watched the ball drop at Times Square. Simultaneously they blew their cardboard horns, and hugged one another, wishing each a happy new year. When Gillian walked up to Mitch, he passionately kissed her, with Chase looking on.

"My turn," said Chase, walking over to Gillian.

Mitch nudged him aside. "You have to have been married to her first."

"If I were, I would still be her husband."

Gillian looked at them both, rolled her eyes, walked over to Dixie, saying, "They're like babies."

Dixie finished her last drop of champagne. "I told you not to invite Chase and Leslie, but you wouldn't listen."

"I thought you were friends with them."

"I've said a thousand times to stay away from them, that I only met them that one time when they gave me a ride here for Cy's grand opening. Look, Gil, just stay away from them. They look like trouble to me."

Gillian stared at Dixie. "You seem pretty sure about that."

"Just a feeling, that's all. The less you know about them, the better."

"How about more champagne?" Wally interrupted Gillian and Dixie.

"You sure you're old enough to drink, kid?" Gillian reached for the bottle on the end table. "With that acne, you look like a teeny bopper."

"What would an old maid like you know?" He winked at her.

She enjoyed sharing barbs with Wally, making Cy howl with laughter.

"We have to go," Chase said, approaching Gillian, with his sister at his side. "I'm sorry for my bad manners; I guess I was a little jealous."

Gillian shook his hand first, and then Leslie's, noticing how rough it seemed. She wanted to steer Leslie to a good doctor to help her, but Leslie seldom spoke. Instead, she usually let her brother do all the talking. Once, when Gillian tried prying into Leslie's job, Chase answered for her, saying she was currently unemployed. Gillian's task became one of trying to get Leslie alone to talk to her.

Gilly watched the pair, thinking it was going to be one interesting new year.

Chapter
8

Mitchell Frey studied all the real estate reports and property plats laid out before him at the deeds office. Nowhere could he find any record of the surveyed property he had sold to Dr. Hammond several years ago—the property where Hammond had built an "invisible" lab. Nor could he find the plat site of the property where Hammond had wanted to expand the so-called existing lab.

Mitch rubbed his eyes, looked harder to discern the tiny type and numbers on the plat. Still he couldn't see where any buildings had been placed; surely the town of Easton would have a record of that, especially through inspections and zoning, and other agencies. Well, he thought, the government agency behind those labs certainly had power.

He said to the deeds clerk, "I'm the real estate agent who sold the northerly branch of the Gwen Estate where the client had said he was going to build some kind of research labs. Yet, I don't see any buildings on the land. Could you check the zoning applications?"

She rose from her desk chair and walked over to the counter where he stood on the other side. Pulling the plat to her, she slid it around so she could read it, copied down numbers. "Let me look it up." She went to a file cabinet and yanked out drawers.

He watched. In his mind, something wasn't right. He noticed how quizzically she looked at the folder in the file cabinet, then walked back to her desk where she hit a couple of keys on her computer, studied the screen, and said, "I'm sorry but the records on that piece of property seem to have been misplaced."

"Misplaced?" He knew then that if he sold the additional property to Hammond that, that, too, would somehow end up "lost." He pushed his hair back from his face. "Could you get Salyer Basse for me, please? He's worked in this office for the last ten, eleven years."

"He resigned a few weeks ago, saying retirement would give him some much needed free time."

"Retirement? The man's only forty-two years old!"

Chevy Chase, Maryland

For the third time over many months, the couple sat in the examining room with Meg stripped and lying on the table wearing a thin, papery gown. Her husband Ben looked bored and frustrated as he sat in a chair near the head of the examining table. As the minutes slipped by, Meg closed her eyes, recalling the day Dr. Byers had first told them about this procedure she was waiting to undergo yet again.

It had started last December, barely over a year ago. She and Ben had tried for years to conceive but with no success. They finally sought out a fertility specialist where they underwent many tests and procedures to determine their problem. Finally an answer came that one cold, wintry day nearly a year ago. She remembered it well, how nonchalantly Dr. Byers had said "I'm sorry"—and then looked at the stack of papers in front of him—"the problem is with Ben's sperm. Quite simply, they're inadequate for fertilization."

Meg had felt Ben's hand grasp hers as if to say he was sorry, and then heard him say, "Is there nothing you can do, doctor?"

The gynecologist leaned back in his expensive leather chair, slipped a pen in his mouth and nibbled on it as if in thought. "There is one alternative."

Meg recalled how she and Ben scooted forward in anticipation, not wanting to miss any of the doctor's words. "Anything, anything," Meg had said, her voice barely above a whisper as she held back the tears.

She saw Dr. Byers lean his elbow on the desk and clasp his hands together. "Of course, there's artificial insemination." He looked at her husband. "Since your sperm are impotent, we'll implant another's sperm into your wife's eggs." He looked at Meg. "You can now choose the traits of your baby: Blue eyes, brown hair—"

"In vitro fertilization?" Meg heard Ben say as he glanced at her.

"I can pick the traits of my baby?" Meg wanted to make sure she understood.

The doctor nodded. "Then we fertilize the egg with a sperm carrying those dominant traits you list. Of course, sometimes the dominance of the ovum's traits take over and the baby looks more like the mother."

"Just a minute," Ben had interrupted. "You mean the father won't be me?"

Dr. Byers had explained, "If Meg selects genetic features that are similar to yours, with your sandy brown hair, brown eyes, dark skin, high forehead . . . then the baby might very well grow up to reflect both of you." He rose. "Think about it, but I have to tell you that we have a long list of would-be-parents waiting for this opportunity. I pick only those couples who are the best candidates. The precursor for this procedure is the taking of a couple of tests . . . nothing major, a physical, some scholastic assessment things, and—"

"Why?" Ben's voice rang with wariness.

The doctor had opened the door indicating he was in a hurry to leave. "It's standard. You wouldn't want to select genes that would direct your child to be inferior any more than we would want to have parents contribute such traits." The doctor looked at Meg. "You do know this procedure is, well, costly."

"How much?" asked Ben.

"Thousands," Byers said softly.

Meg gasped; Ben shook his head.

After a long silence, Byers offered, "there is a way—"

Meg remembered how she would have agreed to anything that day.

"If you're willing to donate some of your eggs, and," here he looked at Ben, "some of your sperm, and deliver the baby in our fertility/delivery clinic, in our special birthing rooms, I'll call it a wash."

The couple looked at each other. Ben asked, "but what about complications?"

"Our birthing center is equipped with expert nurses, physician assistants, nurse practitioners, and myself. It's even set up for in-patient care, if need be. Plus, I'll make sure you're not billed for the procedure. But you must understand that pregnancy doesn't often happen on the first try. It'll likely take several attempts."

"What will you do with the . . . our eggs and sperm, especially since my sperm are impotent?"

"We'll pull out the DNA from your sperm and store it. Meg's ova can help other women who don't create viable eggs. Science today is very advanced in this area." Dr. Byers waited but when neither jumped at the opportunity, he quickly added, "There is no other way for you two to conceive. No other fertility lab will give you the deal I just offered. But you must keep this on the q.t. because if other couples hear about it, they'll want a free ride, too." He grabbed the door knob.

"Giving up a part of us, a part that could make other humans, isn't what I call a free ride, Doc," Ben said.

Meg recalled hearing Byers mutter under his breath only loud enough for her to hear, "You ungrateful S.O.B.", then said in a normal tone, "what I'm offering you gratis will cost you thousands and thousands of dollars elsewhere, assuming that other fertility clinics are as advanced as we are." He reached for the door.

Meg remembered thinking that he was just going to walk out of their lives because they hadn't agreed, and any possible chance of their having a baby would be vanquished as soon as he left the room. She had given Ben a look which Byers must have picked up on because he had remianed at the door, adding, "The procedure is simple. We combine Meg's ova with viable sperm, injecting the traits you desire your child to have. And, we store your sperm, Ben, to keep the nucleic acids—RNA and DNA—operative."

Meg had looked at Ben who shrugged and said, "All right, we'll do it."

"Fine," said Dr. Byers, using a sweep of his hand to usher them out the door and down the hall to a lab, while adding, "this is my Christmas gift to you."

That was last Christmas; it must have been a few months later—around March— when Byers had told her she was pregnant. She and Ben were ecstatic and began planning for their baby's future, only for their bliss to turn to devastation when the baby had arrived so prematurely that Dr. Byers had to deliver their son without even letting them see him. She had cried so hard that Byers repeatedly assured her that she was healthy and could try again as soon as she was psychologically ready. The emotional and psychological readiness had taken time to return, but when she and Ben finally felt confident enough to try again, they had made another appointment with Byers.

And now here they sat, again in his examining room—a year behind them—and waited for Byers to enter, knowing what she and Ben had to go through. "This is ridiculous," she told herself. "This time, I'll just tell Byers that if I don't get pregnant within the first few months, the heck with it."

The door clicked open and the second Byers stepped ino the exam room was the same second she gushed, "Oh, Dr. Byers, thanks so much for not giving up on us. If it takes ten years before I become pregnant, I'll do it!"

Byers smiled, a gesture which did not quite reach his eyes, and said "I don't think it will take that long, my dear." He got right to work, and inserted an instrument into Meg's vagina while saying to Ben, "You made your deposit today?" What Byers dragged out of her cervix, he touched to a vial that the nurse held open for him.

"How many times am I going to have to give my sperm before I've paid my debt?"

The doctor looked over at Ben. "As many times as I tell you, young man." He took the other vial from his nurse's hand and with a different instrument, placed its contents inside Meg's vagina.

Ben groused, "I hate doing it."

"Too damn bad." Dr. Byers stood, patted Meg on her knee. "I'll keep my fingers crossed that the next time you call you'll be telling me that you haven't had your period yet." He exited, leaving Meg to dress. Ben stood fuming.

****

The nurse followed Byers out. "You have Mr. and Mrs. Banner in room two. I'll be in as soon as I take this to our lab."

"Mark it for Enolc 1. Meg and snotty Ben are good specimens. By the way, how much did the government pay us last month?"

"Ten-thousand"

"We're down from the month before."

"Well, you've been telling me to keep for our own needs nearly all the eggs and sperm we've been collecting. Theirs," she beckoned with her head toward the room where Meg and Ben were, "is the first this month you said to ship to Enolc 1."

"Remind me to collect more. We need the money. By the way, I didn't check the vial contents you handed me to implant into Meg. It was 't-natum', wasn't it?"

"'T-natum-Wen', the new and improved version."

"Hmmph. I hope so, for their sake." He went to the next examining room to see patients, thinking that he might ask Hammond to increase payment.

3:00 p.m.; Worcester, Massachusetts

Hilda stood on a step-stool, washing the back windows of her bungalow, hating the tiny grids inserted into each window because it took so much time to snap them out, wash the window, and then snap them back in. The brisk winter air enervated her, and washing windows in the winter served as a metaphor for her life: Getting rid of last year's grime and starting with a fresh, clear view. But never again would she buy windows with built-in grids, and, hopefully, never again would she build a home, as she and her ex-husband had done ten years ago. She remembered the divorce had happened suddenly.

What was that? She turned her head in the direction she thought she saw a shadow. It looked like the blurred form had come from inside her house. Maybe it was just the glare from the clean windows.

She recalled it been a painful severance; he had left her for his secretary. When Hilda and her ex had bought the bungalow, they had decided to use it as a starter home, then get something larger when the kids came. But then she had learned she couldn't have children. She cried, tried every kosher and unorthodox method she came across. Finally, her doctor had sent her and her husband to a Boston fertility expert who had just opened shop.

A noise! She was sure she heard something. She stood absolutely still, waiting for another sound. Chill out, she told herself. It's a perfectly nice day, sun's out, warm.

The Boston fertility specialist—a Dr. Thatcher— she remembered, had seemed a bit dazed the entire time he had worked with them. She knew it was because he was new at it. She did get pregnant eight years ago, and was sick every single morning while carrying the child. Then the doctor had said her tests indicated an abnormal nine-month fetus that would most likely die at delivery. It did. When she asked to see the fully formed but abnormal baby, they refused. Five months later, her husband left her.

She did see something inside the house! Could someone have gotten into her home? Came through the front door while she was in the back? Hadn't she locked the front door? She stepped off the ladder and went to check the patio door. The second she slid it open was the same second she heard a noise in the adjacent room. She froze. Did the breeze from opening the patio door knock something off the buffet, or was someone really in there? She was so scared she was certain she had quit breathing. Her mind reeled in fast forward, trying to determine if she should grab a knife out of a kitchen drawer, or turn and run back outside. She decided to softly step through the patio doors to the outside, and speed to a neighbor's house where she'd call the police.

Her foot poised to pivot, she gingerly touched her fingers to the slider's frame and ever so quietly applied force to slide it open along the track.

Out of nowhere, a form charged from the dining room, stormed at Hilda, tackling her. She went down hard on the kitchen floor, her head smacking the edge of the breakfast table. He squatted his husky body on her chest and began pummelling her face with heavy blows that shattered her left jaw, preventing her from opening her mouth to scream.

In between his blows—her eyes closed to protect her vision—she tried pulling his ski mask off his face. If she lived, she wanted to remember his every feature to make sure it was eternally seen only from behind bars. His pulverizing fists warded off her outstretched fingers at his face.

She neared unconsciousness when she managed to get the tip of her nails under the mask's cloth. With one last moment of sensibility, she yanked off the disguise and, instantly, horror filled her. The mask was a gift. The bulging eye, partial nose, split mouth, and lack of chin made him the ugliest creature she had seen. Those tumor-like weals all over his face repulsed her so much, she could feel the bile rising inside her.

They stared at one another for a minute.

Suddenly he lurched forward, bit her cheek with his long, canine-like teeth, then perforated her skull.

Easton

With his good arm, Dr. Hammond removed the phone's mouth piece from its cradle. Hitting a programmed button, he waited for someone to pick up at the other end in Chevy Chase; then, wedging the mouth piece between his chin and cheek, he touched his hand to the limp arm at his side.

"This is Hammond at Enolc 1. Put Byers on, and tell him not to make me wait." The very small act of patting his bad arm with his good one caused excruciating pain. He remembered how he had barely made it underground to his lab where one of the physicians on staff patched him up while saying, "Look, you ought to be in the hospital on antibiotics to prevent infection." Hammond had waved him off, pulling rank by insisting that no record of the event be filed anywhere inside or outside the clinic.

A voice came to the phone. "Hello, Dr. Hammond? I'm sorry to keep you on hold but Dr. Byers is right in the middle of a procedure and—"

"You tell that idiot that I don't care about his procedure and to get his rear to the phone now!"

When Hammond had left the lab the day he had been attacked while surveying the ground with Mitchell Frey, he had remained up and hurting all night and the next morning, even with the pain pills he had been on. Now, here, eight days later, his arm was still tender and useless. Hammond knew that wasn't a good sign. He suspected an infection, especially with the red streaks striating from the wound.

"Don't ever talk to my staff like that again," were the first words out of Byers' mouth when he finally came to the phone.

"You're not in any position to tell me what to do! If it wasn't for my office, your practice would be kaput." Hammond winced in pain. If he'd stay calm, he wouldn't hurt so much. He could hear Byers taking deep breaths. "I'm waiting for another shipment."

"It's on its way. You'll be pleased with vials marked Miles ten-ninety-two. Excellent specimens. Ben Miles is an MBA, and Meg's an elementary teacher; both health freaks. Wonderful bodies and minds. His sperm are impotent but his DNA and RNA might come in handy; her nucleic acids and ova are very viable."

"Miles, huh? Well, I haven't been pleased in the past. Look where your other specimens have put us."

"The error's from your lab, not mine, and the problems aren't limited to Enolc 1; labs and clinics all over the country that were modeled after yours are showing the same kind of problems. In some cases, even worse ones."

"It's the specimens we're getting from clinics like yours, but in the end, Gamblin will put me on the hot seat, even though I'm only in charge of Enolc 1."

"But yours has served as the prototype for all the others. Why don't you quit and come work for me, providing you can still get me money?"

"Now why would I want to work for a two-bit quack!"

Wilmington

Mitch stood when Gilly entered the restaurant. "Hey," he said softly, pulling out her chair. "How's the detective business?"

She looked at him, liking the smell of his new after-shave, relishing his aristocratic nose, loving his smooth, patrician face, pointed cleft chin. "This better be good, Mitchell Frey."

They sat at the table. "Salyer should be here any minute. The info he can provide will be of help to you in your hunt for the killers of Dixie's sister-in-law, as well as what you call 'the flashing eyes men.'"

"So, you do believe me, and you do think there's some kind of connection between my search and your real estate business client who was attacked?"

"I think there are some unusual things going on but I wouldn't go so far as to say there's a connection between anything." He looked thoughtful for a minute. "The two giants with flashing eyes that you saw, the big man I saw attacking Dr. Hammond I told you about, and there being no record of the property I sold to the government, as well as Salyer's retiring—all seem strange."

"Don't forget Leslie and Chase."

"They're weird, too, but I don't think they have anything to do with what you and I have seen."

"Maybe we should notify the police or the mayor or—"

"What mayor, Gil? Did you forget that last year the city went the route of replacing administrators with computers. Interested citizens go to town meetings and voice their opinions and vote on what they want. The computer director—who now essentially runs the city—feeds in the votes against the city budget and up comes an answer, whether it deals with roads, public zoo, city infrastructure, or whatever. Ironically, it's worked so far. Wilmington has saved a ton of money by not having to payroll personnel, but it does seem inhuman."

"It is," carped Gillian. "As inhuman as those goons I've seen."

Salyer Basse entered and strode over to the table.

"Hi, guys. Long time no see." He shook his old friend's hand and pecked Gillian on the cheek. "I thought the marriage was dead, and here you two are again."

"Mitch and I are just old friends conversing." Gilly looked at Mitch.

They ordered their meals and drinks, chatted about old times, how they often had doubled—with Sal always asking the least attractive woman out—and the things they had done together: Theater, bowling, miniature golf, sailing, camping, billiards. They talked about Gilly's job, how the city was becoming unsafe to live in, how society as a whole was growing more aggressive and frightening with each passing day.

When the waitress set down coffee cups, Mitch began, "Sal, I asked Gilly here because you may have info that could greatly help her." He sipped his coffee. "The other day, I went to county records to look up a piece of real estate my clients had me sell to the government through its agent—Dr. Hammond—who had returned to buy more property to expand his operation. When I had met him near the original plot I originally had sold him, I saw there were no structures which made me wonder why he needed to extend his operation." Mitch dabbed his mouth with the cloth napkin, noticing Salyer moving uneasily in his chair. "While standing and talking with Hammond, a huge form suddenly attacked him. Hammond refused medical care, saying he'd get it at his clinic. I followed him but where he stopped his car had no structures, either. He and his secretary must have known I was behind them because neither got out of the car, so I left. But since Hammond was so elusive about the missing buildings, I tried researching building and zoning records but the clerk said no records existed on it. She seemed nervous about the whole thing." Mitch looked at Gillian eyeing Salyer. "I was just as surprised to learn that you retired."

Salyer pursed his lips. "I needed a change. I don't know anything about plats, the government and research labs, and expansion of those labs, or—"

"I didn't say they were research labs, Sal. How did you know that?"

Salyer's gaze went from Mitch to Gillian. "Just a guess."

"You've worked in the deeds office for over a decade, recorded my first transaction with Dr. Hammond, so don't feign ignorance, pal."

"Can't help," he mumbled.

"Come on, Salyer. This is me, Mitch, your old friend. Don't try to put me off!"

"Mitchell." Gillian's voice was soft but stern.

"I don't care, Gil. Salyer's treating us like we're stupid. I know he knows what's going down." Looking at Salyer, he said bitterly, "If you can't tell me, say so, but don't pretend that nothing's going on!"

Salyer stood, scraping back his chair. "I'll pay for my coffee on the way out."

"Wait!" Mitch grabbed his arm. Leaning in closer to his friend, he asked lowly, "Sal, what's going on? Are you all right?"

Gilly watched Salyer take in a quick glance of the restaurant, shifting his eyes from one table to the next. Then in a hushed tone, he warned, "Stay out of it, for your own good." He stomped out.

Chicago

Carol Givens screamed so loud, Dr. Sorian thought she had broken his eardrums. Carol's hubby, Charlie, stood at her side, gowned and masked, squeezing her hand, thinking that he should have forced his wife to deliver in an accredited hospital in downtown Chicago instead of at this tiny clinic in the outskirts of Waukeegan. But, "Oh no," she had said, it had to be at the clinic because that was part of the deal the fertility doctor made with them.

At her spread-opened legs stood Dr. Sorian feverishly working to deliver the breech baby. "Push, Carol, push."

Charlie stretched to see what Dr. Sorian was doing. "What's wrong?"

The nurses assisting the delivery elbowed Charlie back.

A loud groan, and out plopped the infant. Sorian grunted, looked at his assistants. A slap resounded but no cry.

"My baby!" Carol screamed, trying to rise from the

examining table.

Among all the hub-bub surrounding the silent child and the screeching mother, Charlie managed to sneak around the table to looked at the baby. "My God! What's wrong with it!"

Sorian hurriedly covered the infant by pulling its face close to his chest. "Get this man out of here," he growled.

Instantly two assistants bulldozed Charlie from the room.

"What's wrong with my baby? Let me see his face!" wailed Carol.

Sorian said, "I'm sorry, Carol. You'll just have to try again." She sobbed so noisily that he had to whisper loudly into his nurse's ear, "Take the baby. Call Chicago's Enolc director; tell him to get someone to pick up the infant; it's another T-natum."

Wilmington

Chase made a fist he pumped in air. "Yes! A strike!" He turned to the trio watching him in the large bowling alley. "Who's the best bowler?"

"What a bore," his sibling Leslie mouthed.

Gilly glanced at her and Leslie smiled. Turning to Dixie, Gilly whispered, "Just my luck—a woman who's falling in love with me!"

"She has a nice mustache." Dixie giggled.

"Hush, she'll hear you! Here comes Chase."

Coming up to them, Chase boasted, "How many strikes does that make for me?"

"That was your ninth. None of us have a chance against you." Gilly looked at the computerized score. "This has to be a record."

"I'm as strong as he," Leslie said.

Everyone turned to her.

Gilly saw the dirty look Chase gave his sister while

saying, "You're a mere female."

She watched the exchange between the two, listening to them berate each other. Then, in one fluid motion, Chase struck a light blow across Leslie's face, his eyes going steel gray, then bright, his lips curled.

"Play time's over," he snarled, grabbing Gilly by her arm and forcefully escorting her to the outside, with Leslie and Dixie following.

"Ow! You're hurting me, Chase." Gillian pulled away.

Chase released her.

Coming up from behind, Dixie whispered to Gilly, "I told you to stay away from him. He has a brutal side to him. With his strength, I'd be afraid of him." Dixie whispered even lower, "I'm sorry I ever brought him to your house, and I can see I'll regret it for a long time. Just keep your distance."

Thursday, January 3; 1:30 a.m.; Washington, D.C.

In the dark of night, the vice president stood at a window in Blair House on a portable phone to Marcus Cinzan, saying, "They're unloading the tanks now."

Cinzan answered gruffly, "Remind Williams that we leaders have the private supplies. If your people do it right, the Atlantic Ocean will be affected enough that I won't have to send my guys out. My advisors say that if the ocean's tributaries are contaminated, the ocean itself will eventually be infected. It's simple science. Make sure you and the others have your fresh water sources preserved and available when this project gets going."

The vice president walked away from the window, the portable phone still attached to his ear. "I hope the boys supervising this project know what they're doing, that they make sure we don't die with the rest."

"An ugly death at that. It's all been planned out. We here in the European Community are in as much danger as you are, Greenman, but the edict has come down to cut the population, and so we must. It's just too bad we couldn't limit our target to our enemies."

"All I know is that Williams and I are doing as you directed. He's implementing NAR, and soon he'll come out with the bill to eliminate the churches."

Cinzan chuckled. "Now there's irony, don't you think, that you—the symbolic environmentalist—are directing the very contamination of the water."

"That environmental stuff is what you and your people told me to promote. It looks good for the president, too. I only do what you order, Mr. Premier."

"And I give you orders based on the committee's decision."

"Right . . . a committee made of your hand-picked, ten most powerful men in the world."

"You don't have to worry about serving on it."

Chapter
9

Old Mark Daniels liked early mornings, though rising at dawn to milk cows and start farm chores in the bitter weather of Amish country was making him consider retirement. The morn's darkness broke to let sun beams dance to a winter song, but not enough light entered for him to see through the barn's dimness. "Hey, Millie," he called lowly to his prized cow while tightening his black coat and pulling his brimmed black hat down over his ears. "Let's go; it's cold, girl." He sat on the stool, placed the bucket underneath the cow, but she yielded nothing. He looked under the mammal's belly. Millie only refused giving milk when she was sick or spooked. He looked around, saw nothing out of order.

Suddenly a noise. He turned. Aaah, a shovel hanging on the wall had dropped to the ground. He thought about how easily one could get unnerved being alone in the dark. "C'mon, Millie. Give a little. You're be'en stubborn this morn." He pulled harder on each nipple but only drops of milk dribbled out.

Again he looked under the bovine's belly, his body bent at the waist, his head cocked at an angle to see if his old cow was sick.

A crunching noise, like heavy shoes crushing straw on the barn floor, made him turn. His eyes shifted to the right to see mammoth-sized boots standing next to him—boots so large that Mark Daniels figured the form standing in them had to tower seven-feet. Just as he started to slip his upper torso out from the underside of the animal, he heard a SWISSH, and felt a pain so intense that his brain couldn't synapse to open his mouth in a scream.

The massive figure reached down with one long enormous hand, picked up Mark Daniel's head with its mouth still opened in shock, and put its lips to the gushing blood from the head's stem, and began sucking.

10:00 a.m.; Washington, D.C.

Gamblin sat at his desk, his hands cupping his head. Things were rapidly falling apart. He wanted to leave his position but knew the second he did, he would be a marked man. Williams and Greenman would have their brutes on him. He removed his hands from his face and again read the brief article:

(API MA) A Worcester woman, 49-year-old Hilda Dillon, was brutally attacked and viciously mauled yesterday in a house break-in. Police discovered a ski mask in the corner of the room and have taken it in for analysis. No motivation was given for the act.

"Cripes," whined Gamblin. "Where the hell are the checks and balances in this project? Not long ago it was that woman who left the mall, then Hammond who was attacked by his big ape who went wild; then there was

Zakowicz, and all those other reports. Now it's a maniac ripping into middle-aged women." He picked up the phone and dialed the Worcester Enolc lab, ordering, "Put Dr. Thatcher on; this is Secretary Gamblin."

Seconds later, Thatcher said, "Sorry to make you wait, Mr. Secretary. I have a good guess why you're calling."

"Do you have any idea how much damage you've caused, how much you've breached governmental security by letting your freaks lose?" Gamblin didn't wait for an answer. "And don't try telling me that it wasn't your lab!"

"No, sir, I won't say that. Any one of our mutants—even violently strong eight-year-olds—have the power to mutilate the victim, tear right through her ligaments and nerves with its bare hands and teeth. Protocol was violated somehow, as we found the specimen not caged and not in the sanitarium anywhere, so we suspected it had escaped. But we're—"

"What happens when the police capture this . . . this monster and the whole world finds out what we're doing? Jeesh, Thatcher! You really screwed up!"

"What about all those giants running free in society that are capable of mentally snapping at any given time, attacking citizens, sucking out their brains?"

"Worry about your own project and find that ghoul!"

Early Thursday Afternoon;
Salisbury, Maryland

Mitch shifted his stance, hoping that Salyer hadn't changed his mind. Having to beg his old friend to meet with him—even if for only briefly—was beneath Mitch but he would have done anything to get Sal to talk, especially after Sal had just upped and left the restaurant yesterday. Salyer agreed to meet in a safe, public spot where enough people would serve as shields for him, so Mitch chose the men's section in Salisbury's Boscov's department store. They had decided to drive separately to the small hub of the Eastern Shore from Wilmington to make Salyer feel safe that the two-plus hour drive would likely deter someone from following him. Mitch had commented to him on the phone, "Gosh, Sal, you sound paranoid."

Mitch's eyes scanned his surroundings, taking in displays of brown shoes, colorful ties, Hanes briefs and t-shirts, all the while wondering what he and his beautiful Gilly had innocently gotten themselves into.

"Make it quick," said a voice behind him who was pretentiously fingering polo shirts. The dark sunglasses below a straw, wide-brimmed hat did more to call attention to Salyer than to conceal him. His face bared an unkempt beard from negligence rather than style, while his overgrown mustache nearly covered his entire mouth.

Mitch smiled. "Sal? You look like a nineteen-seventies Mexican peon."

"Ssshh!" He put his finger to his mouth. "Don't say my name. I think I'm being followed." He looked suspiciously around. "Get on with it. I don't want to be here; I only came because of our friendship."

"How are we going to talk like this . . . over a bin of polo shirts and your constantly yelling 'quiet!'?"

Sal beckoned with his head for Mitch to follow him upstairs to the store's men's room.

"Look, I need to ask a few things." Mitch stopped when Sal tip-toed over to the single stall to make sure no one was in the bathroom. When he returned to where Mitch was standing, Mitch asked, "What happened at your job?"

"I was released. The upper echelon didn't appreciate my being privy to so much info." Salyer's eyes scanned the austere tiled bathroom with the single black-door stall, and various urinals flush against the wall.

"How did you get cozy with the government?"

"I was promoted to a high-level liaison position among the local, state and federal governments. So I knew a lot of stuff that was going down. Let me tell you, friend, it's scary. Then, out of nowhere, my supervisor said I was being released and never to divulge—"

He stopped when in walked a peculiar-looking man with his eyes timidly lowered to the floor. He couldn't have been any taller than five-feet and was painfully thin, and yet carried a heavy-looking Samonsite suitcase. Dressed in an old style powder blue leisure suit with a black top hat, he looked like something out of a James Thurber book. Without even a glance at either Mitch or Salyer, the little man went into the stall, shutting the door.

Sal tried to keep his voice down. "All I'm saying, man, is to stay out of it."

"It? It, what?"

"Everything connected with whatever you think is going on." He looked around the bathroom again.

"What about the land in Easton—Gwen Estates? Where are the structures?"

"Underground . . . research and medical-scientific labs."

"Why underground?"

"They're making life."

Mitch felt his heart leap. "What kind of life? How?"

"All kinds of life: One-celled, multi-celled, viruses, bacteria, primates—"

"Primates!"

"Enolc 1—is the world's prototype. They've made a lot of mistakes in the process." Sal turned when he heard a toilet flush.

The little man exited the stall, washed his hands, then left the bathroom.

Salyer watched him. "Look, I've got the jitters here. Let's call it quits."

Mitch grasped his arm. "What kind of mistakes?"

"Some of the experiments have resulted in mutant forms."

"Like rats with three tails?"

"Worse."

"Humans, right?" Mitch stared.

"I'm out of here." Salyer started to leave.

"And Hammond?"

Salyer sighed. "He's in charge of Enolc 1; there are directors for each lab. I don't know much about the others."

"Where exactly is the lab on Gwen Estates?"

Salyer glared. "Don't go and do something stupid, Mitchell."

"Look, we've been friends for decades. You can trust me."

"If I didn't, I wouldn't be here now, risking my life."

"What are you afraid of? Who's going to hurt you?"

"Who do you think?" He nervously shifted his stance. "Don't trust the government. They'll go to any length to do what they believe has to be done."

"Those huge fellows with flashing eyes that Gilly and I have seen?"

"It started with Enolc 1 but quickly went awry. The first generation is what's out there now and assimilated into society. The mistake or genetic fluke that happened with them has been found in many of the progeny of that generation in all the labs. There are a few that seem to be okay, but who knows."

"What is this fluke?"

Salyer raised his eyebrows. "They just go berserk." He snapped his fingers for emphasis. "Everything's hush-hush. What information I have comes from the grapevine."

"How do I get to the underground lab on the Gwen grounds?"

"I gotta go, pal. I'm really getting unglued here." He said in a whisper, "A copy of the plat is in my apartment in the fireplace hearth. Enolc 1 is marked on the plat. If you decide to go to my apartment, let me know first so I can leave."

Mitch noticed Salyer's hands visibly trembled. "Any info you can give me will help stop these people from the evil they're doing."

"Yeah, sure, like the government can be stopped. Stay out of it, Mitch, for your own good, and Gilly's too."

Mitch studied Sal's eyes, and instantly he felt a deep passion for his very frightened old friend.

"We can't walk out together. You go first. I really wouldn't want anyone to connect you to me."

"Thanks." Mitch shook his friend's hand. "I appreciate it. Maybe we can get together some time . . . socially, I mean."

"You're better off staying away from me and anyone associated with this insanity."

Mitch stared at his overwrought friend, nodded his thanks again, and left the men's bathroom, leaving Salyer to stare after him.

At the south exit of Boscov's, Mitch heard a roar and a WOOOOSH, felt the hardwood rumble. He saw kids knocked to the floor, packages fly out of shoppers's hands. Smoke seeped through the air, and Mitch instantly realized it was a bomb. He spun around, detected amid the ruins behind him, flames shooting upward. Pushing against the stampeding crowd exiting the store, Mitch dashed for the men's room.

Mid-Afternoon, Thursday;
Wilmington

Gilly and Cy stood glued in Cy's office near a radio screaming *BULLETIN BULLETIN.* Cy turned up the volume as Annie and his nephew Wally hustled inside, an expressions of puzzlement plastered across their faces.

"Ssshh," Cy ordered when Wally opened his mouth to say something.

"Dimethyl mercury," the President of the United States went on, "is a very lethal poison that causes carcinogenic fatalities within a short period. A mere microscopic drop would transmute the body's cells within weeks. Those living throughout the western and eastern shores of Maryland and Virginia, all of Delaware, and the Susquehanna basin, as well as the Carolinas, New England, and all their numerous tributaries, are advised not to drink the water. Boiling has no effect; the water will remain lethal. Because of this crisis, I am forced to enact Executive Orders 10997, 10998, and 11001. If we cannot find a solution for this very serious disaster, I will also have to enforce Executive Orders 11000, 11002, and 11004 which will allow me to relocate non-U.S. citizens in order to provide more supplies and food for our own people. Should panic, hysteria, riots, looting and other types of anarchy and chaos erupt, I will then enact Executive Orders 10995, 10999, 11003, and 11005. Do not be mistaken in thinking that I will not take such severe action in order—"

"Good lord," Cy whistled.

Gilly looked at him. "What's he talking about?"

"The abolishment of our rights, especially the First, Second, Fourth, Fifth and Tenth Amendments." Cy shook his head disbelievingly. "Having worked security for the government many years ago, I know that Executive Order 10995 empowers the government to take control of all communications; 10997 gives the President the authority to control all fuels and minerals, while 10998 permits him to command all food. Orders 10999, 11003 and 11005 commission the government to seize every form of transportation, including privately owned vehicles. His reference to what he called 'relocating' people means about the same thing as when our government interred the Japanese during World War II. He could do that with the disabled, the infirmed—"

"What about people on Green Cards, and—" Annie asked.

"Anyone he darn well wants."

"My God!" Gillian stood frozen. "And 11001?"

"That empowers him to seize all health and educational facilities."

Stunned, she stuttered, "B-but how? Doesn't Congress have to approve such—"

"Not an Executive Order."

"How can Williams get away with this?" She noticed the expression on Annie's face mirrored her own outrage and shock.

Cy puffed on a cigar. "Gilly, grow up. The way our government and the One-World-Society in-the-making is manipulating us, anything can be done. No one groused back in the early-Nineties when Bush allowed UN operations to use U.S. troops. That was accomplished via a Presidential Decision Directive called PD225, which is like an Executive Order. Look, Executive Orders have been written and implemented since the 1940s, but those were pretty innocuous back then. However, in the last twenty years, presidents have been creating EOs that are eliminating our constitutional rights and giving them dictatorial powers. As long as the President or the Premier proclaim the state of affairs, an emergency—whether real or contrived—nothing can be done to stop these power mongers."

The room went stark quiet.

It was Wally who finally broke the silence. "I don't believe the water's contaminated. It's a scare tactic."

Everyone looked at him.

The radio bulletin continued: "That was the President of the United States. A Special Report by Premier Cinzan may come in later. We'll keep you posted but currently, from the information we're receiving, it appears that the contamination seems to be limited to the Chesapeake Bay and Atlantic costal waters. The cause has yet to be determined. More on this breaking news as—"

Cy interrupted, "The Bay is near us and D.C., so it would affect the president, but likely he and his key people have a private supply of water."

Gilly nodded." The thing of this is that the Chesapeake Bay is not only a major tributary of the Susquehanna River but also of the Atlantic Ocean."

"We're doomed." Annie snapped her gum.

"Stop overreacting." Wally sighed.

Late Thursday Afternoon;
Easton

Hammond turned around from grabbing his lab coat off the clothes tree to find the figure standing at his office door. "Oh, it's you. At least you're not the other. I told my secretary not to let either of you in."

"My 'other'—a   result of your doing—is ruining me."

Hammond hit the intercom button. "Ms. Azar, send security."

The figure accused, "That's your answer to everything, isn't it? Just get rid of the problem—not deal with it."

"Look, I'm sorry the project went haywire. But be grateful. Your 'other'—who was one of the first progeny—isn't as menacing as what's out there now."

"That's supposed to make me feel better?" The form stepped near Hammond. "You don't call 'abusive' menacing?"

"I never knew 'evil' until they came along." Hammond looked off into space thoughtfully. "I don't know what happened. The original specimens' genes—yours and the few others like you—should have been identically transposed into—"

"But something didn't get transferred over, did it?"

"Maybe something **extra** did. Whatever, we have a real problem world-wide. Enolc 1 is the prototype lab internationally. We thought we had it right until we put them into the military—"

"And let them loose in public, getting them employed in public and government jobs."

"Our intent was good, you know that. You worked here as a research scientist. . . . You knew our goal had been to engineer genes to eliminate disorders, and diseases like cancer, CP, MS, AIDS, and to breed healthy, brilliant citizens of the future who could run a world that would have the best and brightest to fight off any enemy. We had every intention to create a futuristic world of only the healthiest, biggest, smartest, strongest and youngest. Look at the good we were doing by giving barren couples the opportunity to have children of their own . . . but then came the edict to create special breeds for the military. We've come so far. Now we even have the capabilities to chemically produce DNA—imagine artificial nucleic acids."

"You're using barren couples as unknowing donors, stealing their DNA from their sperm and eggs, and making the women receptacles for the hideous. Had I known you and your top brass were trying to create a military filled with vicious, amoral, callous fighting machines, I'd have left long before you used me. Now not only have you ruined me—my identity, career, personality, and my future—but soon you'll have destroyed the entire world. All because of the government's greediness, which you're a part of."

"I'm not to blame; I only take orders. You knew that the Illuminati, Bilderbergers, and all the others wanted a one world government, one world economy, a global religion. Enolc 1 was just the beginning. More is on the way. So don't condemn me for what's developed. Yes, You have losses but at least you still have your life." He tried slipping his lab coat over his bad arm; flashes of hot white pain zinged through him. "Feel proud that you were chosen for the experiment based on a number of criteria. You should have expected all along that when the government runs a project, something goes wrong and someone usually gets hurt. Live with it." He winced.

"Thanks to demons like you, this world's crumbling."

"We'll improve with continued practice."

"It's not man's place to do God's work."

Guards appeared at Hammond's door.

"Go before I have Security literally pick you up and throw you out." Hammond left the lab coat hang off the shoulder of his throbbing arm.

The form softly added, "You're going to lose your arm, Doc. It looks and smells gangrenous . . . just like the gangrene running through our government."

Washington, D.C.

On the White House lawn where a fancy table was set up aside a podium bearing the seal of the American eagle, the grayish-haired president, with the younger premiere, stood between the Israeli prime minister and the representatives from Palestine and the Middle East. The president watched as they signed on the line, then shook hands. Everyone around them applauded and sang shouts of "peace" and "shalom."

President Williams looked up at the overcast sky, hoping the storm held off until the event was finished. He worked too hard and waited too long for anything to mess this up. Glancing at the group behind the table where they sat signing papers, Williams said on cue, "Now I present Premiere Cinzan."

Everyone in the audience stood and applauded. The noted diplomat took a modest bow and went to the podium where he said in perfect English while looking at the former adversaries who had just signed the treaty, "Always the United Nations and our global world will stand behind your two wonderful countries against any attack. This is our pledge, this is our vow, this is our peace promise."

Williams looked over at his vice president; Greenman stood wildly nodding and breaking into another round of plaudits, a thin sneer on his lips.

"At last," responded the Israeli prime minister to Cinzan, in his broken accent, "A peace treaty has been signed with the blessings and protection of the two greatest entities in the world: America and the U.N., both soon to announce the New World Order." Williams grimaced, realizing America as an independent sovereign would soon be history.

In a congratulatory motion, President Williams slapped the two men on their backs, and turned both leaders towards the dozens of cameras where he mugged a broad smile while endlessly pumping their hands. "It has finally been done: the beginning of the end . . . of centuries of war, hatred, crime, hurt."

Flashes popped and more applause rang out.

"Yes, the beginning and the end; the alpha and the omega," Cinzan whispered to Williams while continuing to absently shake hands.

Philadelphia

Dixie and her colleagues watched the late afternoon televised peace accords from the lounge of her workplace. To Gordon, her fellow employee, she muttered, "What nonsense. I'll bet Israel and the PLO will be back to fighting within a week."

"All of this has been planned." Gordon turned to the others in the room.

"Meaning what?" Dixie looked at him. She liked his intelligence, his wit, and his skill as a the company's computer whiz.

"You don't think peace treaties like this just happen, do you? The government is orchestrating everything."

Grins and snickers resounded throughout the breakroom.

"You have plans tonight, after we get off work?" Gordon huffed as he got into step with Dixie.

"My friend Gillian's meeting me here so we can do dinner or something."

The crack of thunder echoed outside. "Not much you can do on a day like this. Sex seems old hat after working in a fertility clinic all day."

"Gillian is a girl, dummy."

"I know that," he laughed. Walking to their respective labs and offices, Gordon added, "Recently I've heard things about this lab that give me pause."

"We'll have to talk about that," she said under her breath. "Don't make waves right now; the work here pays well and keeps us fed, clothed and housed. Besides, if anyone here knows what's going on, it must be you, Gordie, since as the computer director you have access to all the files."

"Here all along I thought it was you who knew what was going on."

"Don't stir up trouble, Gordie." She entered her lab

station tucked in a back corner, thunder crashing over head.

The second she stepped into her office, she was met by her boss. "Dixie," he said. "I saw you sitting with Gordon. He's trouble."

"And you're not?"

"My authority stretches over all this lab."

"Mine, beyond."

He glanced out into the hall. "No one knows that, so I'm in command." He stepped out of her office, "The big-whig called; wants you to call him back. Do it, so I don't look at fault for your not calling." He pivoted, saying, "Stay away from Gordon; he already knows too much."

5:00 p.m.; Wilmington

Mitch sat staring at the television, his mind recording none of the images except those repeating in his head of his old friend Salyer standing in the bathroom when the bomb went off. The horror embedded itself into Mitch's brain like a hot branding iron.

He stood, his eyes focused on a spot on the wall, his mind reeling in reverse. In it, he recollected seeing the Samsonite valise the little man had carried into the bathroom stall that must have exploded inside the restroom. My God! **They** do know everything; **they** had followed Salyer. **They** were brutal, heartless buzzards. Mitch would go right after them and fix them good. He paced his apartment, trying to piece things together.

Get your mind off it and do something constructive. Nothing seemed sane anymore. Something was happening in his once endurable, even lovable, world. Out of nowhere order had morphed into chaos.

Zombie-like he left his apartment, got into his car, and headed for Gwen Estates.

Philadelphia

The rain pummeled in torrents as Gillian drove up to the building marked "Traditional Fertility Clinic." The guest parking pass Dixie had gotten her came in handy whenever Gilly wanted to visit. The guard at the steel gray booth tipped his hat, electronically lifted the gate while saying, "Near closing, ma'am; make your business short."

She nodded and drove on. Dixie better be ready, she thought as her car splashed through a deep puddle. At the clinic's entrances, she got out of her car, driving rain soaking her, the wind battering her face, and met with couples and handfuls of workers exiting while popping open umbrellas and commenting on how miserable the day was. Gilly slipped inside the opened door when several workers stepped out.

The building looked deserted. Office doors were closed, labs empty, the receptionist's chair vacant, and the semi-circular counter void of activity. She looked around for the correct wing leading to Dixie's lab and office. She hadn't visited enough to be certain where it was, and with the place nearly abandoned, she felt all the more confused. She tried the door lighted with a sign reading, "North Corridor."

Where were the guards? Normally she wouldn't be allowed access like this. She looked into the first lab where she saw only one employee who was replacing his lab smock for his winter coat. A lab next door was locked tight and dark inside.

Half way down the long narrow hall, thunder snapped so loud, she jumped. Within seconds, the entire place went black. "Darnit!" she said into the dark.

At a hallway intersection, she took a few steps to the left, her hand feeling the wall to help grope her way around. She was completely disoriented now. Her only hope was that Dixie hadn't left work thinking Gilly had changed her mind about going to the lab. Her breathing echoed in the hallowed corridors, bouncing off the silence in the building. Her soft-soled suede loafers gave no sound, and the absence of others anywhere around added to the hush. She shuddered, thinking how eerie the place was. Maybe if she yelled Dixie's name, she'd magically appear. But Gilly wasn't even certain if she was in the right passageway.

More lightening lit the building followed by loud booms. She kept walking.

Abruptly her eyes caught a glow or a light—some form of brightness—emanating from down the hall. Being the detective she was training to be, she skulked toward it, walking in a hunched over position as she neared the half-solid-half-windowed unclosed door. She peaked in at an angle so as not to be seen.

Between the lightening and lowly-lit battery flash-lights on the lab counter, she could see the forms, though only dimly. Inside, stood a white-coated, bespectacled balding man leaning over a small figure. Right before her eyes the scientist jabbed a large syringe into the skull of the little figure—an infant, toddler?—and drew something up inside the syringe. The tiny form screamed, curled in pain, its wee hands and feet quivering into convulsions.

Gilly gasped. She wanted to charge the man, grab the baby and run.

In the next flash of lightening, her eyes took in the scientist carrying the filled syringe over to the huge form seated on a stool, all the while the baby squealing in agony. The doctor mumbled to the big man who rolled up his khaki shirt sleeve for the syringe to prick his skin with whatever was drawn out of the infant's brain. Although the mad scientist looked pretty stereo-typical to her, the large male struck Gilly as unusual, like someone afflicted with acromegalia—a disease that abnormally enlarges a human's head size and height as well as facial features, and nearly all body parts and organs. In a khaki shirt and camouflaged-designed pants, the patient sported an expansive nose; big, thick lips; an ample neck with cord-like veins, and eyes so wide that they looked as if they occupied most of his enlarged face.

"If you keep takin . . . ser . . . nin . . ." the scientist said between thunderous cracks and pounding rain, making Gillian listen all the harder, "your person . . .ity . . . not get . . .olent . . . ."

Again thunder fractured overhead. She wished she could hear them. She crept a little closer to the window.

While talking to the scientist, the patient turned his large head slightly and looked off in the direction of the door. Just as he did, lightning cracked so shrilly that Gilly jumped, her shoulder accidentally slamming against the door. She saw his eyes: Big, unfocused, flashing. Her heart beat fast.

He vaulted to his feet and within a few strides was almost at her side.

In roadrunner speed, she tore down the hall, her feet turning so fast, they barely touched the tile floor. She could feel him right behind her.

Chapter
10

Having followed Hammond and Azar the day Hammond had been stabbed, Mitch knew exactly where Enolc 1 was. He arrived in his Bonneville feeling disoriented from exhaustion. He pondered why residents of the area—though many miles away—didn't question the existence of a tall iron fence surrounding acres of barren land with no buildings, no obvious paths, no signs of civilization.

Mitch turned the ignition key to auxiliary, cracked open his window, and played the radio, his fingers drumming against the steering wheel, staring at the grounds, wondering if this was the main entrance. But where were the cars? Was the garage underground? He began driving around the terrain for signs of parked cars.

Not having found any entrance or cars, he left after a few hours to go into downtown Easton for a cup of coffee.

Philadelphia

Gillian felt the floor rock as she slammed the steel door to create a barrier between her and the thing chasing her. He was gaining; she could almost feel his breath.

Inside the stairwell landing, the heat and pitch blackness rammed into her like a speeding car into a brick wall. She stood, trying to catch her breath, make out the location of the steps in the dark. She heard the thing ram the door. In a second he would be at her. Quickly and softly she hustled up the stairwell, thinking that if she ran down a flight he would be able to see her easier. She was panting so hard, she feared he had sonic ears that would hear her no matter where she was. But "up" was at least in the direction of Dixie's lab on the third floor . . . or had Gillian already gone beyond the third story and was too confused to tell?

She darted up another flight, breathing harder, faster, feeling as if she were going to faint. *Hold on! Hold on!*

BOOM! It crashed through the steel door, one large foot stepping onto the landing.

She stood numb on the third step from the top at the second flight of stairs, knowing if she made a sound, he would find her. Frozen, she listened. He must be stalled, she thought. She could envision his eyes roving up, down, to the extreme corners of its sockets as he intently listened.

She heard him sniffing. *He's trying to smell me! What is he—a hunting dog?*

He took a step towards the upstairs.

Don't move, don't move! Yet she wanted to slam her feet on the steel risers and sprint up the stairs, away from him. Her fingers jittered on the handrail, urging her to sprint. Then she heard what she feared the most—a footstep coming up the stairs. He had figured out she was above him.

Another step, then he paused.

Please, Lord, don't let me die this way.

He was getting so close now that she could **feel** him. *Move, moVE MOVE!* What if she started to run and tripped on a step in the blackness? Her heart thumped so fast that her chest hurt; her blood pressure rose like a gushing volcano.

He remained halted on the step.

Please, God, let me run, and run hard and fast.

He grunted, and shivers spread over her entire body, wrapping themselves around the back of her neck.

Then she smelled his breath—as foul as week-old dead fish—and she knew he was near her, steps away.

A door slammed from somewhere below her. Her body jerked in surprise but she held back from making any noise. She remained silent in the inky stairwell.

The big monster grunted again, stood motionless as if listening, and then in a surge, he clamored down the steps towards the noise.

She stood shaking so long that she was sure he had enough time to discover the noise below wasn't her and then race back to the stairwell. But her legs were like mush. She could feel herself collapsing nerve by nerve while biting down on her arm to mute her hysteria. She sank to the steps, sat there weeping, her head in her hands.

From above her a door crashed open and feet sprinted towards her.

She looked up from her sitting position on the steel risers in the stairwell, saw two men who began pulling her up from underneath her arms.

"We're security," said one. "Saw you on the surveillance monitors before the electricity went out; we just now located you. What're you doing here?"

Overhead lights flickered on. "Generator finally kicked in," said the other.

Gillian looked at them, relieved to see human faces and forms. She sucked in sobs. "I-I-I got lost when the lights went out. Something chased me."

"Why are you here, lady?" asked the first one.

"I was supposed to meet Dixie Morris."

"It's against the rules to have visitors loose on the premises. How did you get in here if Technician Morris isn't with you?" He and the other guard led Gilly upstairs to the next landing and out the door to the third floor.

"There was so much confusion in the storm that I just walked in while workers were leaving. I'm telling you," she barked, "something big was chasing me!"

"Things can look strange in the dark during a thunderstorm." The second guard walked ahead towards Dixie's office.

"Gilly!" squealed Dixie as she exited her lab while slipping on her winter coat. "Where have you been? I've been waiting for you, and was just now getting ready to leave!" She peered closer at her friend. "You look terrible!"

After the guards exchanged I.D. verification on Gilly, they departed in a rigid manner. Dixie shepherded Gilly into a seat in her office. "Just tell me everything; stay calm, go slowly."

Wilmington

Cy stood in the cashier line juggling a loaf of bread, a six-pack of Millers Beer, large jug of bottled water, and a bag of chocolate chips which he ate like peanuts. His cholesterol at 396 urged doctors to use him as an example of what not to eat. But he managed to pass all his stress tests, and his one and only cardiac catherization a year ago confirmed what he believed all along: That his oily arteries had allowed nothing to stick to them. So he kept munching potato chips, chocolate chips, popcorn loaded with butter, and Hershey Kisses.

He wanted to get home, read and listen to the reports about President Williams and Premier Cinzan's signed guarantee of alliance to Israel. He feared this and all those accounts of mammoth men with glowing eyes heralded more than what was on the surface—just one more sign of how the world would evolve. He wasn't a religious man but he was well-read via his studies of the Torah through a formal Judaic education as a child. Later, as an adult, he had enrolled in a Christian correspondence course that focused on the New Testament, with emphasis on Revelations. So, he thought, the Lord was releasing the scrolls, vials, and woes.

What's taking this express line so long?

He peaked his head around the back of the person in front of him who was holding a box of cigarettes and a pack of spring water. Four people ahead of him, all shaking their heads yes or no when the cashier asked each a question. His turn came.

She said, "Please take this application form for your mark."

"Mark?" He looked at the cashier. "What are you talking about?"

He watched her glide his groceries across the laser beam and the register tally it. "The mark the president talked about on T.V. at his press conference." Blowing the bangs off her forehead, she added tiredly "Next time you buy groceries, you have to have your identification mark. Six-forty-nine. Plastic or paper?"

"What press conference?" He scratched his head in puzzlement.

She put the groceries into a plastic bag. "The press conference that came on after the signing of that treaty thing." She yawned widely. "Six-forty-nine."

He pulled bills and coins from his pocket. "And this mark?"

"The Premier said it'd help er'one buy and sell things easier. Ya know, like passing yer hand 'cross the scanner instead of using money?"

He frowned, handed her a ten, waited for his change, then grabbed the bag with his groceries, and hustled out. He was more determined than ever to help Gillian with her research on the men with glowing eyes. It was all coming together.

Easton

Hammond rested his hand on his folded arms, sweat rolling down his face, his body wracked with shivers.

Ms. Azar opened his office door. "I've been buzzing you on the intercom but you're not answering." She studied him. "Are you all right, Doctor?"

No response.

She walked across the spacious office to his desk, touched his quivering body. "You're burning up!" She picked up the phone, dialed a three digit number. "Dr. Rin, this is Ms. Azar. Please come immediately to Dr. Hammond's office. He's very ill."

7:00 p.m.

Having returned from killing time over a cup of coffee, Mitch went back to the lab grounds, and again tried finding the main entrance. Fifteen minutes later, frustrated from driving around the vacant complex and not seeing any signs of cars, parking garages, lots, or even a structure or two, he slammed his fist against the steering wheel and headed for home, giving up on his idea of trying to seize Ms. Azar and pump her for information.

Well, he decided, whatever crazy things were going on, he was better off not knowing. He turned the car around toward home, driving north on Route 13. It was then that he remembered what Salyer had told him: "In my fireplace" were the plat and documents. Why hadn't he thought of it before? He stepped on the accelerator.

Northwest Pennsylvania

In the hills of northwest Pennsylvania, about fifteen miles from Erie, quartered the del Rey family around a fire where they ate marshmallows and sang songs of both their native Spain and their adopted United States. Since having become American citizens, the family had taken up the sport of camping as an affordable way to vacation and see the country.

Miguel del Rey loved his new homeland where he had managed to acquire a job as an engineer at Highwater, Inc, in Niagara, New York. In Spain, he had lost a parallel position due to political cut-backs, so when he had emigrated in hopes of finding work where his brother and family had long lived, he felt lucky to get one that paid well. Now, three years later, he and his wife were finally becoming adjusted to Yankee life, though his wife was still struggling with the idioms of the English language. Their children, though, had learned it swiftly through school.

"May I have another marshmallow, Papa?" asked his twelve-year-old daughter in Spanish. She smiled, her eyes bright and dancing by the firelight.

Miguel wished his son, seventeen-year-old Javier, wasn't so sour, much of which was due to missing his girlfriend back home.

"Where we go next, after we pack up camp tomorrow?" his wife Lucia asked, wrapping her coat closer around her to ward off the cold.

"We go home. We stay near home when camping because it cold, and we can't be gone long 'til my company give me summers off." He turned when he heard a noise in the woods behind him, but no one else seemed to notice. He thought, three days of camping in a motorhome wasn't such a hardship, even if it was frosty. Besides, his family should feel lucky they had money to have recreation.

Again, another crunching sound . . . as if someone were walking over sticks and twigs. When Miguel glanced at his family, he could tell by their fearful expressions that they too had heard it this time.

"It be fine," he reassured them. "Maybe just a animal." He gave serious consideration to camping in the future in established grounds where others romped. In the past, he had saved admission and parking fees by going somewhere less civilized; and this location in particular offered a spectacular view of the lake, crisp, fresh-smelling air, and wild flowers and evergreens all around the grounds. One sprawling tree supported a tire swing which Javier had enjoyed all day; and nearby, two trees proudly held a hammock some fishermen had rigged. Way in the corner of the property rested a sole, splintering port-a-john that Miguel figured tent campers must have had trucked in. So it seemed that enough people had made these isolated campgrounds their home.

A THUD sounded behind him that reminded Miguel of the noise Godzilla made when tromping Tokyo in all those funny movies he had seen when younger. How his daughter's eyes got big and his son drew back, made him say, "No worry. I look." He went in the direction he thought the sound came from, the fire still roaring and crackling behind him.

Another crunching sound. But from where? He stopped, listened to locate the source, then resumed walking in the direction where he first heard the noise.

"Aw, nada." He stuck a blade of grass in his mouth as he hiked the earth in search of the sound, his back lighted by the fire, his front growing black as the flickering glow receded behind him. "Animal," he thought, his eyes searching the high grass. The farther he walked from the fire, the colder he got; he envisioned crawling into the motorhome bed with the warmth of his wife in his arms. He loved her so much he would die for her.

He blindly walked aimlessly in the dark trying to find the cause of the noise.

A heart-wrenching scream paralyzed him. When he turned to the campsite, he understood something ugly was happening.

Screeches sliced through him, punctuating the silent air. He wanted to run to the campsite, but instead he instantly dropped to the ground and crawled in the cold, high grass toward the motorhome, his hands curled into fists, his heart racing.

From fifty feet away, his eyes caught in the glow of the blaze what seemed like giants hooting and rampaging around the fire, holding guns and knives, even machetes. One form picked up something, held it overhead and folded it top to bottom, cracking it into two, breaking it the way a firestarter snaps a twig for kindling. The squeal rent the air so piercingly that Miguel felt it ricochet inside his lungs. He gulped, sank to the ground when he realized they had severed his son's spinal cord. He howled into the earth.

The next time Miguel's eyes opened, he saw, at ground level through blades of grass, one of the behemoths gash a hole into his son's skull and suck from it; the other brute threw his wife on the ground so close to the flames that Miguel feared she would catch on fire. Like a swarm, they were on top of her, gnawing on her breasts, ripping her slacks off. He saw a fifth shadow tower over his wife's head with a machete in his hands poised to strike, its eyes glowing. Miguel instantly was reminded of fiends from hell.

Inside his head, a force so powerful built that he prayed it would slam him hard enough that he would die right there of a stroke. Instead it pounded, pounded, pounded, like an incessant hammer striking an anvil.

Violent shrieks bellowed from the motorhome, startling him. He twitched when he stole a look, saw an enormous form grasping his daughter by her hair.

Miguel climbed to his knees to stand, wanting to run to his baby's rescue, but he stopped when he saw another gargantuan grab her by the left leg while the other reached for her right leg. They sneered as each strode in opposite directions, pulling her apart. She screamed loudly, madly.

Mio dios, mio dios! He lowered his head into his hands and wept silently in the echo of his little girl's sinew ripping, bones cracking. When he felt a wetness in his pants, he knew he had lost all control. His mind went blank.

Wilmington

Wally looked around his efficiency apartment from his old sofa that he used as a bed. He just didn't have the energy to get up. It seemed as though the few weeks after he had started working with his Uncle Cy to learn the detective business, he had begun feeling badly. Maybe Cy was just working him too hard. He ought to go back to bed, especially since no one complained when he had left work early. He stood unsteadily, wobbled his way into the kitchenette across the room. Gosh, he felt awful, like his guts were in his mouth and his head was split in half.

At the sink, he turned on the cold water, and drank two glasses, realizing he was feverish. *Must be the flu everyone was talking about.*

He lay back on the sofa, closed his eyes and instantly fell asleep between waves of nausea and cramps.

11:00 p.m.

Gillian sipped sherry from a snifter to warm her. She was all talked out about what she had seen at Dixie's lab. Dixie had listened intently, graciously, but Gilly sensed she didn't believe a word of it.

"Are you hungry? We missed dinner." Dixie fussed over her friend, soothed her, since they had left Traditional Fertility Clinic and arrived at Dixie's home.

"A little. It's cold in here, Dix." Gillian rubbed her eyes. Though feeling exhausted, she was in a strange way, energized, having for the first time experienced the fear and yet thrill that private investigators go through. "Let's just order out."

"Only Dominoes delivers this late on a weekday. I'll jump into my jeep and go to Imperial Palace. It's only two blocks away, and open until midnight, though they don't deliver." Dixie already had her coat on. "You still cold? Take off your wet clothes and put on a pair of my jeans and a blouse. In my bedroom closet are blankets. Grab one, lie on the couch, and I'll be back in a jif."

"I'm not sick, Dix, just soaked and traumatized for the rest of my entire life. I'll probably need psychotherapy."

Dixie rolled her eyes. "You're just not private eye material . . . too girlish."

"Just get the food, Dix."

Feeling chilled, Gillian crossed the room into Dixie's bedroom looking for a blanket. Rummaging through clothes, shelves, and shoes, Gilly found an afghan that she grabbed. Her eyes caught site of a key card sticking out of one of Dixie's blouses. She read the

engraved lettering: TRADITIONAL FERTILITY LAB
MASTER. Underneath was typed on a label: "Duplicate
2, only; store securely."

If this is a spare key, Dixie probably won't miss it.
Gillian argued with herself over whether she should
take it, but her eagerness to become a good detective as
well as her feeling a need to prove that a goon had
chased her, made her decide to "borrow" it. She slipped
the card snugly into her back jeans pants pocket.

She turned to leave, throwing the afghan over her
shoulder. The blinking light on the computer sitting
atop Dixie's bedroom made her pause. The monitor was
asleep but the computer was operating. Out of curiosity,
Gillian took a step toward the set-up, touched the
mouse button, and on popped the screen. Instantly Gilly
realized she was looking at an official report on Traditional clinic and a lab with the name "Enolc 1." Gillian
skimmed the screen. Several places in the report were
encoded which she suspected were the most important
passages.

She rummaged through Dixie's desk, found a box of
formatted disks, and took one out, slid it into the drive
slot, and copied the other disk. Her fingers jittered lest
Dixie walk in. She hated doing this to her friend, but
she had to know.

When she heard the jiggling of the front door handle, she pulled the disk out, put it into her back pocket
with the card key, then dashed out to the den area where
she speedily lay on the sofa with the afghan covering
her.

Dixie entered. "Wake up. Food's here."

They sat in the kitchen, talking, with Gillian beginning to regain her strength and get her mind off the
goon. Manipulating the chop sticks, she teased, "So,
Dix, any active love life? Didn't you mention someone
named Gordie?"

Dixie laughed. "He's a co-worker. Obese but nice.

We're friends, not lovers."

Gilly stabbed a piece of chicken, plunged it into her mouth. "What's he do?"

"He's in charge of computing. Very bright, but he needs to do more than sit on his rear all day at a computer console. Activity will help him lose weight. I get my exercise in bed." Dixie giggled.

Washington, D.C.

President Jackson Williams stood before shelves of books in the Oval Office with the phone held tightly in his hand. He could picture Premier Cinzan at the other end, sitting behind his desk, his feet propped on the blotter, his hand holding a glass filled with martinis. "I'm here," responded the president on the other end.

Williams heard the Premier drag on a cigarette. "It's time."

"But when you were here, you didn't give any indication that we were going to add this so soon after the contamination. Don't you think people will catch on—"

"Williams, Williams, Williams. I, and only I, do the thinking. Not you or your flunkie Greenman." He sighed loudly for effect. "First order of business—"

"Really, Mr. Premier, I think we should wait."

"Williams . . ." came the warning tone of Cinzan.

"We just signed a pact with Israel . . . . how will we explain to the world that all churches and synagogues have to be closed?"

"It's all part of the game plan, you know that. You sold your soul to attend top colleges, become a Rhodes Scholar, senator, and president. Until now, you've served us sufficiently. Don't ruin it with your righteous drivel."

"All I'm saying, Mr. Premier, is that the timing seems bad. You of all people, who's part Italian and part Jewish, shou—"

"I am **not** Jewish, no matter what anyone claims!
Do what I say, you wimp!" A long stretch of silence
hung in the air. "Okay, Williams, one more time: I said
now we infuse the new religion. Close them: Each and
every worship place, except those I approve. Now, let's
make our call to Prime Minister Rubin Steinmetz."

Minutes later, the connection among Williams, Cinzan, and Steinmetz went through.

"Yes, Mr. Premier?" said Israel's Steinmetz the second he realized the heads of states were on the line.

"I want you to close your synagogues and bring in
our New Age religion. His Eminence is ready to broad-
cast his prepared statement."

"But, Mr. Cinzan," objected Steinmetz, "that's
impossible."

"You knew there would be a trade off for our protection. It's politics."

"B-b-but," sputtered the Israeli leader, "surely not a
trade-off of this magnitude. Our country is our faith.
We have lost soldiers in wars for the right to live and
practice our fai—"

"I don't want to hear it. I said, close the synagogues."

Williams grew uncomfortable with the conversation.

"If I don't?" The Jewish ruler's voice was a mixture
of fear and defiance. "Just where is this protection you
promised in front of millions of people?"

"Well," started Cinzan, "I hear tell that Russia,
which has always wanted your little country, is in prep-
aration for a visit."

Indignantly, Steinmetz said, "We will be prepared
for this so-called visit. Russia will try to overtake us
whether we bow to you or not. Right, Mr. Premier?"

"Close your synagogues, Steinmetz. It's my order."
He exhaled loudly. "Same for you, Williams!"

President Jackson Williams gingerly replaced the phone's headpiece in its cradle, stood staring at the floor.

Chapter 11

Having returned from Easton's Gwen Estates last night, Mitch had decided to go to his apartment first before breaking into Salyer's apartment to find the materials. He was so exhausted though that he conked out the second he sat for a sole minute. Mitch hadn't awakened until an hour ago, and soon after, he was en route to Salyer's.

As soon as he neared Salyer's apartment, Mitch saw that the lock and jamb had been busted open. He entered.

Gosh! Mitch looked around the ransacked place. On the floor, papers covered the carpeting, pillows stretched from one end to the other, some split open. End tables were upturned, their drawers twisted out, some broken and splintered. Mitch shook his head, walked into the kitchen where he was greeted by smashed glasses and plates, pots and pans strewn on the floor, food morsels in the sink, the counters and stove.

Cabinet drawers hung open, their contents emptied on the linoleum.

He left the kitchen, walked back through the disheveled living room, looking around, and entered Sal's bedroom where he was met with the same kind of bedlam. He returned to the living room, cleared a spot on the couch, and sat, thinking how useless it was to search it. "Oh man," he groaned, wondering what was happening in the world. He ran the palm of his hands over his eyes. Then he stood and began inspecting every corner of the small apartment.

An hour later, Mitch found nothing of value, certain that the government had taken whatever they thought was useful. He explored every inch of the fireplace, but found no plat with information. "In the fireplace," Mitch repeated aloud the words Salyer had said. He stared at the fake fireplace, stooped over, looked up inside it. Nothing. Walking around the tiny four-room apartment, Mitch went back into the closet-sized bedroom, looked under the bed covers, under the bed, in overturned drawers, everywhere.

Perspiring and dispirited, he stood in the bedroom, wiping his face with a hanky. *He didn't tell me it was a fake fireplace!* Mitch looked around the room, remembering how Salyer used to laugh easily and frequently, how he did little things for others, and loved going to work, making him feel fulfilled.

Fake fireplace? Mitch dashed out of the bedroom and back to the mantle, looked atop the hearth, and then tore into the guts of the fireplace, lifting the synthetic logs attached to the metal grate. There, in a black envelope—of all things—matching the grate and floor—was the very thing he was looking for. Or was it? He ripped open the 9 X 13, black painted envelope and found a paper folded in fours, along with thin-lined notebook paper that had journal-like entries.

Carrying the material, he went to the front door of

the flat and checked to make sure no one was around, then drove home to sit in his recliner and read.

11:00 a.m.

In her apartment, Gillian wiped the blurriness from her eyes. Sitting at the computer screen so long made her feel light-headed and headachy from eye strain. Why couldn't she figure out how to read Dixie's disk? She tried everything but it was so well coded that the few areas that did come through gave her no sense of continuity. She sensed that Dixie was involved in something but was unable to determine exactly what or how serious it was.

Disgusted, she threw open the White Pages, and, finding the number she wanted, dialed. "Gordon, in computing, please," she said to the clinic's receptionist who answered on the first ring.

When Gordon came on the line, Gillian went right to the point after explaining who she was. "I fear Dixie is in trouble. I know she speaks highly of you, so I was wondering if you could give me a little of your time."

He seemed hesitant.

****

Cy sat in his ragged recliner, munching on three PBJ sandwiches washed down by large cans of root beer, while alternating his attention between CNN on the wide, rectangular, flat screen built into the wall, and reading yesterday's paper on a hand-held computer. But his mind kept wandering back to the incident at the grocery store. First it was ugly looking men killing innocent people, then contaminated water, and a peace treaty that no one in the world seemed to know was coming, and now it was identification chips under the skin for scanner machines. "Global conspiracy. Didn't

think those guys were smart enough to pull off something so complex. Where do the brutes fit in?"

He wiped peanut butter from his face with his
sleeve, remembering that these "glowing" forms ranged
from six-feet-six-inches to eight-feet, and were inhumanly strong, with rugged features, big hands, massive
bodies, but not ugly looking.

"Height, body mass, and eyes," he said, grunting
again. He stared at the television in thought as if waiting for a bulletin to come on the way it did decades ago
when Cronkite had announced President Kennedy had
been shot. The power of television to give instant
notices that forever changed people's lives and alter
history, had always stayed with Cy, making him
impressed one second, and scared the next.

"Now a report from the Center for Disease Control
on the rise and preponderance of the flesh-eating bacteria," started the anchorman.

Cy bit into a second PBJ sandwich, getting jelly on
his chin. "That's it!" he squealed. He slammed the
remainder of his sandwich on the paper plate and was
up and out of his chair searching for his computerized
phone directory to call Atlanta.

Noon; Easton

The physician at Enolc 1 studied the medical chart,
then looked at the figure lying in the clinic bed. He
shook his head, turned to the nurse, and said matter-of-
factly, "We'll have to amputate, though I'm not sure that
will help."

"The pain must be extraordinary," said the nurse.

"The gangrene has spread throughout his system. I
doubt if amputating his arm now will save him." He
shrugged. "Let's try."

"Shouldn't we send him to a hospital—Johns Hop-
kins University Hospital? We can't give him what he

needs here, in this small clinic for employees."

The doctor wrote something in the patient's chart. "Secretary of State Gamblin said to definitely not send him to any public hospital. He even said no to taking him to the Veterans' Hospital. Afraid Hammond might say something in his delirium."

"Isn't his health more important?"

"Not when it comes to government matters." The physician flipped the chart closed. "Prep him."

3:00 p.m.

Mitch sat in his car near the location indicated on the map he had found in Salyer's apartment. He had parked in a secluded spot that allowed him a view of the site. Looking around the grounds, he still didn't see any parking lot or cars. Yet the map showed that some structure existed directly in front of him. Mitch waited patiently for full daylight to help him make out what was supposed to be there.

He badly needed sleep. His clothes smelled, his breath tasted bad, and his stubbly face cried for a shave. Quickly, he realized, he was becoming fixated—obsessed—with avenging Salyer's death, and putting an end to whatever the government's plan was.

Bright sun rays rolled across the sky. "Stay awake." He opened his car window to let the frigid air blast his face, but the more the sun beamed, the more he wanted to squint; squinting meant closing his eyes . . . going to SL . . .E . . . e . . . p.

His eyes popped open. He shook his head like a horse. "Stay awake."

VROOooooom sounded a car engine. A glance at his watch told him it was seven a.m.: Shift change.

He peered harder. Still couldn't see where the car went. Several more vehicles drove down the road. He watched each go over the graveled road, turn right onto the dirt lane and seemingly disappear into nothingness.

He decided to sit and wait until he was sure the shift change was done, and then he'd drive up to the disappearing spot. He turned the ignition key to auxiliary and the radio volume to low. He reached an oldies station and drummed his fingers to "Wipe Out," a song he knew would keep him awake. A noise sounded from the radio much like a rapid moving ticker tape. "This is a bulletin from—"

Mitch raised the volume: " . . . here is Pope John Paul III's official announcement:" In broken English, the Pope said, "Today mark a new era of good will, unity, love, and the sharing of God."

Mitch listened intently, unaware that he was hardly breathing.

"Today," continued the pontiff, "we stop all division among religions through-a efforts for united faith. Today," his voice resonated as though he were speaking in a hall, "we open our arms to the new Spiritualism— the religion of the whole-a world—the only faith that speaks for-a all us."

Another voice chimed in: "This holds true, too, for our synagogues," said Rabbi Andrew Rosenberg, a well-respected, widely honored religious leader who spoke for Rubin Steinmetz at the Premier's orders.

"The Islamic community will abide as well," broke in a Moslem chief, who was instantly followed by concurrence from other world leaders.

"Jeesh!" swore Mitch. "This can't be happening."

Indiana, Pennsylvania

In a lab in the hills of Indiana, Pennsylvania, near Pittsburgh, two doctors, three scientists, and several technicians and nurses hovered over a lab table holding a small form.

"We did it," said one doctor, turning and shaking

hands with the other physician and personnel, and slapping them on their backs in congratulations. "Secretary Gamblin will be very pleased."

A scientist nodded. "Hopefully this model won't grow disproportionately like its earlier genotypic parallel, though it is already large for its age."

"No signs of irradiated orbits. Cornea and rods appear normal," said the opthamologist. "No apparent facial disfiguration or mutation."

The first doctor nodded. "If the eyes remain normal, and the body stays within the desired height range without contorting into some kind of anomaly like it did in T-natum, then we have created the first successful female engineered prototype from adult cellular transmutation and proliferation."

"It's more androgynous than feminine," rebutted the second doctor. "It's just like the other few females out there. I don't see how we've accomplished anything."

"Don't forget the serotonin," reminded a nurse. "We wouldn't want to go through that again with this strain."

A scientist shrugged. "We'll draw a cerebral sample and test it for quality before performing the BCI procedure. Even then we may not really know until the specimen matures like the others have, which is when we first became aware of the problem."

"But this sample appears to be a victory," countered the first scientist.

"Shall we began the duplication and multiplication systemic propagation?" asked another nurse.

Said the doctor, "Not until I contact Secretary Gamblin about this. Who knows . . . maybe he'll nix the whole idea since things have gone wrong."

4:00; Easton

Mitch followed the dirt path to the plexiglass gate to a transparent barrier where he got out of his Bonneville and went over to it. "So that's what that is."

He touched the plastic, semi-circular-bubble covering the graded path leading into the bowels of the earth where, figured Mitch, it went to an underground garage that no one would have ever discovered because of the dome. "I'll be darned," he whistled, amazed at the technology. He wondered if he should follow the path inside the bubble, realizing though, that even if he got onto the down ramp, there was no guarantee that he could get past security; yet, it was late afternoon Friday, and maybe not a lot of people would be around near quitting time on this shift. He decided to return to his hidden parking place and continue watching.

8:30 p.m.; Lockport, New York

In the small town outside Buffalo, paced well over 5,000 Catholic parishioners in front of St. Patrick's church, carrying signs reading: GOV'T HAS NO RIGHT CLOSING CHURCHES; KILL THE GOVERNMENT, NOT CHRIST; WITHOUT GOD, THERE'S NOTHING; GETTING RID OF GOD MEANS THE END.

Across the country from Buffalo, in Bel Air, California, rabbis from the region met to discuss the imminent destruction of their temples. One offered, "We can appeal to the president but the edict comes from higher up. We must fight this. All places of worship are being destroyed or converted into heathen centers."

Far from them, in Atlanta, thousands of Fundamentalists surrounded their churches, arm in arm, in protest. They turned at the sound of cranes starting engines with wrecking balls already swinging toward the stone cathedral.

Easton

Ms. Azar walked into the lab's medical clinic and looked at her boss lying flat on the hospital bed, his armless shoulder wrapped in gauze, his nose supporting an oxygen hose, his chest holding cardiac leads, and his good arm propping a blood pressure cuff.

The doctor standing next to Azar leaned over and said, "Knowing you've worked with him for a good while and that you've been a faithful servant to him, I called you in from home in case you want to say your goodbyes."

She looked at the physician, shifted her gaze back to Hammond. "No hope?"

"We thought the amputation would improve his condition but the gangrene is coursing through his body. No amount of antibiotics will prevent its consumption."

She had come to know this man, worked with him for several years. She would miss him, and his passing would only bring about a new supervisor, and not necessarily a better one. What was going on in all the Enolc labs was evil and should be terminated. But she was only one individual.

She couldn't stop tears from spilling over onto her cheeks. *Why am I crying? For him, or for our country, our world?*

The doctor put his hand on her arm.

"If you don't mind, I'd like to sit with him for awhile," she said sadly.

5:30 p.m. PST; Albuquerque, New Mexico

In Albuquerque, Mr. and Mrs. Ripley kissed their twenty year-old daughter, Eileen, and hugged eight-year-old Brandon. The father said to Eileen, "We have to sit through all the speeches at the banquet so we'll be gone awhile. Make sure your brother's in bed by ten; he has scouts in the morning. Page me if you need us."

The mother chimed in, "Go to the neighbors if that predicted storm gets nasty."

Eileen locked the door behind them. To her dimple-faced brother, she said, "Okay, whadda ya wanna do?"

"Let's tell spooky stories." Off he dashed, running around the house, shutting lights to make the setting more conducive. She wondered what story he would tell this time? His were better than hers which made her get on her mother about what she allowed him to watch on television. She threw a bag of popcorn in the micro-wave, and listened to the kernels burst in the bag.

Her thoughts drifted to the upcoming wedding when she would promenade down the aisle decked in an old-fashioned white, handmade, laced gown with matching hat. She and her fiance had good jobs at her father's computer business. Her only worry was where to hold the service. Under the government's edict, her Method-ist church had closed.

She grabbed a plastic liter of Pepsi and a couple of paper, thinking she ought to be drinking something other than soda to make sure she fit into her wedding gown. But with the ban, and the jug empty of store-bought water, she decided to drink only a small glass of Pepsi.

When the two had situated themselves comfortably on the sofa, with popcorn and drinks near them, Bran-don said, "Let **me** go first!"

She threw a handful of buttered kernels into her mouth. "None of that gruesome axe murder stuff."

"Once upon a time," began the child, "there was a forest that everyone was warned not to go into because a Frankenstein scientist was creating—"

"Oh, Brandon, enough of the Frankenstein stories. You have to stop reading that junk." She took a sip of

Pepsi, recalling how much he had liked stories on were-wolves, vampires, and monsters.

"There was a private power plant in the forest that supplied electricity to the lab where these things were made—"

She rolled her eyes.

"Just as the scientist slammed high voltage into the monster on the table—"

"What did this monster look like?" She yawned, took another sip of soda pop.

"They had skin like—"

They both turned at a noise behind them. "Probably that storm Mom told us about. Go on." She tousled his hair. "

Again came a noise like the shuffling of feet.

She turned quickly enough to make her think she saw a figure in the doorway of the kitchen. But was it a form or something glowing? *I'm spooking myself.* "Let's put the lights back on—"

"See see! I did scare you!" He squealed with glee.

"Did not. Let's prepare for that storm; get flash-lights and—" She stopped when she saw her brother jump at another sound. Chills raced through her. "Brandon, run to the neighbors. Do it now!" Her voice quivered.

"I'm not going to leave you," he whined, his voice low but bordering hysteria. "I'm scared, Sis."

She grabbed him by the shoulder and pulled his head into her chest so she could whisper into his ear while eyeing the kitchen doorway in front of her. "Do what I tell you. No matter what happens, don't stop!" She pecked him on the head, gave him a little shove, watching him sprint for the door while she stood guard of him, intending to stop any intruder who tried to chase him.

She saw her brother turn around to look at her before dashing across the yard, the wind kicking up. In that split instant, something stupendous in size jumped out of the shadows, grabbed her by the throat and squeezed so hard that she felt as though her neck would pop out of its socket.

Chapter 12

Gilly sat on the floor of her flat, her back against the couch, and her feet touching stacks of books, magazines and newspaper photocopies from the library, wanting to prepare herself for her interviews with the survivors. She was tired of reading, tired of life's turmoil, and equally nostalgic for Mitch who she hadn't seen in days. Nor had she seen Dixie since the incident at the clinic. She decided to take a break and call both to make sure they were okay. The phone rang just as she climbed to a standing position.

"Hello?" she said while glancing at the floor with the literature spread out. As soon as the voice on the other end spoke, she knew it was Chase, and a part of her was glad that he had called. He asked her to dinner the next night, and she agreed. She hung up, smiling, and returned to her work where she weeded through available accounts on the goons and the mutated people. She began a list of survivors' names. She knew right off the project was going to be trying.

The phone rang again.

"Gil? Dixie here. Where have you been?" They chatted. Dixie ended the conversation with, "I took another look into your claim of a giant man chasing you at the clinic and a mad scientist piercing an infant's skull, but nothing I investigated substantiates your report."

"You sound like a programmed robot. Weren't you the one who told me your sister-in-law was murdered by the very same kind of killer? Now you're changi—"

"I'm not changing my mind, and I do believe there's something strange going on, but honestly, Gil, my clinic is not involved. I think the storm spooked you and you thought you saw something that just didn't exist."

"Some best friend you are."

"Gillian, stop! I am your best friend. I just don't want you to give my clinic a bad reputation for something that never happened."

"Your clinic's more important than our friendship."

"Whatever you think is happening isn't going on at my clinic."

"I'll talk to you later." Gillian slipped the mouthpiece back into the cradle.

A second later, she dialed Mitch's number. But getting only his machine, she hung up and returned to her spot on the floor to continue her research.

Her eyes caught an image on T.V. of protestors in front of churches all over the world. She listened more closely. Flashes of Jews entering synagogues in Israel infused the screen while reporters uttered, "Here, in Jerusalem, and elsewhere in this small country, the synagogues are open and welcoming. In spite of orders by the United Nations for all religious places to close, Israel has done otherwise, angering authorities who— reports have it—intend to send troops in to enforce the closure edict. This certainly does not bode well for

Israel's Rubin Steinmetz, who, until this mandate had been issued had rested comfortably in the knowledge that the U.N. would come to Israel's aid if ever placed under attack."

Gillian went back to scanning magazines, pausing at various articles.

"In world news," said the anchorman, "comes a report from Premier Cinzan."

Gillian looked up at the screen, her eyes taking in the tall, slender but muscular Mediterranean who stood before a television microphone. "We have finally managed to put out a debit card for all Europe." Cameras swung to a plastic card Cinzan held in his palm, with one side profiling Cinzan and the other, showing a banner with stars fluttering above a woman on some kind of animal—dragon, bull, whatever. Gillian couldn't make it out on the screen.

Cinzan continued, "It's our intent to implement the card in the European bloc, then worldwide, so that every nation on Earth will be trading in the same form."

A reporter asked, "Isn't that what the implanted chip is supposed to do?"

Cinzan recited, "Again, some day in the near future, we'll all be talking the same language, buying and selling in the same currency, working from the same base, so that the differences existing from nation to nation will no longer be a barrier. We will then truly be a united planet, a one-world society."

Gosh. Somewhere in her mind she sensed connections to everything but was incapable of gluing them together. She returned to studying the materials before her.

Easton

Mitch slammed a fist on the steering wheel. He had dozed off. Wiping sleepers from his eyes, he ordered himself to stay awake to watch any incoming or outgoing cars. He looked at his watch. What should he do—wait around to see if someone came down the road and then follow them to the grounds?

He rubbed his eyes again. He had to get sleep. *Wait—a car!* He heard an engine revving. His eyes scanned the horizon and after focusing, realized it was coming from the transparent structure. He watched a female behind the steering wheel pull out of the underground ramp, roll down the window, and punch numbers into a box he hadn't noticed until now. Suddenly, out of nowhere, more invisible structures opened. He saw the gates were made of glass or some specially fabricated form of plastic that prevented anyone from driving up close to the semi-circular bubble. "Heck, I couldn't have gone down that ramp if I wanted to," he mumbled.

He leaned forward at the wheel, trying to discern the driver. It was odd that someone would be leaving at this hour. He squinted harder when the car passed him. "Aha!" he exclaimed, recognizing the driver. He turned the key and stepped on the accelerator, ripping out of his hiding place after Ms. Azar.

Wilmington

Gillian reached over to grab the ringing phone. "Where are you?"

"Listen," Cy said on the other end. "I'm getting ready to meet a gal I know at the CDC who might be able to tell us about the bogeyman with glowing eyes."

"Good, but I have something to tell you." She went into the explanation about what had happened at Dixie's lab.

"What's the name of that place?"

"Traditional Fertility Clinic."

"There's probably nothing traditional about it. The

only thing I know is that there are too many strange things going on."

"What do you want me to do here?"

"On the flight over, I heard that a Hispanic family—the del Reys from Niagara, New York—went camping in Erie, Pennsylvania and were attacked by these goons. The father survived and is living with his sister. See what you can find out. Also, I learned that an Albuquerque boy witnessed the death of his sister by something enormous. Track the kid down, as well as the woman who was attacked by a teenager with facial deformities. Research the library's fiche for any articles on this, and then hunt down survivors and interview them."

"I'm ahead of you. I've already done that."

"Good. Take someone with you; I don't want you to go alone. Try Wally; he needs the experience. And get a gun like I've been saying. With the banning of all firearms going through, even P.I.s are going to have problems registering; do it before the law passes."

"Wally didn't come in to work today."

"He left early yesterday, too." Cy paused. "Check on him, Gil; maybe he just slept in. Listen, I gotta go. Don't wanna miss my appointment." He hung up.

Replacing the mouth piece in the cradle, she mused, "I've got to go to Wally's, get on the Net to make flight arrangements, pack, and continue my list of phone numbers and addresses of people to interview." She hustled to her car.

Washington, D.C.

Secretary Gamblin entered the Oval Office when given permission. He dreaded times like this. He should have gotten out when he could; now he was in too deep, and the administration—all the way up to Cinzan—

would never let him leave with all that he knew. Worse, his family was at risk, too. He had to do something, he thought, as he walked into President Williams' office and saw him standing behind his desk, looking out the window, his hands crossed behind his back.

"Mr. President."

"Sit down, Harry." The commander-in-chief turned, pulled out his desk chair.

Gamblin noticed the redness of William's bulbous nose from drinking.

"Do you know why I'm unhappy, Harry?" Williams sat. "I'm unhappy because of the kind of department you're running. I put you in charge of one of the most prestigious cabinets, and you're blowing it! I'm hearing stories about mutants and monsters running wild, killing people. . . . Are they now in other countries?"

Gamblin wet his lips. "The project seems to be out of control everywhere."

The president slammed his fist on the expansive desk. "What good are you? I put you in charge because of our old friendship and your illustrious background— Harvard grad—and you screw it up." He let out a loud sigh in between curses, then re-crossed his hands. "Which labs are out of control?"

"I'm unsure of that status, sir."

"Which specimens are on the loose?"

"Both."

"Both what?"

"Both T-natums and the C's."

"Great, just great." He drummed his fingers on the mahogany desk top. "All right, all right." He exhaled loudly for effect. "We had success with them . . . in the beginning, right?"

Gamblin wringed his hands. "Never with T-natums. They went sour from the get-go. But the others were our hope . . . until they started to snap, which we think is due to the serotonin. The project is still too new to have any definitives to it, but there are a few out there who seem stabilized because of their ability to get the chemical replacement. They're in productive positions in society and assimilating, but we don't know how long they'll remain that way; the BCI is quite unstable."

"You don't know much of anything, do you?"

"We're learning."

"At the expense of my presidency!" The president rose, walked around his desk, and, looking Gamblin in the eye, said, "These reports I'm hearing about glowing eyes . . . this is limited to the C's, right, from the lack of the chemical?"

"I believe so."

"It's your job to know!" Williams let lose with a string of profanity that made Gamblin blush. Then the president sat on the corner of his desk and crossed his arms at his chest. "When I had you appointed to office, you told me you had experience with genetic engineering."

Gamblin shifted in his seat. "I had . . . but not on the level you wanted. My experience, as I told you before, is limited to genetic manipulation for the betterment of society: To improve crops, find ways to eliminate diseases, inherited disorders—"

"Don't give me that!" He got up from the corner of his desk and paced the large office. "You knew from the beginning what Cinzan and his people wanted our country to do, and I had entrusted you with doing it."

". . . huge, strong, robust soldiers as fighting machines, obedient robots—"

Williams leaned over Gamblin and pointing at him, said, "You ruined the entire project, and now you must take the heat for it!"

"I'll gladly resign."

"Sure, the easy way out, you wimp. Do you have any idea how bad this makes our country—makes **me**—look?"

"My resignation will be on your desk first thing in the morning."

Williams glowered. "I'll have you shot first! You will not resign, do you hear me? **You're** going down with this—not me! You're going to take the heat for this screw-up. Your running away leaves me holding the bag and I won't let you get away with it. I have my political future to think about, you jackass!"

Gamblin stood.

"Sit down!" Williams pointed to the chair.

"Excuse me for saying this, but regarding your political future," began Gamblin who realized he had nothing to lose now by voicing his opinion, "there is none with Premier Cinzan in office. There's no room for you to move up in this New World Order you and your predecessors have been creating for the last fifty-plus years."

Williams inhaled-exhaled loudly. Now in a calmer tone, he said, "You're right: This one-world order **has** been in the making for decades. Everything's been planned and arranged. I was put in to make us the leader until Cinzan took over. I was groomed for this from the beginning of my college years to obey those in charge—Cinzan, Rockefeller, Rothchild—"

"As I said, there is no place for you to move up to."

Williams hissed, "You think so? I may not be able to again hold the highest office in the world but I can become a global leader. In time, I'll replace Cinzan."

Gamblin stuck his hand into his pocket, absently fingering his keys. "Mr. Cinzan won't be going anywhere. The devil is immortal, Mr. President. I'm afraid you, too, sir, are condemned to hell, and—I fear—I along with you." He watched Williams' mouth drop open. "You'll have my resignation shortly."

With that, Gamblin turned to walk out, hearing Williams order over the intercom: "Send in the 'Discontinuation Command Team.'" He looked over at Harry, saying, "If you want to behave like an ass, I'll make sure you become one."

9:00 p.m.; Easton

When Mitch forced the car in front of him off the road and onto the berm, he knew he was taking a chance getting out of the driver's seat. After all, she could have a gun or a knife, or have even made a call to lab security who might already be on their way. Still, he had to do this; he had spent too many days watching the lab in hopes of finding a way in or catching up with someone to talk to.

As soon as he approached her window, he put his hands up in a surrendering position while mouthing through the glass, "I'm not going to hurt you. I just want to talk to you, Ms. Azar. Remember . . . we met when Dr. Hammond was attacked?"

Seconds later, she rolled down her window and said, "He died an hour ago from that arm wound."

Mitch stood staring, stunned.

"He had septicemia, which is a poisoning of the entire body through the blood. His wound turned gangrenous. The antibiotics didn't save him. We all feel badly, Mr. Frey, but Dr. Hammond was a stubborn man. We did it his way and he died for it."

Mitch said absently, "A lot of people are dying for 'it.'" He looked her in the eye when he added, "We both know strange things are going on, only you know a lot more than I. Somebody's got to stop whatever is happening. My dear friend was just murdered; he used to work in the deeds office in Wilmington. The only reason anyone would want to hurt him is because he knew too much."

She started to roll her window up.

He jammed his fingers on the glass rim. "Please, tell me what's going on. I need to do something to avenge my pal's death and to stop the government."

"I don't know anything." She tried harder to get the window all the way up but his fingers remained on the glass. "Just let me go."

"You're not the type of person who would let anyone hurt another, and yet, that's exactly what you are doing."

"The less you know, Mr. Frey, the better off you are. Release your hand from my window unless you'd like your fingers severed." She started to pull the car off the berm with him still holding on.

"Please, please, just give me a few minutes. I'll meet you anywhere. I beg you." He started to run alongside her vehicle, not wanting to let her go.

"Stop it!" she snapped, scrutinizing the front windshield, side and rearview mirrors, to see if anyone was watching. "I have to go home now to my little bungalow in Cambridge at Nineteen Reed Street. Take your hand off my window or you're going to find yourself airborne in a minute." She revved the engine for effect.

What did he care about her plans to go home? All she had to do was give him five measly minutes. "The heck with you," he yelled to her as she took off.

He got behind the wheel of his car and started the engine. There wasn't another vehicle in sight, though he knew the powers of the government's surveillance capabilities. He took his time getting back on Route 13 North, not caring if a thousand cars passed him. He had failed in his attempt to learn something from the only source he knew could help him, and she wouldn't. Oh no, she was too interested in going home.

He hit the button, automatically opening his window to let the icy breeze in.

When the clues hit him, he almost slammed his car into the moving van in front of him. She did say Nineteen Reed Street, right? Why hadn't he figured it out sooner?

Wilmington

Gillian banged on the apartment door several times before the figure emerged and clicked open the lock once he saw who it was.

"Are you okay? You look terrible," she said.

Wally answered, "I feel like my guts are being wrenched out of me." He felt his forehead, reeled over to the kitchen sink. "I've got a temp again, and I'm so thirsty."

"Maybe it's the flu." She watched him.

"Tell my uncle I'll be back as soon as I'm over this."

"Cy's in Atlanta meeting with someone he knows at the CDC."

Wally tossed some ice into the glass and stuck it under the cold water faucet. "On which case?"

She shrugged. "The goons." She blinked, shouted, "Don't drink that!"

He stopped, the glass suspended in mid-air. His eyes shifted to her face. "Oh my God," he said slowly, with emphasis. "I forgot. The contamination."

"How long have you been drinking the water?"

He shook his head. "I never stopped."

"You better go to the ER. Dimethyl mercury is toxic."

"I don't have medical insurance."

"Your uncle's cheap."

"He's trying to get me on his policy."

"Come on, get your coat. I'll take you to an immediate care clinic and pay whatever the visit is." This was going to be a long night, she realized.

Hours later she returned to her apartment after Wally had been given band-aid repair, taken tests, and then sent home. The clinic doctor hadn't seemed too encouraging but he did give Wally something to make him comfortable through the night. Gillian got him into bed, medicated, and then went home.

Chapter
13

Sitting on the wrought iron chair on a restaurant terrace, Cy ordered a martini, then zipped up his jacket; it was chilly even for the deep south. Looking around, he instantly spotted her coming his way. He stood, gave her a bear hug, and pulled out her chair. She looked lovelier than ever, with her bronze skin, striking gray eyes, dark, dark curly hair hanging at her shoulders. In every way, she was model material, and he should have married her years ago when he worked as a detective in Atlanta. But being over eighteen years older than she, he nixed the idea so as not to embarrass her—though at first she had thought it was a racial thing. He had rued his moronic decision ever since; she would have made him a wonderful wife.

"Hello, Dr. Reid. You're as beautiful as ever, and haven't acquired one wrinkle in the years since I lost you." He rose, gave her a hug, then motioned for the waiter to bring her a glass of wine.

"Now you've found me, and I'm starved. I don't like

late dinners but it's the only time our schedules connected, so let's order immediately. That way I'll better digest my food and not gain weight."

"You haven't put on an inch of fat."

They chatted awhile about the good ol' days and what each was doing: That he was still unmarried and playing detective, and that she had been married, divorced, and remained childless, and still worked as a scientist at the Center for Disease Control.

After he finished his veal, and she her steak tartar, she said, "For you to fly down here on short notice means you must have some serious concerns."

He started with the huge goons and numerous reports surrounding them, adding Gillian's experiences; then went on to the water contamination, and the mark under the skin. He got so caught up in his narrative, that if it hadn't been for her interrupting him, he might have gone on for another ten minutes.

"Whoa! Back up, Cy," she laughed. "Let's start with these giants you're talking about." She sipped her wine. "I've heard the same myself. It's been in a few selected newspapers but not on the air. From what I've read, there are actually two different specimens out there: The huge men, and a much younger group that have distorted facial features and extremities. To me, it sounds like a mad experiment."

"The glowing eyes?" He sipped his seltzer.

She looked pensive, her hands cupping the wine goblet, her eyes staring absently into space. "When specimens look similar and have the same defect, only one explanation comes to mind: Duplication." She brought the glass to her mouth, paused, then said. "My God, Cy; maybe those things out there are clones." She shook her head. "No. There's no way any lab, any institution, any one person could get away with something like that. Why, the ramifications of this would be—"

"The government can," he stated.

"For years the government encouraged scientists to clone as a means of creating better produce, ridding our society of hereditary diseases, as—"

"I've heard all that before. But why duplicate humans?"

"If the government's behind it, then why not? After all, the strongest, bravest, most cunning soldier could be created and duplicated so that an entire army, navy . . . could be built from just one or several perfectly designed specimens."

"It makes perfect sense. But how?"

"Now this is all speculation on my part because I don't know the actual mechanics behind the engineering process but my guess is that DNA was removed from the original—"

"You mean, if these are clones, they all come from the same person?"

"Not necessarily," she continued, "though through genetic engineering, scientists could have changed the clones' traits to make them look different. Maybe they coded for body mass, eye and hair color—anything they thought was desirable. In the mid-Nineties, scientists were able to manipulate cell cultures to contain targeted genes they could mass produce in 'designer' form. With Dolly they had used somatic or mature cells, but they learned soon after how to clone with fibroblasts or fetal cells. They removed the cells' nuclei, fused it with eggs, and, voila!, created embryos which were placed in wombs of unrelated maternal animals that gave birth at the end of their full term. Cloning with adult cells was miraculous back then since such cells are differentiated and thought to direct cellular reproduction only for their correlative types."

"Huh?"

"What I am saying is that Dolly was a duplicate of a living, adult sheep, while the newer technology in 1998 allowed scientists to create duplicates of calves that weren't even born yet. Doing this, gave science more flexibility in gene manipulation."

"Good God." He whistled lowly. "Is that what you think they're doing now?"

"I think the full grown specimens—what you call 'goons'—were cloned from an adult male, while the younger, deformed ones—the mutants—were done the newer way. I wouldn't doubt it one bit that scientists are taking fetal cells from mothers-to-be, either willingly or covertly, to produce an even newer strain of human." She leaned forward. "My guess, though, is that these scientists use different human sperm and eggs so they won't be discovered. Who knows. Today they could even take the DNA from eggs and sperms and grow them in petri dishes—so to speak—though the womb is the best receptacle, even today."

"Why?"

"Humans need it for growth, cell differentiation, nutrients, and a slew of other things that artificial settings can't provide, though today, the technology exists for the production of petri dish babies from which the mother delivers a gene-engineered, cloned specimen."

"But how does the hospital get the delivered infant from the mother without her knowing, to the government center raising the clones?"

Stella shrugged. "I doubt if non-government hospitals are in on this. I suspect that when the infant is born in these government facilities, the doctors either substitute another child for the engineered infant, or that they tell the parents the baby died from an illness."

"Where would they find these substitute infants?"

She pulled at her bottom lip in thought. "They likely locate pregnant teenagers and pay them well for their unwanted babies, whether they're healthy or not."

"And the mutants came from genetic engineering?" He wanted to be sure he understood.

"Playing with nucleic acids—DNA, RNA—allows

room for lots of mistakes, like facial deformities, mental deficiencies, maybe even 'glowing red eyes.' But as far as the clones go, their height was most likely deliberately trait-engineered via inbreeding or duplicated by the incorporation of HGH—Human Growth Hormone. But the eyes and mutations must have resulted from an anomaly, maybe something that happened to a gene that was multiplied each time a specimen was cloned. Or maybe it's due to a lack of some chemical. On the other hand, it could be a trait researchers think is desirable and so they masterminded it."

He called for the check while asking, "What do you make of the water contamination?"

"That will be the ruination of civilization. Dimethyl mercury is extremely carcinogenic. In fact, in 1997 a forty-eight year-old research scientist was studying the very effects of this chemical when she accidentally pricked herself—through her gloves—and died within a few mere months . . . that's how lethal it is."

"A pin-prick."

"From what I hear, our drinking water has a much greater concentration than what this researcher had been working with. The CDC is looking into the situation now, trying to determine how mercury invaded the water and what, if anything, can be done. It's beyond me, Cy, how it could have gotten into the drinking water."

"Three guesses."

"But why would the government want to do that?"

"To control us, make us compliant."

She set down her glass, and, leaning across the table, whispered, "It has to be intentional; dimeth merc isn't found naturally in water. It's unlikely any factory would have dumped it—if they had it at all on the premises—knowing its lethal toxicity."

"Isn't your CDC a part of the government?"

"You have that smug, teasing look on your face."

She rose, grabbing her purse. "Of course, my feedback is purely guess work. I'd have to investigate everything."

"Speaking of which . . . is it too late for us to continue investigating each other?"

"Too much time has passed, and too many things have gone between and beyond us." She kissed him sweetly on the cheek. "But always you'll remain special to me, Cy." She turned and strutted away, calling over her shoulder, "I'll ring you up as soon as I learn anything more."

"Wait." When she turned around, he said, "I'm not scheduled to fly out until tomorrow. I was wondering . . . well . . . if you'd like to . . . come back with me to my hotel—Sheraton . . . get a drink at the bar . . . ."

She considered it. Looking undecided, she offered, "If you see me there later, you'll know the answer." She blew him a kiss and walked away.

Washington, D.C.

Harry Gamblin locked his car door after sliding into the passenger's seat, turned the ignition key, hoping to get home within forty minutes. With his resigning from his secretaryship, he would be able to spend more time with his wife, daughter, and son. He pulled away from D.C.'s downtown loop and got on the beltway.

Oh sure, President Williams made it very clear that he wouldn't permit Harry to resign, but, if plans went right, Harry would be long gone before Williams could do anything. His intent was to shepherd his family to Canada during the middle of the night, call a real estate agent from Manitoba to sell their Bethesda home while he and his family hightailed it to Australia. Harry would have his wife and kids pack and leave immediately. Williams shouldn't see the resignation letter until the next day, at the earliest, if not on Monday when he then would send someone to Harry's home. But by then, Harry and his family would be in flight to Australia.

Harry smiled. At last he would be away from the political hell-hole where the devil ate people whole and then threw their scraps to his legions of demons.

His pager went off. He brought it up toward the steering wheel so he could read the number. It was home. He picked up the car phone and dialed.

"When will you be home?" asked his wife. "No doubt you're still in your office and we won't see the likes of you until midnight."

"I have a surprise for you," he said into the mouthpiece stuck between his ear and shoulder while listening to surrounding traffic. "Not only will I be home for dinner, but I want you and the kids to start packing for a trip."

"Is everything okay?"

"Now it is. I'm free."

"You quit?"

"Just start packing, hon. By the way, why did you page me?"

"Williams' aides called looking for you. I told them you were still at the office."

He was pleased that Williams thought he hadn't left the White House.

He found himself humming to radio tunes. With the political machinery behind him, he suddenly felt stripped of heavy loads. At last, he was his old self again: The Harry who joked with people, played tag football with his son, teased his daughter, celebrated his love for his wife over wine and roses. He was the Harry who had at one time thoroughly enjoyed his job—the rise in the political arena from city councilman to mayor, to lieutenant governor, to deputy secretary at the White House, and finally to Secretary. But with each step higher he had taken, he had lost a little bit of his soul, his freedom, and his zest for life. He was glad to be liberated from orders, immorality, and lies. Working in the city all day, fighting traffic to and from, was what had prompted him to move his family out of downtown D.C..

He slowed when the sleet and wind picked up. A shadow at his left made him jump. "Hey!" he yelled through closed car windows. The black BMW that had been behind him suddenly was at his left, pulling up close, trying to squeeze him off the road.

THUMP came a sound from behind his back bumper. His grip on the steering wheel tightened, and he looked into the rearview mirror. Another black car, this one tapping his tail fender in attempt to force him onto the right berm.

When the car at his left clipped the handle of his door, Harry instinctively veered the wheel to the right, which forced him onto the berm where he hit a branch and came to a halt.

Both cars stopped next to him. Out of the passenger sides of each, stepped two colossal sized men. "Oh Lord no." Frantically he tried jettisoning his auto off the berm while hitting the car's automatic locks. But already they were at his door. In an even motion, one ripped the driver's door right off its hinges while the other yanked Harry out of the seat.

The second he saw the machete was the same instant the goon lifted it in the air—sleet glistening off it—and swiftly rent it across Harry's waist and head.

9:00 pm; Cambridge, Maryland

Mitch hit "end" on his cell phone as he rolled up to Azar's front curb in the revitalized town located about fifteen miles from Easton. He tried Gillian's phone number again but still no answer. Either she was sleeping or out somewhere. He just hoped she wasn't sick. Running his hand through his hair, he looked around before getting out of his car and walking up to Ms. Azar's residence. The second she admitted him, he thanked her for seeing him so late. Pointedly, he asked, "What's going on in the Enolc labs?"

"It goes against God. Creation should be His realm."

"Why are the labs underground?"

"So no one will know." She shifted her stance, not inviting him to sit.

"Is it true the labs are cloning humans?"

"It's more advanced than that."

"More advanced!"

"Sssh." She looked around her apartment. "I wouldn't be surprised if there are bugs planted here." She walked over to the blinds on her windows and turned the rods to make sure each slat rested tightly against one another. "That day Hammond was attacked, it was by a highly engineered clone gone mad. They're ferocious."

"Good God." He had fifty-thousand questions but didn't know where to start. "Not only is Hammond dead, but so is my best buddy, my ex-wife's friend's sister-in-law, and a slew of other innocent people. If you don't help me, more will die."

She stuck her nose in the air. "You don't know what they'll do if they find out I'm talking about them. They have spies and surveillance everywhere. Dr. Hammond was always on the lookout." Again she nervously glanced around. "It's the global government."

"I won't put you into jeopardy, but we've got to stop those who are destroying our freedoms, our rights, our world."

"It's too late, Mr. Frey."

"If we don't do something to end this corrupt tyranny, then we'll have only ourselves to blame." He looked her right in the eye. "Especially you, Ms. Azar, who's known all along what's been going on." He paused. "I've read the journal of my friend, Salyer Basse." He held up the papers as testimony. "In them he talks about the labs. How many are there?"

"A couple dozen. We're preparing to open some in other countries. The cloning ones are called Enolc labs. The word is 'clone' backwards."

"Their purpose?" He glanced at Salyer's notes. "I know . . . better food, better—"

"A ready-made U.N. military composed of super powerful, immensely strong, intelligent men to serve on the battlefields and in key governmental positions to be yes-men. And don't forget immortality, Mr. Frey. The Enolcs have genetically identified the aging gene, and now all they have to do is remove, reverse, and inbreed it. Plus, high level genetic engineering that's being done in government labs eliminates the need for organ donors and transplants, and can eradicate osteoporosis and other diseases. Also top secret is that the Enolcs have figured out how to regenerate nerve cells so that permanent spinal injuries will be passe. It's all a matter of the government publicly revealing its scientific discoveries, which it hasn't done."

"And won't, especially if it benefits us 'little people,'" Mitch snorted.

"Clones are also used as spare parts, but all of this has fallen into satanic hands that want to breed a Nietzchean/Hitlerian race. There's no one to stop the wicked government from achieving its fiendish goal."

Mitch puffed up his chest. "Well, I'll do it."

A little smile cracked at the corners of her mouth. "I respect your gumption but **no one** can stop them; it's not some rinky-dink operation." She glanced towards the windows. "When Dr. Hammond originally started cloning, the first group was fairly normal but—"

"Explain 'first group' and 'normal'." He skimmed Sal's handwriting.

"The first group wasn't the true clones—more like

the old 'test tube babies.' These men are out in society functioning in near normal capacity, and though they have negative attributes, they aren't as violent as the real clones. But nor can they be programmed like true clones, either, which was the goal all along. Dr. Hammond was working on that, striving for programmable duplicates through high-technology."

"The thing that attacked Hammond was a Progeny Two?"

She nodded. "A chemical or a couple of chemicals appear to be lacking in their brains—serotonin and maybe dopamine. There is another group out there, too, that's a result of Secretary Gamblin's dictate to encourage women to be breeders. To do that, couples are given the incentive of picking their babies' traits—babies they'll never see because the fertility clinics would take them to be raised as clones."

"Clinics? You don't mean the Enolc labs?"

"Of course not; Enolcs are top secret but certain fertility clinics are fronts for Enolcs, meaning that couples go there to get pregnant and then the Enolcs use their zygotes in cloning. So not only are the traits genetically engineered, but the fertilization process is a bit different because it's based not only on DNA transfer but also on cytoplasmic exchange and the shuffling—addition, deletion, and rearrangement—of DNA without regard to natural law. In theory, it should work; in practice, it's been disastrous. Our fertility clinics usually take the deformed infants from the parents under some pretense and replaces them with abandoned or unwanted babies so that the parents won't know the difference, and the clinic won't get a negative reputation."

"Then the engineered infant ends up at an Enolc near that fertility clinic?"

"Such fertility clinics are paid well for the infants or T-natums."

"T-natums? 'Mutants' spelled backwards." He shook his head.

"No parent wants a mutant child, so those babies are shipped off to specific fertility clinics where their serotonin and dopamine are removed from their brains and injected into clones that show promise."

"What happens to the infant?"

"It dies, or is put away in some institution. The end result is that no one wants these T-natums because of their disfigurement and violent behavior." She walked over to the window and peaked between the slats in the blinds. "Hammond was studying this when he died. Our best transgenics techs think it has to do with certain traits that when selected together somehow create a grotesque effect. But I've also seen reports that indicate that not only was the DNA rearranged, but the RNA was also transmutated."

"This sounds like science fiction."

"None of this should come as a surprise. Over fifteen years ago we could grow body parts—human organs—inside animals."

"Are there mutants or T-natums that aren't grotesque in appearance?"

"I don't think so. Those fertility clinics that assist Enolcs aren't more than eight or nine years old, so we don't have solid data yet; besides, the T-natums aren't old enough to yield long term results. Supposedly they're grotesque looking because of genetic foul-ups; yet, they're very intelligent, with IQs in the 150-180 range. The one who attached Hilda Dillon had broken into the computer files and located her address."

"You mean Dillon was his natural mother? What about the adult clones?"

"Progeny Two have genetically engineered IQs in the 170-210 range, with near photographic memories, powerful vision and sense of smell, and unequaled eye-hand coordination. The next progeny—currently under development—will be even more brilliant and skilled. I'd say as it is now they're already smarter than their creators. The problem is the brain biochip—the government's idea of having dual control over them: One through genetic engineering, and the other via the programmed chip." She quietly added, "I've heard that there are female clones but I don't know for sure; and nor do I know if they're healthy even if they do exist."

"Our government is behind all this?"

She looked uneasy. "Via the U. N.. The U.S. is the only nation that's advanced enough to carry this out, although it has begun in other countries now."

"What fertility clinics are part of Enolc One?"

"I think Delaware Gap, Pitt-Valley, and Traditional, though I could be wrong about Traditional because that one might have been a conversion clinic." She read his eyes. "By conversion, I mean a clinic that originally may have been legit but the government got it to come on board. Money speaks loudly."

He stared into the air, repeating the word 'Traditional, Traditional, Tradi-' Suddenly it hit him, "Traditional! Dixie Morris works there! She could be in danger!"

Azar's brows raised.

Mitch pressed: "You did know Salyer Basse, didn't you."

"I only knew of him. If he hadn't met with you, he might still be alive today. You and I are equally doomed. The world will end in a burning hell with the global government dictating to us, making and dispensing life. Its plan is to eliminate humans who are aged, diseased, handicapped and disabled, mentally slow and dysfunctional, as well as all criminals, welfare-mongers—"

"If we're not productive, we're gone. Right?"

"It's all in the chronicles of the CFR, the Bilderbergers, Illuminata, and all those other top, shadow associations, some of which society isn't even aware of." She gave him a gentle push and shoved him toward the door.

He turned around, asked, "What will you do?"

"I can't ever return to work. I know they'll find out I talked to you. I'm going to pack the second you leave."

"You can't run forever. Get the police to protect you."

She laughed mockingly. "If you were a local or state officer, would you believe this story? Besides, the government has them in their clutches, too."

"If you're leaving here, then give me whatever I need to sneak into Enolc One to collect documentation as proof of—"

"You'll be caught."

"If I don't get any records, no one will believe me. With proof I can go to the media and rat on this operation." He paused before suggesting, ". . . unless **you** go back one more time to copy documents for me. They wouldn't suspect you."

"I won't risk my life returning. The few times I worked the graveyard shift, I know that between five and seven in the morning, everyone's in report. That shift has the least number of employees. Hammond's office has a copy of all the documents. Just grab what records you can and then get out. But know this, whether you're caught while there or they learn later what you did, they'll come after you. Once the media breaks the news, the government will track down the source—meaning you—through bribery, blackmail, threats, and executions. You will be a marked man." She glanced out her front windows. "We're both marked now. Going to the media won't help; most are puppets of the omnipotent one-worlders. Your work will be all for naught."

"Where are these records in Hammond's office; will

someone be there then?"

"There's no replacement yet for Dr. Hammond, though Dr. Glazier is 'acting.' The documents can be found in his back room file cabinet. The key is taped to the back of the cabinet. Grope with your hand between the cabinet and the wall and you'll find it. The code to his locked door is double-oh-seven. Yes, double-oh-seven. Just know that you're about to take your first step into hell."

"How do I get into the underground parking lot and the clinic itself?"

She gave him detailed directions which he wrote down. "Drive down the dirt path about 150-feet where you'll see a vertical, plastic tube with a touch pad computer. Punch in 3-18-10. The plastic semi-dome will open to let you drive down the ramp. Park in a far corner in the garage, walk to the entrance, and again punch in 3-18-10. You'll be admitted to an elevator; hit three to go down to Hammond's office. Walk down the hall, make a right at the first hallway intersection, and the first office on the right is Hammond's. His number is double-oh-seven." She smiled for the first time. "He was eccentric like that." She stepped out of the foyer and went into a room that looked like a bedroom. When she returned, she was carrying a white lab coat. "Wear this. You might get away with it, though that late shift has so few people that most know each other." She wet her lips. "I wish you luck, but I have no illusions that you'll get through safely."

"Is there another entrance to the garage besides the transparent dome?"

"Where we stood the day Dr. Hammond was attacked by a clone is an emergency escape through a manhole. Inside this camouflaged shed is a hydraulic switch to lift the lid, as well as a specially-made wrench for when the hydraulics aren't working."

"That will get me into the place . . . can I get out

that way if I have to?"

"Yes, but describing how to access the passageway
leading to it is difficult. You either have to stumble on
it, or see it on a very detailed computerized map."

"Thank you," he mumbled, then bussed her on the
cheek, and turned to leave.

She called, "Just know that if you get caught, no
one will come to your aid."

He grew worried about her. "Would you like to stay
with me?"

"You think you're safe?" She shut the door, turned
all three inside locks.

Washington, D.C.

Exhausted, President Williams sat behind his desk,
rubbing his eyes. "I should be with my family now—it
is Friday night—but instead I've called you in here
because we have a mini-crisis. We must find a way to
graciously explain Gamblin's death and find a replacement for him by Monday morning before the press
makes mincemeat of all this."

The White House spokesperson said, "Gamblin did
hold one of the highest cabinet offices. You can make
an 'acting' appointment, and then stall the selection
committee's search for a new secretary until you're out
of office. By then, we'll have lined up someone who we
really want, and whose background we can clean up
enough to pass the committee's nomination."

"To think a pansy like Harry would put the media in
an uproar. Give me names of potential candidates to
replace him, and I'll make the appointment." He
thought a second. "Names whose background—no matter how unscrupulous—won't likely come out under
investigation." He rose from his seat.

"Awful the way Gamblin died—his body sliced,
with only his buttocks left."

President Williams yawned. "Yeah, he behaved like an ass in here."

Chapter
14

By his wide girth, Gillian recognized him the second he stepped into the cafe. She waved to him. "You're Gordon?"

He sat in a sturdy bistro chair. "I don't know why I'm here, Ms. Montague, but I came because Dixie has spoken highly of you in the past." He wheezed from the excess fat his body toted around the way it would if carrying heavy suitcases.

Gillian explained how she felt about Dixie, how many years they had been friends. "But I fear she's gotten herself into some serious sticky situations, that she's hooked up with the wrong people. I worry about her."

He blew his nose into a white hanky when the steam from the hot, frothing latte cleaned his sinuses. "I like Dixie a lot, and I wouldn't want her to be in trouble or have something happen to her. When I get up my nerve, I'll ask her out, but I know she won't date me because she's so attractive, and all the guys at the clinic want her."

Gillian tried picturing Dixie as the glamorous type. "Maybe I can put in a good word for you in a nonchalant way so that she doesn't know we met."

"What will this cost me?"

Gilly shrugged. "I just want you to decode a disk for me, and for me to be with you when you do it."

"Why me?"

"It's Dixie's disk from the clinic."

He visibly pulled back.

I could be making a big mistake here; what if he's part of all this?

"I could lose my job," he blew at the rising steam from his tall glass mug, "especially if you're there."

"I just want to make sure she's not into trouble."

He coughed as if trying to clear phlegm from his lungs. "If you're such best friends, why not just ask her?"

Instantly she realized that not only was he not going to help her, but that he'd probably tell Dixie, too. "If you cared about her, you'd do everything you could to make sure she wasn't into something over her head."

He looked at her, sipped his coffee, set it back on the saucer, took another sip, and looked at her again. "Ironically, I did say something to Dixie once about whether what we were doing at the lab was really helping infertile couples."

She jumped at that. "So you've had doubts, too?" Leaning closer to the edge of the table, she said, "All I want you to do is see if you can decode the disk."

He shrugged as if that wasn't a tall order for him. "When?"

"It's Saturday; the lab slows down on weekends. Why not now?"

He looked up from the coffee mug, glimpsed his watch. "This is crazy." Blowing his nose again after sipping his coffee, he said, "You'll set me up with her?"

"I'll do my very best. If not, I'll go out with you."

It was the first time she saw him grin. "Work on Dixie."

9:30 a.m.

When Cy got home from Atlanta, he went straight for his answering machine. One message after another rolled out—from bill collectors, potential and established clients, salespeople, and Wally. The kid sounded awful: "Uncle Cyril." Pause. "I don't feel so hot. Can you" pause "come over?"

"What the hell am I supposed to do?" Cy asked himself. "I'm no nurse."

He stood motionless, trying to decide what action he should take first; he considered the flurry of chores he faced, and overwhelmed by it all, he remained frozen. Then a mental picture of his nephew came to mind. He put his coat back on and went out the door.

With snow piling, it took him longer to get to Wally's apartment than he expected, and even longer for Wally to make it to the door and let him in.

"You look ghastly, kid." Cy's eyes roved his nephew's face.

A wave of nausea swept through Wally and instantly he put his soiled hanky to his lips. "I'm sorry, Uncle Cy; I've been sick to my stomach. Gillian took me to the Immediate Care Clinic and they ran tests, gave me some medicine to settle my stomach and take the pain away. We didn't get home until really late last night."

"Where is she now?"

He scrunched his shoulders together. "She said she had an appointment this morning with some guy about the goon case." He belched again into the hanky.

"What did the doctor say? The tests?"

"No results yet."

Cy unbuttoned his trench coat in spite of the cold. He felt inexplicably flushed, as if his body were raging in conflict with the fight or flight instinct. Something was definitely wrong, and he was fearful of trying to pin-point it. "Why didn't you tell me, Wallace? You know you're my responsibility."

"It just got worse the last day or so. My stomach's been balling up with horrendous cramps, and my head feels like a hammer's in it."

"So you haven't eaten in days. Jeesh, Wally, you should have told me you were feeling this bad. Get your coat. We're going to the emergency room."

The boy tried protesting but was too weak to argue. When he finally struggled outside to the steps of his apartment building, the cold rushed his belly and made him so sick that he puked right off the side of the stoop. Cy picked him up and carried him to his car.

9:30 a.m.; Philadelphia

After having passed through the guard booth at the clinic's front entrance, with Gillian in her car following, Gordon punched in numbers to the alarm system at the entrance, and then slid his key card into the metal slotted box. When the light blinked, he nudged the handle and the door opened.

"Are all the doors on the key card, and with the same alarm code?" she asked as if impressed with the set-up, just to get him to respond.

"Yeah, unfortunately. It's a terribly unsecured way to do it. It should be more computerized but no one here listens to me."

Gordon went up to a monitor, hit a button, identified himself to the guards in their booth, and said, "With me, I have Kate Shadduck from Adelphi Computer Consultants." He motioned for Gillian, wearing a full-brimmed hat and sunglasses, to step before the monitors.

With approval granted, they headed for Gordon's computer center, their footfall echoing in the deadly silent halls.

"Just remember you're Kate Shadduck—a specialty tech from Adelphi—who's here to help me with a computer software problem," Gordon lowly mumbled out of the side of his mouth. "You said the guards might know you from some incident you had when visiting Dixie the last time you were here; if so, then keep a low profile."

"That's why I put the hat and shades on." Casually she said, "You must have a pretty tight security system if everyone has to present themselves to the monitors."

"They don't if they enter in the back way. We couldn't go in that way since the front gate registered my car entering. The back isn't that well secured at all."

"What about my car?"

"They link it to mine, so when I leave, they'll know you have, too. That's what I'm saying . . . it's not all that secure; just looks that way."

They walked up a flight of stairs.

Gordon ventured, "You don't want to go into that 'incident' you referred to?"

"I told you that it had to do with a giant-sized man chasing me—someone who was being injected with something taken from an infant."

"Never mind; it's better I don't know." He blew out air. "I sure hope I'm not getting involved with some lunatic." He glanced nervously around the halls. "I'm going to scan the disk, and then we're going to get right out of here. I'm not doing a print-out or anything else."

She nodded, entered his computer room after him.

Wilmington

The young, chunky, mouse-brown, curly-haired woman hung up the phone after talking to her doctor who arranged for her to have a CT scan of her head to determine if there was a sinus infection. She jotted her January 8, 8:00 a.m. appointment on her calendar, and then looked over at Mitch who sat at the desk across from her. She glanced around the newsroom from her portable cubicle, and asked, "You just now left your source? Well, I'll need proof."

He handed her seven typed sheets. "I've typed up an overview on everything I read. I also have the originals, such as Salyer Basse's handwritten documents. You'll find clues in my typed overview where I'm going to hide Sal's materials if anything happens to me." Mitch's eyes met hers and he wondered how much he could trust her. She was a novice reporter, but that she was, made her all the more daring and eager to prove herself. He only hoped she would believe him, and he prayed she wasn't some plant for Big Brother. *Stop it, Mitch; you're being paranoid.*

"Why can't you just tell me where Basse's documents are, Mr. Frey? Why must you be so dramatic and secretive? You're the one who called **me** at home to meet you here, and then you expect me to believ—"

"Haven't you heard a word I've been telling you? The government has plants everywhere. Look, all I'm asking is that if something happens to me, you'll follow up on my investigation, starting with my overview and then studying Salyer's documents." His typed sheets gave clues on how she could locate those papers. He didn't trust putting the exact location in writing. "You'll get your proof, Ms. Carter, after I sneak into a top secret lab."

She looked questioningly. "Oh? So why don't you let me go with you?"

"I can't put you at risk; I wouldn't want us both to

get killed. And I need to know I can trust you. Your name came to me from recommendations but still. . . ."

"Likewise, Mr. Frey, I, too, will check you out, and if I find you're on the up and up, I'll do my best at my end. I'm young and a bit inexperienced, but I'm a very good reporter who's not afraid to expose any wrong-doing on any level. You do your job, and I'll do mine."

He leaned toward her, saying under his breath. "You might not be afraid now but there are horrors beyond human imagination. I know; I saw Salyer Basse die, and after you read his documents, you won't be able to sleep at night. I've talked to people who are so afraid of the evil, that they can't move. What you'll uncover—if you do your job right—will shake this world to its core. You've got to promise that you'll go after them if anything happens to me."

She raised her eyebrows, flipped through his over-view. "I'll do what I can."

"The future may very well rest in your young, smooth, lily white hands."

"I don't know whether that's a slam or a compliment."

"Following through on this story, Ms. Carter, will not only make your name known all over the world, but you'll be saving every citizen on this earth."

"Now that's a hyperbole."

"This is no joke. I'm not a screwball."

"If I thought you were, I wouldn't have driven here to meet you on a Saturday." She rose, and he, with her. "I'll start with studying your typed pages, checking out your background, and doing my own research. It would really help if you could give me a list of references on you."

He leaned over her desk and wrote out names and numbers of people she could call: Gillian, his office staff, his pastor, business colleagues. But he was hesi-tant about giving the location of where he put Salyer's documents. He straightened from his stooped position, saying, "Look, if you can't figure out where Salyer's papers are after you're read my journal, I'll let you know because by then I should know you well enough to trust you. But if you're as hot of an investigative reporter as I've been told, you should be able to discern this. The only thing I know, miss, is that we don't have much time."

"I'll need time to go over your paper." She settled into her chair as if for a long period.

10:00 a.m.; Philadelphia

Gillian impatiently tapped her foot, waiting on Gordon. Standing behind him as he sat at the computer console, she noticed how adeptly his fingers moved about the keyboard as he switched this disk, slid that one in, moving his wheely chair from one side of the long desk to the other.

She glanced around the room to see if there was anything she should be investigating. The place gave her the creeps even with the well-lighted computer room, the humming of the machines to break the eerie silence, and a normal human being sharing the same room with her.

She did a double take when she thought her vision caught sight of movement outside the computer room door.

"This is what I have so far," Gordon said lowly.

She eyed the screen, saw zany marks integrated into text. "It's still coded."

"That's all that's been read and translated so far. It's going to take me awhile to do more, and I'm not comfortable sitting here on a Saturday doing this."

"Who would know what you're doing? You yourself said that you come in all hours." She interpreted the document on the screen. "It says something about infertile couples coming in and having babies switched? Is that right?"

Gordon shook his head. "There are names there: Miles, Givens, Dillon—"

"Dillon?"

He looked at her. "I don't know these people." He hit a couple of buttons, tried bringing in a correlative document. "It's all encoded."

"Cross-reference the names Miles, Givens, Dillon. I need addresses." No sooner was that out of her mouth when she slightly turned her head and again caught sight of movement at the door. "Gordon, there's a goon out there."

He spun around in his chair. "I didn't see anything."

"Just watch."

They went stark quiet, with only their breathing reverberating in the room.

Suddenly Gordon said, "I saw it . . . big faced, exaggerated features."

"That's what I'm talking about."

"We've gotta get out of here." He yanked the disk out of the slot, and hustled Gillian and himself out of the computer room. "I don't see anyone in this hall."

"Halt!" came a voice around the corner.

Both jumped.

"I'll take that." The normal-looking and average-sized guard took the disk out of Gordon's hands.

Gillian's heart sank. She hadn't made a copy of it. If they told Dixie, Gillian knew their friendship was over. She looked over at Gordie when she felt his eyes on her.

11:30 p.m.; Wilmington

Cy walked from one end of the emergency room to the other, then back again. He needed a cigar but didn't want to go outside to smoke in case the doctor came to talk to him. Why did these things take so long? He hated emergency departments for that reason alone—always took forever to call the patient in and then another forever to examine them and arrive at a diagnosis.

He thought about going back to the nurse's counter to ask about Wally but he had made such a pest of himself that he decided to wait. He continued pacing.

"Mr. Collier?"

Cy turned at the sound of his name.

A nurse motioned for him to follow.

In a small cubicle cordoned off by a curtain hanging on a rail, hovered an older doctor over Wally, listening to his stomach through a stethoscope. Seconds later, he patted the boy's leg, said he'd be right back, and led Cy out into the hall.

"Well?" asked Cy, irritated with all the delays.

Philadelphia

Sitting behind the fertility lab on a treed lane, Gillian scrutinized the back door. Earlier, she and Gordon had had the disk taken from them and then had been escorted off the clinic property and had driven away.

Gillian was half-way home when she remembered what Dixie had told her years ago, about how she once had lost her admission credentials to the lab but had gone down to a lane overgrown with trees and foliage and got onto the grounds that way. It had taken Gillian a good hour to locate the lane based on what she remembered from Dixie's description, but then she did locate it in an area where the lane had a severed rusty, tightly knit barbed wire enervated with high voltage.

From her distance, watching through binoculars, she saw four huge guards walk their rounds at shift

change. When they had gone inside, she quietly left her
car, and sneaked to the back door using trees as cover.
Recalling Gordie having said security was about nonex-
istent at the back entrance, she punched the alarm code
in to temporarily dismantle it as she slid into the slot
the master key card she had taken from Dixie's bedroom. The minute she got into the back foyer, she
looked around for concealed cameras, but saw none.
While having waited for the computer to translate
Dixie's disk, Gordon had talked about his computer and
what it did for the clinic, explaining how it was connected to cameras in the building and where the cameras were located. *Maybe he told me all that for a
reason.* She began to wonder about Gordon and what
role he really played in the entire operation.

Looking at the mounted, laminated wall map at the
back entrance, she matched up the route to Dixie's lab
to areas where Gordon said there were no security cameras. Softly, in the dimly lighted halls, she made her
way. Only once did she have a close call when a tech
walked down a hall to enter a vaulted room. She looked
around when she reached Dixie's lab, then swiftly slid
in the key card.

Where to look, she wondered—in the lab itself with
all its apparati, or in the office adjoining it? Staying
away from anything resembling a security camera, she
slipped into Dixie's office and began looking through
desk drawers and file cabinets, gingerly shoving open
and softly shutting drawers after fingering through
files. She couldn't decide what she wanted: Everything
she could find on the fertility projects, anything on the
clones, or, specifically, on the files of Miles, Givens,
Dillon. Were there reports on Ripley, del Reys, and others? And what was Dixie doing with those files anyway?

She focused only on those files of people listed on
the partially translated disk, intending at some other

point to return to the fertility clinic and gather more information.

Thinking she heard a noise outside the office door, she looked up, searching for an intruder. Apprehensive now, she quickly leafed through the manilla files in search of familiar names and jotted down addresses and phone numbers.

At a folder marked, "Neurocerebral Chemicals," she paused long enough to glance at a few lines with such words as "serotonin," "brain stem," "brain bio-chips," "electronic cerebral programming," "BCI," and other unique terms.

Again the noise.

She closed the file cabinet, tip-toed back through the lab, stood at the door, her eyes scanning for human or goon figures. Minutes passed before she felt confi-dent enough to venture out in the hallway and hug the walls away from the corridor cameras. She was sur-prised how easy it was for her to get to the back entrance without interference from authorities, and even more shocked that she made it back to her car and was off without having been noticed.

11:40 a.m.; Wilmington

When the doctor sat, Cy plunked into a hard back chair with a grunt. He rubbed his nose nervously, sensed the tension in every fiber of his body. "Okay, Doc, get to it."

"Your nephew, Mr. Collier, is very ill. All our water fountains are shut off."

"I don't give a horse's ass about your water foun-tains. Tell me about Wally."

"Why did he drink the water?"

"Maybe I shoulda kept better tabs. . . . but he was there with us in my office when the radio announced not to drink the water. I figured he knew better."

"Whether twenty or ninety, Mr. Collier, we should all look after each other. We've been seeing many cases like this. People just don't listen. Everywhere, emergency rooms are filling up with the very ill who ignored warnings and drank the toxic water, or the toxin infiltrated their systems through the skin from taking baths and showers, washing their hair, and whatnot. They just don't seem to put it together that any contact with dimethyl is deadly."

"We can thank our government for that."

The doctor gave him an odd look then glanced at the metal chart. "Your nephew has at the most a month."

"A month!" Cy could feel the blood drain from his face. "A month!"

"More likely weeks, maybe even a few days. He's ingested so much water that his cells are hypertonic—saturated with dimethyl mercury. We'll admit him and do our best to keep him comfortable. We have only a few beds available because like other hospitals everywhere, we're admitting a patient every ten minutes. When your nephew's brain becomes infiltrated, and he becomes comatose, and if he should, by chance, continue to demonstrate vital signs, you'll have to decide whether to cease life support or have him admitted to a long term nursing institution. We don't have enough beds and manpower to take care of him and other dimeth victims when we're already near capacity with regular med-surge patients."

Cy's focus lowered to the floor.

"I'm sorry to be so blunt, but your nephew could linger for weeks, maybe months, or go suddenly."

"Is he in pain?"

"His cells are bursting with suffused toxic levels; the cancer is rampant. We're trying to ease his discomfort with pain injections. We're doing all we can."

The veteran emergency room physician turned and

walked away, with Cy watching his white coat flap as he walked.

3:00 p.m.; Philadelphia

Dixie arrived at the clinic sorely angry and put out. Of all things . . . having to go into work on a weekend. She waved to the guard at the gate and hopped out of her car at the front entrance, sliding her key card into the machine, then went straight up to the fifth floor where the security office was located.

The guard tipped his hat on seeing her. "Sorry to call you in on a Saturday, Ms. Morris, but we need you to see the tape."

"This better be good, Dallas, or I'll have your job." She saw the other guards in the security room stiffen at her words. She watched him rerun the videotape from the hidden security cameras, then eyed the playback, her teeth gritted, lips tight, as she saw Gordon and Gillian at the camera with Gordon introducing Gillian as someone else. Livid, she viewed a guard removing a disk from Gordon's hand, and then ushering them out. Equally unnerved, she watched her best friend on camera cutting across the grounds to get into the clinic—using what Dixie figured was her card key—and then skulking down the halls to Dixie's lab and rummaging through her office.

"What was on the disk?" Dixie asked over her shoulder.

"Most of it was encoded but each page had your name and I.D. number on it." The guard handed her the computer disk he had removed from Gillian and Gordon's possession. "We let her go because we have the goods on her, and we didn't want to alert her to our being on to her until you directed us as what to do."

"I'll take care of it myself." Dixie turned and left the clinic.

6:00 p.m.; Wilmington

Gillian let Chase give her a quick, light hug when he opened the door and saw her. He gushed his pleasure at her arrival, and shepherded her inside his small rancher, talking about the chicken cordon bleu he had made, and what a nice evening they would have.

She watched him pour two glasses of wine, then seat himself next to her on the couch. She asked, "The stockbroker company you work for, is it a branch office or a franchise?" She wouldn't let her eyes meet his, but she felt him staring at her.

"It's a small office; you wouldn't have heard of it." He leaned over the coffee table and absently examined the bottle of chardonay.

"I might have; I've been in Wilmington a long time. And you?"

"Aaah, I see, Gillian. You're back to playing your detective games; trying to get the low-down on me."

She figured he was ticked off, but instead of losing his temper, he set the bottle down on the glass table, and leaned back in the couch, his one arm going around her, and his other hand holding the goblet. Without making a transition to his former statement, he said, "So, tell me more about your detective job, since you seem to be 'on' every minute of the day."

"You don't like that?"

"I don't like being made to feel as though I'm a criminal. You've been checking up on me." With the glass to his lips, he shifted his eyes in her direction.

"I always check out guys I'm interested in. It's part of my nature as a detective."

He chuckled a light, sweet laugh. "So, fine, you're a detective. I have no problem with that. In fact, I'd love to learn more about what you do."

Well, she thought; that was more than Mitch had ever done. "I started out doing rut stuff like checking out insurance fraud, tailing adulterers . . . but now I've got this exciting case requiring lots of research on my part: reading, interviewing—"

"Researching what? It's hard picturing someone as gorgeous and fragile-looking as you, as a detective."

"I can be tough when I have to." She made an exaggerated bulge on her bent arm, and he playfully felt her biceps, acting as though her strength was astounding.

Downing another glass, he asked, "What kind of stuff are you researching?"

"I told you I'm looking into all the murders by these so-called goons with flashing red eyes."

"Goons?" He glanced at her. "Those you claim are colossal sized?"

"They're barbaric savages. I'm going to interview the survivors of families who have been attacked by them."

He looked at her. "Who will you be interviewing?"

She explained about the del Reys, the Ripleys, Hilda Dillon.

He excused himself to go into the kitchen to fix a vegetable dish. Returning minutes later, he poured himself another drink while Gilly was still on her first one. Ten minutes later, after more drinks, endless chit-chat, and Chase running in and out of the kitchen, he was finally ready to serve dinner. He kissed her on the mouth and headed for the kitchen.

Running her tongue over her lips, she wondered what he had eaten before she came; he had a certain recognizable smell on his breath that she couldn't place.

She heard him curse. "What's wrong?" Entering the kitchen she saw how upset he was.

Slamming the oven door shut with his foot while holding dinner between pot holders, he swore again. "Look at this: Not cooked! Something must be wrong with the damn oven!" He dumped the chicken into a garbage bag. "Can't even save it because it's been sitting in the oven for hours and chicken shouldn't be left sitting out. Now what?"

Smiling, she said, "I love pizza."

"You sit here and watch TV while I run down the block to Pizza Hut." He threw on a jacket and dashed outside.

Well, she thought, what to do? She turned on the T.V., heard a reporter on a news documentary interview a young man who was given a dishonorable discharge from the service for refusing to fight for the U.N. when, he claimed, he thought he had enlisted to serve America. Gillian knew he'd end up court-martialled; that was how the government had come to handle such things in the last several years. She rose and walked around the bungalow, looking at pictures. Studying them, she realized that there were no shots of Chase and Leslie together. In fact, all of the photos seemed to be only of Chase, and, yet, in a way in each, he looked just a bit different than now: Less intense, even smiling, and less bulk and height. Maybe since the photos were taken, he had undergone body-building. If anything, she thought, he had looked more like his sister in those photos. She wondered what had happened between him and Leslie that made them such dire enemies. Obviously Chase's parents had favored him more than Leslie. Suddenly Gillian's heart went out to the peculiar woman.

The door opened. She walked toward it to help Chase carry in the pizza.

It was Leslie. They stared at one another.

Gilly spoke first: "I didn't expect you."

"Why not? I live here?"

"Yes, of course. . . . I'm sorry. I just thought—"

"I think we were both taken by surprise." She stepped inside the foyer and shut the door behind her.

It was then that Gilly wondered why she hadn't noticed Leslie's wig before. Did she have some kind of health problem to cause her to lose her hair? It made sense, thought Gilly.

Footsteps outside. Leslie turned, whispered to Gilly, "Stay away from Chase."

Gilly's mouth flew open. "But he's your brother! Why would you say that?"

Leslie walked past Gilly, saying under her breath as Chase started opening the door, "Just keep your distance."

Chapter 15

In the kitchen of his brick rancher, Chase poured more white wine into his glass, and then into Gillian's while muttering, "White goes with chicken, but now that we're relegated to eating pizza, I should have gotten red."

She studied him. A look crossed his face, making her uncomfortable. He gulped the alcohol as if he were on some rugged trek and hadn't had fluids in days.

He stopped drinking when he saw her staring. "What's wrong? Do I have wine dribbling down my chin?"

"Of course not." She patted his hand. "While you were out getting the pizza, your sister ran in to me."

He swore.

"She didn't do anything wrong. She said hello and went to her bedroom."

"I've told her a hundred times not to bug my guests. What did she say?"

"We didn't have a conversation." Gillian waited a

few minutes before pressing him since he was rapidly moving into a bad mood: "Why does Leslie wear a wig?"

He slammed his fist against the table, stood, and adjusting his belt, walked around the room. "Can't she even dress right? What a retard."

"Chase, really, that's a terrible thing to say about your sister."

He returned to the table, reseated himself. "You're right. But you ought to know that Leslie has some serious physical and mental problems. She wears a wig because of an endocrine disorder that—"

"What?"

"What what?"

"What kind of disorder?"

"Some medical term. It's why she seems masculine—hormones. Mentally, she has the brain of a fifteen-year-old."

"I find that hard to believe. Your sister comes across a lot brighter than that. She's not repulsive, either. After all, she does look like you."

He shot her a dirty look.

She watched him pour garlic over his third piece of pizza. "Did either of your parents have a glandular problem? Maybe you have it, too, since you're twins."

"Enough, Gillian."

"Why must you be so private about your past, your life, your—"

"Why must you be so nosy?" He looked up at the ceiling in dismay. "Look, I'm sorry but every time we're together, I feel like you're trying to trip me up."

"Why would that come to mind if you have nothing to hide?"

"Oh for pete's sake! That's exactly what I'm talking about. Stop playing your detective games!" He threw a pot holder on the counter. "You've made me lose my appetite. In fact, you've made me lose any desire I had to be with you this evening."

"You're making a big deal out of nothing. I'm just trying to get to know you but anytime I ask about your sister, you just go off." She pushed her chair out, knowing he wanted her to leave.

"When it comes to **her**, she bothers the hell out of me! Always I was the one who took care of her, who defended her when the other kids ridiculed her."

"It's what brothers do." She could tell by his fist that she ought to back off.

He looked off into space. "I didn't mean to lose my temper."

"If we can't talk, Chase, we can't have much of a relationship."

"You're right. Go on, ask me anything."

"Is Leslie gay?"

His surprised look made her smile.

"Gosh, what a question. I . . . I don't know. Maybe that's part of her problem. Maybe she's jealous of the women I entertain. Now there's a thought."

And maybe too convenient a one.

"But **I'm** not gay." Out of nowhere, he came around the table to where she sat, and planted a kiss on her lips.

There was that odor again, but negligible.

He must have noticed her reaction because he pulled back and slipped out a small packet of Lifesavers, dropping a lemon one into his mouth, while saying, "Must have been the garlic." He kissed her again, his tongue searching her mouth; his hand resting temptingly below her right breast.

She stood to meet his lips, his searching hands toying with her breast. She arched her back, every one of her muscles responding.

He lifted her with one hand, and carried her to his bedroom, his fingers still massaging her nipple through her sweater.

She thought she heard Leslie's bedroom door open and then close. Chase lay her on the bed. She protested, "Please, let me up."

He straddled her. One button at a time, he bewitchingly undid her blouse, and then unsnapped her bra, exposing her bare chest.

"Perfect; beautiful." He said it almost in an analyzing tone. His lips came down and wet her skin, cupping her nipples.

"Mitch, please, don't."

He stopped. "Mitch?" he repeated angrily.

She closed her eyes. "My ex-husband. Sorry. But please don't." She regretted having drunk the little wine she did.

He grunted. His hands kneaded her breasts, then pulled down the zipper on her jeans, sliding them down past her hips, off her feet.

"Don't, I said!"

His hand went between her crotch.

"I said stop it!" Anger rushed inside her. She struggled against his bulk.

He ripped off his shirt, undid his zipper. With his tongue in her mouth, he stopped her verbal protests. His hands yanked down her panties; his fingers went inside her, hard.

"Ow!" she screamed, twisting to get away from his crushing mass.

His mouth went to her breasts, his teeth biting down on her skin.

She shrieked.

He slapped her hard.

The bedroom door flew open. Leslie stomped in, yelling, "Get off her!" She wrest Chase off Gillian, but in one swift move, Chase—taller, more muscular—belted Leslie across the mouth, knocking her to the floor.

Gillian cried out, crawled up toward the bed's headboard, cowering.

Chase reached over and slapped Gillian again. "Get dressed, whore, and get out of here. Now!" He left.

Gilly remained cringed against the headboard, biting down on the back of her hand, sobbing.

Stunned, Leslie struggled to stand. "Are you okay?" she asked Gillian.

Gillian nodded, began dressing, an occasional whimper escaping.

Soothingly Leslie said, "You didn't do anything wrong. Chase is a bully. He always takes advantage of the women he brings here."

"I thought he liked me." She dressed, tucking her blouse in her pants. "He really hurt me."

"Your face is swelling and bruising. You can turn him in but it won't get you anywhere. He wiggles out of trouble because he knows people in high places."

Gillian stomped out of the bedroom, grabbed her coat on the way out, while saying over her shoulder, "Thank you for coming to my rescue. I hope he doesn't hurt you anymore. How can you put up with him when he's like that?"

She shrugged, then she sheepishly asked, "Can I see you some time?"

Gillian blushed.

"Oh no, I mean as a friend. Maybe over coffee? After all, I am your hero."

"And what a heroine you are! I doubt I could ever be that brave."

"I do what I have to." Leslie opened the door for Gillian, bidding her bye.

9:30 p.m.

Gillian heard the doorbell ring twice before she hustled to it, looked through the peephole, and unlocked it. "Come in, Dix."

"What happened? I came as soon as you called. I knew something was wrong by your voice." Dixie touched Gillian's swollen cheek, bruised eye. "Who did this?"

Gilly shut her apartment door, and the two sat, with Gilly detailing her night with Chase, summing it up with, "He wanted sex, I held back and he slugged me."

"He really clubbed you."

"I'm just glad to be rid of him."

"How can you be sure you are?"

"Tell me again, Dix, how you know Chase and his sister."

Dixie sighed. "How many times are you going to ask me that? I told you to stay away from him." Gillian saw Dixie espy a suitcase on the couch, with clothes around it. "Where are you going?"

Gilly stuffed a comb and brush into it. "I have to leave town for awhile."

"I don't think Chase'll go to such lengths that you have to run away."

"Cy's sending me out on a case."

"Really? What is it?"

Gillian was hesitant. "This is between us, but he wants me to interview the survivors of families who've been killed by the same kind of goons who murdered your sister-in-law." She folded a blue cardigan sweater, which matched her eyes, and slipped it into the suitcase.

"Does that mean you'll be talking to my widowed brother and his children?"

The statement gave Gillian an opening: "Why do you think the goons attacked your sister-in-law?" Gilly wondered if Dixie's brother had anything to do with the fertility labs.

"She was at the wrong place at the wrong time."

"I don't know what your brother could tell me since

he wasn't present when your sister-in-law was murdered."

"Don't you think it's kind of dangerous for you to
go it alone, Gil? Shouldn't Cy go with you?"

"His nephew's really sick, been drinking the water."
Gilly picked up a skirt and blazer and crammed those
into the luggage. "Stores everywhere are running out of
bottled water."

"It's been a boon for soda manufacturers. People
are cooking with Pepsi."

They looked at each other and giggled.

"Just so I know you're okay, Gil, give me a copy of
your itinerary." Dixie tossed M&Ms from the candy
bowl into her mouth.

Now I know what she's after. Gillian looked at her
overflowing suitcase. "I didn't think I had that much
stuff in there."

"So give me your schedule just to reassure me that
you're safe."

"It's not firmed up yet."

"Well, where are you going, who are you seeing?"

Gillian watched Dixie's expression when she said,
"I'm hoping to meet with Miguel del Rey, the Ripley
boy, and Hilda Dillon."

"Do you have your flight and lodging schedule
made out?"

"Somewhere. I'll finish packing and then make you
a copy off my fax machine."

"Great. I worry about you, Gil; you're no karate
expert."

Gillian snapped her fingers. "That reminds me: I
was supposed to buy a gun. Cy insists on it."

"Read the papers: Premier Cinzan and his seven
dwarfs—Williams is Dopey—passed a law banning all
weapons all over the world."

"But I'm a P.I."

"Even if you could get one, you wouldn't get

approval before you left tomorrow. There's a waiting period for law enforcers, too. By the way, where's Mitch been?"

"We've been playing phone tag, but I know he's upset over Salyer's death. He's starting to believe the goons are responsible for the deaths of Salyer and others." Glancing at Dixie, she added, "Do you believe they exist, Dix?"

"Here we go again. I know you claim you were chased by one at my clinic."

"You don't believe me."

"I never said that, but how can one goon be in several places at one time?"

"There must be many of them."

"You're in to this too much." She ate more M&Ms. "When's Sal's funeral?"

"It's only a memorial service; I'll miss it, being away on business. I would have liked to have been there for Mitch, and I would have liked to have had time to talk to him since he keeps leaving hints on my answering machine that he's on to something big that has to do with these goons. He rambled on that he had important information to give me about the government, your clinic—"

"My clinic? Maybe Mitch is just a little strung out over his friend Salyer."

"Mitchell isn't like that; he's a calm, analytical person, demanding proof for everything, and likes it even better if it's in writing."

"What would my clinic have to do with anything?" She heard her cell phone jingling in her purse and reached for it, listening more than speaking. Minutes later, she flipped the phone closed, saying to Gillian, "I gotta make tracks."

"Hey. No good-bye hug?" *She's acting cool. Did the clinic tell her that I had been there? She couldn't have known it was me since I was in disguise.*

Dixie embraced her. "Listen, you be careful. Tell Mitch to get some rest. You should be with him instead of running off on your own doing dangerous work."

"I love Mitch dearly, but you keep forgetting that we're no longer married."

With a wave, Dixie was out the door and on her way.

Gillian stood looking after her, wondering who would have called her on the cell phone, making her leave instantly. "Thank goodness she forgot about getting a copy of my itinerary," Gillian said aloud in her apartment.

Certain that Dixie had gone, Gillian pulled out a sheet of paper from her desk drawer with the names she had gotten off Dixie's disk. She found it odd that Dixie's files reflected specific names from all the fertility labs, making Gillian wonder what kind of power her friend had.

Gilly dialed the Givens' number, explaining that she was an investigator looking into the activities of the various fertility clinics. Mrs. Givens hung up. Gillian re-dialed, rushed her words before the line went dead again: "You had a baby, Mrs. Givens. How did it die?"

"I don't want to talk about it."

"Was it sick?"

A long silence; then: "Grotesquely deformed. My husband saw it." She hung up before Gilly could say another word.

Determined, Gillian rang the Miles' phone. Ben Miles answered, saying, after Gillian explained herself, "That Dr. Byers is a quack. We never got a baby out of it. He even told us we could pick our own genetic traits."

She remembered the brief entry on them in Dixie's file. "But your wife did get pregnant. What happened to the baby?"

"Byers said it was stillborn and took it away. He

covered it up, so we never even got a chance to see it. He collected all kinds of eggs from my wife and sperm from me. I'm gonna sue."

"The clinic is government owned and thus is immuned to litigation."

"I was never told that. Shit!" He slammed the phone down.

Well, now I know. The fertility labs must steal the babies and send them elsewhere. The deformed ones must be what Hilda Dillon met up with. Ironically, the goon that had attacked her was the same age her son would have been had the fertility clinic she had gone to allowed her to keep her baby. Supposedly it had died at birth, but I wonder.

Sunday, January 6; 2:00 a.m.; Cambridge, MD

The wind spat snowflakes against the windows, making Althea Azar pull the covers up tighter around her chin. She could feel the tension weighing down her every cell, and she held her breath without realizing it.

Out of nowhere a sound hit her ears, as if something were rapping against her front door. She could lie there all night worrying about it, or she could rise, check out the sound, and go back to sleep.

The noise rang louder. Her body trembled. *Get up and look.*

Wetting her lips and snapping on her bedside lamp, she rose, grabbed the baseball bat from under her bed, and tip-toed into the family room.

BANG BANG

She stiffened at the sound, heart throbbing. Whatever it was, it was in the family room. She raised the bat above her head, ready to swing at the sign of movement. But it was so dark in the room that she couldn't tell who was where.

BANG!

She turned.

Nothing. She let her eyes adjust to the moonlight's stream and saw something shiny out of the corner of her eye. Slowly she tilted her head toward it.

BANG BANG BANG!

"Aaaaah," she exhaled slowly, loudly, at the sight of the fireplace door banging against the hearth frame. She flipped on the ceiling light switch and instantly saw the problem: The flue was open, creating a down draft that battered the glass doors. She fixed it.

Walking back across the room, she flicked off the switch, returned to bed.

Chapter 16

Gordon was half-asleep when the phone rang.

"I saw the tape of you and Gilly at the clinic," said the voice on the other end.

"I wondered how long it would be before you called." He sat on the edge of the bed. "I didn't give her much on the disk. You really shouldn't leave confidential matters lying around like that. Gillian said she klept it when you went out and got Chinese; read what she could off your bedroom computer monitor and then made a copy while you were gone."

"She and I have been friends a long time so I never gave it a thought when she went into my room to get a blanket."

"You've been with the organization long enough to know better. With clinic security aware of her presence with me at the—"

"She returned right after you two left and went through my office, got names of fertility patients."

"Miles, Givens, and Dillon, right? I thought those

were innocuous enough."

"The Givens husband saw the baby."

"Your friend's going to get herself killed if she keeps this up," he warned.

"It's your job as an AUGA member to see that she doesn't."

"I'm putting someone on it."

No sooner had Dixie hung up when the phone rang again.

"Let me sleep, for pete's sake!" he snapped.

It was Security at Traditional Fertility Clinic calling to tell Gordon to come in to work, that a small fire in the computer room had destroyed some hardware.

"Tell the boss I want double time for coming in on a Sunday," he groused.

A half hour later, running behind in getting to the clinic, Gordon wanted to speed down the icy highway but instead kept his eyes on the road. Suddenly, a hefty man loomed before his car lights. Gordon glimpsed him wearing a suit under a trench coat, and carrying a briefcase, as well as a gas can. *Another sucker out of gas. I know that feeling.* At the last moment, he pulled to the side of the road, waved the hitchhiker on.

The next second he heard the passenger door click open. "Thanks." The hitchhiker folded himself into the front seat. "Too cold to be walking to a gas station this early."

They remained quiet.

"Take the next side road and I'll jump out, and get the gas," said the hiker.

Gordon looked at his watch. "I gotta hurry; need to see to an emergency."

As soon as he swerved down the ramp, he realized the hitchhiker was wrong. "There's nothing here, man. It's desolate."

The stranger pointed to the left, and Gordon obeyed, saying, "I'm late, and my cell phone's dead."

"Up the road is a gas station. Call from there while I get gas." He pointed to the back seat where the gas can rolled on the floor.

Minutes later, Gordon saw the service station. "This place is closed down!"

"Maybe someone's around to get a pump going."

Gordon shut off the engine, got out and went toward the front of the station. He tried the glass door—locked. On a second glance, he saw that the bathrooms had been boarded up, and one of the locks on a bay was completely rusted.

He turned to say something to the hitchhiker when suddenly he felt a thrust so powerful it shook his organs. In a vigorous bear hug, the stranger rammed into Gordon and sent him crashing through the station's front window, shattering glass everywhere. Gordon felt blood ooze from his eyes, nose, mouth. In his attempt to see through his bleeding sockets, he lifted his head toward the sound of grunts. A quick kick to his body sent him slamming into the cinder block wall.

The monster picked up Gordon's plump body with one hand while pulling out a knife with the other; he gouged Gordon's neck and ran it straight across the windpipe to the other ear.

8:00 a.m.

Cy watched his sister Marian hover over her son's hospital bed, weeping so hard that he thought he saw Wally's bed shake in response. He had called her hours ago when Wally had been officially admitted to the hospital and word came down that the boy was critical. She and her husband had hurriedly thrown a few things together and frantically driven the 2 1/2 hours from Baltimore in the dead of night to reach the bedside of their only child. Striding back and forth in the emergency room, worried about Wally, and fearing his sister's reaction, Cy hadn't gotten any sleep since Friday night when he had stayed at the Sheraton in Atlanta. With Stella having surprised him by showing up at his hotel, he got even less sleep. Until he returned to Wilmington to find his nephew deathly ill, he had toyed with the idea of getting back with Stella. Together they would have a divine future, in spite of her being a doctor and he a detective. Now his mind was on Wally and his sister who, hanging over her son's bed, looked as pained as the kid himself. He could feel her wretchedness, the deep pain cutting inside her, and he didn't know what to do to make it right. He pulled out his handkerchief and blew his nose. He would never forgive himself for not watching the kid better.

His nephew lay lifeless in the white sheets in ICU, an oxygen tube connected to his nose, an automatic blood pressure cuff around his arm inflating and deflating at regular intervals, a ventilator hooked to his mouth, and a monitor wired to his chest. Suddenly Wally didn't seem like a cocky city boy; now he lay helpless, and perhaps hopeless. He was pale as porcelain, and his eyes remained open but unseeing.

When he saw his sister pull her son's head to her breast, and wail, "Oh my baby, my baby; please, please, don't leave me; oh dear God, please, please," tears sprang to his eyes and his fists curled into a ball. He walked across the cubicle and over to his sister, certain she blamed him. And why not? He had failed her, let the most important thing in her world slip through his hands simply because he hadn't been paying attention. "Marian," Cy said, touching his palm to her elbow. "I swear, I didn't know he was drinking the water; if I ever find out who's responsible for poisoning it, I'll go after them with everything I have. I promise, sis, I promise."

She turned and glared at him through a wall of tears. While rocking her limp son's upper body in her arms, she snarled, "Thanks so much, Cy . . . I trusted you."

Cy bit down on his lower lip and left the unit.

****

At the kitchen table, Dixie flipped through the Sunday paper over a cup of coffee, her eyes on the words, her mind on Gillian, envisioning her alone in unfamiliar cities, pulling information out of people who, no doubt, didn't want to talk anyway. *Maybe it would be a good idea to have someone see what she was up to.* Stretching for the wall phone behind her, she picked up the receiver, dialed a number, and waited for the rings to stop.

"Hello," came the man's voice on the other end.

"It's me. I don't want Gillian Montague to know I'm checking up, but maybe you could call in your chits for me and see where she is and what's happening."

"You don't know her schedule?"

"I couldn't get it," she lied, not wanting him to know she had slipped up and forgotten to pick it up when she was at Gilly's last night. "I didn't want Gilly to think I was pinning her down, then she'd become suspicious; after all, she is a detective. But her office must have her itinerary."

"You're supposed to be her best friend; you get it."

"A detective agency isn't going to give out that information, and the secretary there doesn't know me well enough to just hand it over."

"How much danger?"

"Lots. She'll go to any length to get info. When she gets it, she'll be even more dauntless in doing whatever she thinks is necessary to expose everything."

"The Collier Agency, right? I'll take care of it."

She heard a dial tone.

11:00 a.m.; Upstate New York

Gillian arrived in Rochester, New York, earlier in the morning. Having been told that Señor del Rey, who was in bad shape and unlikely to cooperate, had moved from Niagara Falls, New York to Rochester to be with his sister. The Rochester bus stopped at a corner flower shop where the business' slogan, "Say It With Flowers," jumped out at her from its front display window.

She hustled down the snowy sidewalk, her eyes scanning her surroundings, taking in ten-day old Christmas candles hanging from street lanterns, and stores filled with wreaths and other symbols of a passed holiday.

Shortly she saw the number 2453 Goodman on the transom of a deteriorating brick building. When Gilly had called Miguel's sister for an interview with Mr. del Rey, Señora had warned Gilly that her brother could talk only briefly. The Ripley boy—Brandon—had also agreed, providing his uncle was at his side. The supervisor of the nursing home where Hilda Dillon lived told Gillian she could conduct the interview, though it was unlikely Hilda would be coherent. Gillian arranged all the appointments anyway, deciding against taking on any more surviving victims or victims' families for now. The newspapers were reporting on a regular basis the strange deaths taking place throughout the country. *Gosh, they could even program these goons to be world assassins!*

Seeing no doorbell on 2453, Gilly knocked hard on the steel frame of the paned glass door, breaking off icicles hanging above her. She ducked when one fell near her shoulder. *God, how do people live in this kind of polar bear climate?* She was so cold, it seemed her breath froze the second it left her lungs and hit the air. Knocking louder on the door, a small, petite, but wide-shouldered, dark-haired woman appeared.

"I'm Gillian Montague—the investigator who asked

to talk to your brother."

The olive-skinned woman unlatched the outer door and stood aside as Gillian stepped in and wiped her shoes. She introduced herself: "I Martha. Follow, por favor. My brother, he no can talk long. He no well."

Gillian followed the woman.

"He had shock. Doctors no know if his mind go back to normal. He haf no will to leeve." She handed Gillian copies of police records that Gillian had requested from her when they first spoke.

Gilly took them and entered the twelve-by-twelve room that apparently was used as a small office, though it lacked a desk, chair, and books of any substance.

Miguel sat in the far corner of the room on a hard back folding chair, his face ashen, his body painfully thin. If his sister hadn't addressed him by his name, Gillian would have thought he were an old man and not someone in his forties. She took a seat on a ragged chair next to him after setting up her tape recorder and pulling out additional audio tapes and paper for notes.

"No long," warned Martha to Gillian.

Knowing she was going to get only one chance at popping just a few queries, Gillian asked, "Señor, supposedly you were hiding in tall underbrush when your family was attacked. Can you tell me what happened?"

The man lifted his head, stared at her, or rather— thought Gillian—*through* her. She waited.

"I heard noise. Went see. When walking to it, I hear again. I turn back, see . . . all it." He put his hands to his eyes and wept.

She wanted to rush him but instead said, "It's fine, Señor. Take your time."

"I see my son bend backward, broke in half." He sobbed louder. "A hole made in his head and a . . . a . . . . 'thing' suck from the hole."

Gilly felt moisture in her eyes.

"I see my espousa—wife—raped, grabbed by beautiful hair, throat sliced off."

From behind Gillian came a woeful noise—something between a gulp and a wail. She turned, saw Martha shaking and silently weeping.

"Mi hija," he said at last, "was pulled in opposite directione by her legs, like she taffy. Them diablos . . . split her body right-a down middle." He stopped, clasped his hands in prayer, his face tilted up to the ceiling. "Por favor, mio Dios. Stoppa my pain. Por favor," he bawled.

The pressure built in her chest. Gillian whispered "Thank you" and left the building. Outside, she let the cold air wash over her. "I'm a failure for not having gotten more information, and worse for not being able to console him," she said aloud as she hurried toward the bus station.

Poor Señor. Things seemed so out of whack. Even Chase's behavior the last time they were together had been out of character . . . or maybe she just didn't know him as well as she thought she did. She kicked at the snow as she walked toward the bus station, holding the records Martha had given her, her mind re-focused on Chase. Maybe he had been raised by a dysfunctional unit; after all, Leslie was pretty strange herself. But by the photos Gillian had seen in their house, the parents had looked like average, middle-class Americans. So where did this "organization" fit in? Gilly tugged harder on her gloves to keep her hands warm.

Got to get my mind off Señor del Rey.

Glancing at her watch, and breaking into a dash, Gillian made it to the bus station on time to head for the airport for her flight to Albuquerque. The icy air felt all the more frigid as she sped forward. From New Mexico, she had to crisscross backward to Indiana for her Hilda Dillon interview, before returning home. For sure she'd have jet lag. At least she would make good use of her time during the bus rides and various flights by recopying her notes and studying the del Rey police reports. Maybe she would even be able to "read between the lines," as Cy had always said. To her, right now, the lines seemed pretty blurred.

Noon; Cambridge and Ocean City, MD

Having disposed of nearly all her possessions except for the clothes and few sentimental items she had packed, Althea Azar was ready to leave her little apartment and start a new life elsewhere. The problem was the "elsewhere." She remained uncertain where to go. Being an old maid, she had no children and her parents had been dead for years. Her closest friend had been her first cousin Desidera who died a year before from "dropsy."

She thought she'd drive around Ocean City, then across Route 50 to 13 South and right down the shore into Virginia Beach, and settle there, or maybe she'd just keep going south. But wherever, she had unequivocally decided on living on the water—no more cities.

She took one last look through each room, her hand touching a kitchen counter here, a wall she had painted there, the venetian blinds she had put up herself, and the Pergo hardwood floor she had laid in the foyer. All of this was behind her now. It was time to move on. She leafed through a copy of the sales contract she had signed with a real estate agent, and then locked the door and, carrying her luggage, went down the stairs to the outside where she paused to look back at her history. At the car, she opened the door, slid behind the wheel and never again looked back. She believed not in mourning the past but rather in celebrating the future

With her car window ajar, the sun still high in the sky, and the air warming as she drove south, she found herself smiling. It felt good to get away from all the bureaucracy, secretiveness, and helter-skelter, but she had no misconception that what she was leaving behind wouldn't catch up with her because the government's plan was world-wide; there was nowhere to hide.

****

In Ocean City, she lingered to take in the inlet and have a vanilla cone in spite of how cold it was. Maybe she'd even visit some of the outlet shops. Walking on the boardwalk, she crossed her arms at her chest to warm herself. She was nuts, she told herself; it was too cold to be sitting at the water's edge. Yet, the air's briskness felt refreshing, making her feel reborn after her endless stint with Hammond and his clandestine government secrets. She had felt badly for him, worse for how he had died because she sensed a part of him hated his job and what he had been subversively immersed in. She only hoped it wasn't too late for her.

A stocky, bald-headed man with a thin woman walked past her, the woman carrying a miniature dachshund underneath her coat. Althea smiled. She had forgotten about such warm expressions. Suddenly she jerked when she saw a large man turn and stare at her. *My God! They're here!*

She watched him, half-curious and half-afraid. On closer examination, she realized that there was nothing unusual about the fellow except that he was tall and muscular like a weight-lifter or trainer. She chastised herself for conjuring up monsters emerging from every corner.

She wondered if the experiment would have worked had it been done right. No longer did the clones look like that sole original specimen; now they had their own features and personalities, save for the part of their minds that were controlled by computer chips. *Just think, these mammoth men can easily win any war, and not one human life will be lost because—according to the scientists—they aren't human . . . just replications.*

Yet, they are made up of human material: Genes, carbon. . . . She reminded herself that Hammond's initial intent had been good in that he had wanted to create these clones for spare body parts since organ transplantation had become so commonplace while donors had diminished because of the spread of AIDS, hepatitis, various viruses, blood diseases, drug and alcohol abuse, and an increase in transplantation. But somewhere, Hammond had lost his vision while the government had gained his soul.

Althea sighed, checked her watch. She had been sitting on a dried out, wooden bench too long, contemplating her lot in life in between watching others stroll the sand bundled in coats and hats. Dotted on the beach were groups, individuals, and couples meandering the water's edge or standing and watching the tide roll in. Off to the far corner was a gang of guys playing frisbee in the sand, wearing heavy college jackets. She laughed at their antics.

Around 3:00, she rose and walked down the board walk, stopping in a few open stores, and window-shopping in novelty boutiques where it seemed sea shells were used to make everything. After gorging on hot funnel cake, she walked back to her car, ready to move out. But she had so much enjoyed her relaxation, the beach, people, weather, and all the stores, that time had eluded her. So she decided to get a room at one of the motels and embark fresh in the morning.

Wilmington

Exhausted from not sleeping since Salyer died, Mitch decided that tonight was as good as any other to sneak into the Enolc lab. He would enter looking like a worker with the white jacket Ms. Azar had given him, along with a wig and mustache. For a second, his thoughts shifted to Althea Azar, and he wondered if she

had left the area for safer grounds, or if she had gone
back to the lab, or just decided to stay put for awhile.
He concluded that he'd call her after his adventure
underground, provided he got in and out safely.

He set his alarm clock for one a.m. to give him
enough time to wash, dress, disguise himself, and drive
down to the Easton area. Then he lay across his bed
with the ceiling light on. Mitch knew he needed a few
hours of shut-eye to help him pull off the facade. He
quickly dozed off.

Rochester, New York

Gillian bit down on her lip, distraught that her
flight to Albuquerque had been cancelled and thus put
on a later flight. "Which means I won't get in until
almost two in the morning. I can't visit a kid at that
time," she said to the reservationist, envisioning the ire
of Brandon's uncle at two a.m..

"No, ma'am, Albuquerque's three hours ahead
which means theoretically you would be there at 7:55
p.m., but since you have two layovers—one in St.
Louis, and the other in Austin—you won't arrive in
Albuquerque until midnight their time."

Still, she couldn't call on the family at that hour.
"Whatever." She left the reservations desk, went to
Hertz and re-set her rental car hours, called a hotel and
made arrangements to stay overnight, and then called
the Ripley uncle and rescheduled a new interview time.

"Well, that ought to throw everything off," she
groused to the coin phone.

3:00 p.m.; Ocean City

The clerk at the Silver Sands Inn gave her a bay-
front room accessed via a dark side street. Although the

place had a certain quaintness, with its old style lock and key system instead of the card keys, she preferred modern hotels with superb safety features, excellent service, and fine cuisine, but many of them were closed for the season or too expensive, even for winter time. She heard someone say in the dinky lobby that the inn would be torn down in a year and replaced by a fashionable three story motel.

The room smelled like cigar smoke and gave the impression that though the bed had been made, it needed cleaning and deodorized. Within a few hours, she had washed with bottled water provided by the motel and taken a nap. She awoke invigorated and hungry. She thought how nice it would be to dine out casually, savoring her meal while leisurely reading a magazine, then returning to her room, watching television, and looking forward to getting up early and continuing with the search for her new living quarters—a virgin life, fresh beginning.

By 6:00, she was sitting in Tutti Giusti's, eating eggplant parmesan, and bragging about it to the waitress while patting the sauce off her lips with a paper napkin. She scanned the local newspaper, had a glass of wine, paid her bill, and headed back for her room where she would relax a little, get a good night's sleep to be on the road by seven in the morning, planning on grabbing breakfast on her way out of Ocean City.

"Oh," she mumbled when she opened her room door and saw that she hadn't left a light on. Or had she? She stood in the threshold with her body half in and half out the room. *Stop being so suspicious and childish.* She stretched her arm toward the wall, groping for the light switch. Up, down, her hand smacked the wall in the dark but still she couldn't find the switch. Maybe if she opened the door wider, the dismal hallway's lamp would let some light into the room.

WHACK!

She froze. Stark numbness perfused her. The splat-
tering of blood warm against her cold face jolted her,
and she realized her extended arm had been severed.
She couldn't scream, things happened so fast. She felt
her body yanked into the room, heard someone hiss,
"This will teach you about ratting."

Blood flooded from her body.

When she forced herself to look, she caught his
flashing eyes, evil sneer, in the darkness of the room.

He flicked the light on to dramatize the scene for
her, to see her dismembered limb lying on the floor, her
blood covering walls, the floor, his face, her slumping
body.

"Watch," he said, his mouth open to laugh.

His rotting, fishy odor mixed with cigar smoke
emanating from him. She opened her mouth to shriek
just as he vigorously drove the whetted knife into her
forehead, then yanked it out. Seconds later, he put his
lips over the hole.

Chapter
17

Sunday, January 6, 2011;
9:00 p.m.; Wilmington

Annie sat on the couch with her mother in the den, waiting for Cy to call with an update on Wally, as Cy knew he could reach Annie at home when not working. She sensed inside her that when his call did come, it wouldn't bring good news. As Cy's secretary, she had come to like the kid a lot; he had a wonderful sense of humor and Cy seemed to care a good deal about him, signalling to her that she should, too.

She prided herself on reading clues well—almost as well as her P.I. boss. Not only could she read Cyril, but now, after getting to know Gillian better, she could do equally well with her. In a way, she disliked Gillian—model material, smug prom-type queen of yore with gleaming white teeth—but in other ways, she was fond of her, especially for her intrepidity and her compulsion for following through on a project and keeping her commitments. She liked, too, that Gillian wasn't ashamed to admit that she had been raised in an orphanage—even made the best of it. Annie also admired Gillian's honesty and desire not to hurt anyone, but her moodiness was aggravating which seemed to have gotten worse with everything going on. Maybe, thought Annie, Gillian was just in an interminable PMS state.

"Come on and call, Cy," Annie said to the phone while listening to a special report on increasing worldwide food shortages.

Said her mother, "What's wrong with this world anyway? It's falling apart, what with all the disasters, terrible crimes, water contamination, and now a food shortage that's certain to affect us, too."

Annie pulled out a nail file from her purse. She cracked her gum which popped loose from between her lips, making her giggle over her crudeness. On reflection, Annie thought her mom was the kind of person who had endeavored to perform above her station of life, making Annie's father and older sister feel inferior. But now, years later, Annie thought her mother's reaching for something higher might have been good for the family.

A startling banging at the door made Annie and her mother jump. Opening the door only wide enough for her to speak through the crack, she said in her Brooklynese accent, "Can I help you?" Instantly she was struck by how nice looking the guy was: Smooth, sophisticated, suave, athletically built, and smelling of Brute aftershave . . . probably some jealous husband who wanted a detective agency to trail his cheating wife. "Are you looking for Mr. Collier?" She opened the door wider. "His nephew is very ill and he's with him."

"Is he at the hospital?" the dark-skinned man asked in an articulate manner.

She didn't want him bothering her boss. "Maybe I can help you." She opened the door wider. "Our office opens at eight tomorrow."

"Sorry to bother you. I need to get Ms. Montague's travel schedule."

She turned suspicious. "Why?" What was he doing here at this hour anyway?

"My name's Countee Burrows. I'm an agent for a government watchdog group. My people keep tabs on recent scientific developments. We're concerned about Ms. Montague's safety regarding her investigations into a project."

She had the door opened to talk with him. "What's the name of your group?" *I shouldn't have opened my door; he could force himself in. And how does he know what Gilly's doing?*

"I'm not at liberty to give additional information. Do you have her itinerary? I know she's going to travel, or is already on the road. I've checked her apartment but there's no answer."

"Like you, I'm not at liberty to give information."

"As I said, her safety is our concern. She could possibly be in danger as we talk." He looked behind him. "Can't you just tell me how I might reach her? If you give me the number to her cell phone, I'll—"

Said Annie flatly, "I told you, I ain't at liberty to do that."

The bodybuilder-sized man took a step toward Annie, his face wearing a scowl.

"Who is it, dear?" came a voice behind Annie.

Both Annie and the stranger turned to look.

"It's fine, Mother," Annie said.

The older woman looked at the man.

He nodded to both women, saying, "Sorry to pester you. If there's no other way I can reach Ms. Montague, I'll try her office tomorrow."

Annie shut the door, went back to waiting for Cy to call.

Monday, January 7;
3:00 a.m.; Easton, Maryland

It took him over an hour to reach the grounds and drive down back roads to where the near-invisible gate was. Mitch cracked open his window, hearing the night sounds of weeds rustling, the frigid wind whistling. An eeriness shrouded him, and he gritted his teeth, then drove on. The second his car hit the sensor in the dirt lane that Azar had told him about, a CLICK sounded and up rolled the plastic post with the computerized number pad. Shakily, he punched in 3-18-10. The pole lowered and the semi-domed ramp revealed itself. He drove the Bonneville down the concrete ramp, growing tense inside. "Creepy, creepy place," he muttered to the steering wheel.

The underground parking garage smelled musty and dank, and with its limited number of dim lights, he grew even more jittery. So as not to call attention to his car which didn't feature a sticker with a pyramid symbol like all the other vehicles in the garage, he parked far away in a dim corner obstructed by two globular support pillars. In the darkness, he slipped on an auburn wig, fake black-framed glasses, a mustache attached to a goatee, and the white lab coat. Over the left pocket of the linen, lab jacket, was pinned a laminated I.D. card, reading: "Joseph Johnson, Ph.D.; Fertility Researcher." Mitch thought his disguise nearly matched the man's features on the picture badge. All Ms. Azar had told Mitch was that Johnson, who had owned the lab jacket, had been her friend and co-worker who at times who had visited her after work. Mitch suspected he often had stayed at her place and had left his lab coat there. "Aw, Miz A," Mitch mumbled to the car's rearview mirror, "weren't you a naughty little ol' lady?"

In disguise, he stepped over to the locked door, tapped in the code, and rode the elevator down to floor three. The second he stepped off the lift, a woman in a long white coat walked towards him. She nodded, muttering, "I hate those damned report sessions."

Mitch lowered his head, saying, "Still going on?" He looked at his watch: Almost four.

"Just started." She got on the elevator and, Mitch saw, went down to a floor marked four. *Got to remember that high numbers go down, not up.* He continued ambling down the hall of the austere, chrome and glass building. "Straight down the wide corridor, make a right," was what Azar had told him.

In the dark, a presence collided with him, grabbed his arm. The security guard towered over him, his grip tight. "Show identification." The guard eyed him warily.

Almost immediately Mitch smelled an odor on the man, and though his eyes didn't appear to be the legendary flashing type, they did seem to reflect light differently and pierce right into Mitch. He was huge, immense hands coarse, and his baldness emphasizing an odd shaped skull. *Well, this could be over before it gets started.*

Touching his finger to his I.D. badge, Mitchell emphasized, "Dr. Johnson, researcher on loan from Enolc Three."

The guard's facial muscles relaxed. "Show your pass." His grip on Mitch slackened.

What pass? Azar hadn't told me about that! He was going to be discovered, and he hadn't even made it to Hammond's office. In pretense, Mitch searched his lab coat and pants pocket. "I have it here. Give me a second."

A college-aged kid walked up to the guard, saying, "Dr. Glazier wants you in session. She says you have to give report on the broken glass on lower nine."

Mitch read the boy's name tag. "Hi, Kenny." He hoped the young man would see his badge and react—for his own self-importance—as if he had known Mitch for years. "I haven't seen you since I was last here."

The kid glanced at Mitch, then at his badge and said, "Yessir, Dr. Johnson," and nodded in affirmation.

The guard looked at both and said to Mitch. "Okay, you can go, but tomorrow you better have your pass."

"My work will be done here tonight." Mitch ruffled the boy's brown hair and walked down the hall. *That was close*! He had reservations about going on but knew he had to do it. Each dimly lit corridor threatened his destruction if he were caught.

His rubber soled shoes diverted calling attention to himself. Stealthily he looked around before opening doors to see what he could learn about the place, but most rooms were locked. The place gleamed menacingly, with its shadowy and somber wide halls; glassed labs that housed eerie looking specimens pickled in tubes of preserved liquids; equipment in labs looking akin to something out of an old Frankenstein movie. Over some of the chambers' transoms, he saw flashes of light illuminating the dark halls. He could feel his skin crawl. A sound like a loud puff of air broke the silence, making Mitch jump. More noises: Bangs and thumps, clangs and kicks, and something akin to groans or moans. He could taste his fear.

Tip-toeing around the bend at a hallway intersection, he heard the low mumble of voices coming from across where Azar said Hammond's office was. Mitch stood, listening. Seconds later, he realized it was the report session. What should he do? Eavesdrop to get information, or get the files from Hammond's office and hurry back to listen to their discussions? He opted to get the files.

Double-oh-seven, he punched into the key pad. Hammond's hydraulic door parted and an automated voice sounded: "Security door opened; proper code entered."

The automated voice announced security status at

every door. That didn't bode well for him. He prayed no one in the conference room across the hall heard. Swiftly he scooted inside the office, the door closing behind him, and stood against the inside wall, holding his breath. No one came; Mitch figured they had been talking—or rather arguing—too loud to have heard the automaton voice.

He slipped over to Hammond's desk, and cupping his hand around the rim of the flashlight, he shone it on the surface, wanting to see if any files setting there offered information. One folder on the desk was marked, "Meeting Notes," and next to it another, set labeled, "Planning—Short and Long Term." He removed papers from both manilla folders and stuffed them inside his belt under his crew shirt. Then, seeing a stapled, slim, flexible-backed navy blue book entitled, "Procedures and Policies," he shoved that under his shirt, too, and tucked it inside his belt.

A flicker caught his eyes. Quickly he shut off his own flashlight and crouched in a corner, behind the desk. From where he sat, Mitch could see the beam coming in his direction, and he knew it was a guard with a flashlight. Mitch held his breath, hunkered down even more, his eyes not leaving the moving light in the dark hall. He tried listening but the glassed office had near sound-proof panes.

Oh hell! Another guard appeared; now there were two for Mitch to contend with. One typed the code into the door key pad and, SWSSSH, it opened, the auto-mated voice sounding. Mitch couldn't discern if either guard—who he believed were clones—was the one he had run into before, not only because of the dimness but also because they were difficult to differentiate because of their curiously formed shaved heads, ghastly eyes, and vast size, with each wearing khaki-like pants and jackets, and outfitted with a slew of weapons.

From the doorway, came, "Want me to get the

dogs?" The baritone clone passed his flashlight around the office, settling a shaft of light on Hammond's desk.

"The folders that were on Hammond's desk are still there. Everything's in order. Maybe the door opening was an authorized staffer entering his office. Besides, the computerized voice didn't announce a security breach; it just said the door was opened, which could have been Dr. Glazier or some other authorized person."

The baritone agreed, "If we call the dogs and go in and investigate, we'll be writing reports for hours." He looked at his watch. "It's already five a.m., and I still have to patrol floors ten and nine, and the north corridor of this level."

"I'm behind, too," said the other. "Glazier's management style stinks; she forever has us in meetings. Look, when I go back downstairs, I'll check all the monitors to see if there's any intruders. This way we won't have to fetch the animals and write reports."

Said the partner, "No one can get underground anyway, let alone inside the building, without the passwords, and those are all top secret."

The baritone nodded. "Glazier's style may stink but she has a tough job filling in until the new director comes. Substituting for Hammond isn't easy. His confusion made all of us crazy. Poor es-oh-bee. What a way to go. Lose your arm from putrefaction, then die of it. But I guess he deserved it since he created the mad ones."

Mitch thought his lungs would burst from silencing his breathing.

Said the other guard, "The mad ones resulted from chemical problems. Just be lucky that we're not like that."

"Who's to say we're normal? There's no guarantee we won't go their route. We're fortunate because we work here and the lab can easily supply us with the chemicals whenever our bodies get low. Because we're monitored daily, our levels are adjusted, but those suckers out in the real world explode like time bombs."

"I'd say those out there are the lucky ones and we're the prisoners."

Amazed the two carried on as though they were chatting over coffee, Mitch wanted to shift his stance to ease cramps building in his calves.

"Ever wonder why they don't make females like us?"

The higher pitched voice answered, "Who'd want anyone to look like you?" He laughed. "I did hear they have made females but that they didn't turn out feminine enough to fit into society." Then he asked, "Who's your parent?"

"Some professor who lived in Virginia; he died of a self-inflicted gunshot wound, and the veteran's hospital removed samples of his DNA. And here I am."

Mitch wanted to scream out loud. *DNA replication . . . from adult parents . . . and the veteran's hospitals, too?*

"What about you?" the other asked.

"My genetics came from storage. I'm one of those grown in a 'dish'."

The deep-voiced one closed the door. "Let's finish rounds. It musta just been Dr. Glazier getting something out of Dr. Hammond's office for the report session."

"Too bad. An intruder always makes for a ready supply of fresh serum."

When the door shut, Mitch still didn't move. He was so wobbly that he had to wait until he could collect himself. Horrifying thoughts of how they would have reduced him to mere chemicals—a serum—plagued him. *Why not? We humans are only chemicals and electricity anyway.*

Still squatting, he crept out of the office, leaving

Hammond's file room untouched. What he didn't want to do was call attention to the office again because for sure the guards would return. He decided to take his chances on the materials he found in the manilla files.

He reached for the door, praying the announcement wouldn't go off when he opened it. Hesitantly, he eased it ajar, grimacing while doing so lest the automaton voice sounded.

Silence

Mitch figured the alarm didn't go off when exiting an office . . . only on entering. He was surprised the top-secret Enolc labs didn't use hand recognition for gaining admission . . . or maybe they did in certain restricted areas. Well, one thing was for sure: The government did perfect duplicating real humans to produce artificial and unloving machines. Ha! That, the government had the technology for . . . . *Stupid world.*

Outside Hammond's office, Mitch stood against the wall in the dark so as not to be seen. He listened for the voices he had heard ten minutes ago. Were they still in session? Then he heard a woman say in a muffled voice, "I propose, under the circumstances, that we shut down all Enolc and T-Natum labs so as to prevent—"

Mocked laughter interrupted her.

Another female voice: "The government's plan is right on target. Pulling out now would mean repercussions for us and all the world."

"Besides," said an older man, "we're nearly one-hundred-percent successful with producing fresh body parts; the infallible replication of humans is just a step away. If we stop now, we could lose years . . . why, decades . . . worth of research time. I urge you, Dr. Glazier, not to allow the cessation of this lab and its projects."

Good Lord. Mitch slithered farther down the hall against the wall to get within better hearing range. *"Infallible replication"* . . . *meaning exact duplication with no genetic errors, no chemical problems—*

A vocal fight broke out and a lady's warning rose above the clamor, punctuating the room: "That's enough! Until I'm replaced by a full time director who will make the decision, or I receive word from higher up, we will continue as we had under Dr. Hammond. Let's table this discussion and meet as usual tomorrow. Adjourned." Instantly they began filing out of the conference room.

Ohmigod! Mitch didn't know which way to turn to get out of their sight. Having slid underneath his shirt between his skin and belt the thin manual with Hammond's papers in it, he quickly pulled them out to feign reading them as he tried to nonchalantly walk down the hall.

Lab personnel passed him, most in a hurry, though some glimpsed him and nodded while others barely made eye contact. He continued down the hall, his eyes focusing on words in the book. *Keep walking. No one's stopping me. Just keep walking like I belong here.*

"Excuse me!" came a voice behind him.

He turned, saw standing down the hall a tall woman with one hand on her hip, the other holding a folder and clip board. If he obeyed, she'd realize he didn't belong there, but if he ignored her, she'd call security.

She went up to him. "Who are you?"

"Dr. Johnson." He pointed to his I.D. badge. "I'm on loan from Enolc 3 to help make the transition to the new director . . . " he smiled again at her, "not that you're not doing a fine job of it yourself as—"

She studied his badge. "I just heard a report on you from a guard. I have no documentation that you belong here." She turned and walked away from him.

Mitch exhaled, relieved. He watched her strut down the hall a few feet, pause, and reach for something on the wall. *The security phone!*

In a resonating voice, reminding Mitch of how

announcers spoke over mics in K-Mart, she said, "Code ten, Corridor M; code ten—"

He broke into a run, his lab coat flying behind him, his hands trying to jam the book with papers back under his belt. All through the building he heard the loud, grating alert blaring—a frightening noise sounding more like a nuclear alarm than a security breach. Behind him reverberated doors opening and feet pounding the marble floors after him. With the full impact of his shoulder against the steel door, he flew into the stairwell, ran down one flight, then two, three, his soft bottomed shoes cushioning his footfall.

Momentarily pausing in a corridor, he stripped off his lab coat so his black crew shirt, black pants, and black shoes would blend in better in the dim building. He balled up the jacket in his hands, tucked it in the crook of his back, under the belt, and stood, catching his breath. Everywhere he heard feet racing and doors opening, some slamming, chiming in with the blasts of the squawking siren. He knew what the guards would do if they caught him.

Chapter 18

On level ten, Mitch sprinted down a hall, his rubber bottomed shoes squeaking behind him, but at the intersection of a spoke of six converging corridors, he stopped, huffing hard, and glanced around. The entire floor was almost black except for alarms with flashing lights above doorways. His panting was the only sound he heard. He chose the darkest pathway. Behind him, running feet vibrated as they dashed about in search of him.

He tried every entry but each was locked. Then he saw a figure, dressed in a white jumpsuit wearing a plastic visored helmet, exit a door down the hall carrying a silver metal cylinder in his gloved hands. The form never saw Mitch yards away as he briskly walked in the direction of a stairwell, concentrating on what he was holding. The second he disappeared into the stairwell, Mitch bolted for the door where the figure had come out.

He made it just in time to squeeze his finger in the gap between the jamb and the door. Wanting to scream in pain, he hurriedly pushed open the door with his other hand and entered the dark room, looking for a hiding place.

As soon as he stepped into the murky room, he knew there was something different about it: The clanking, whirring noise, the sense of instruments all around, the feel of light sparking and arcing in front of him. A shiver passed through him when he realized where he was. *What the hell are these people doing here anyway? Maybe it's only a nuclear medicine room and not a nuclear reactor room.* But a nuclear reactor room on the lowest level would make sense because of its weight and its core penetrating the earth.

The door banged open. He dropped to the floor, crawled out of sight on his hands and knees, and made his way toward the center of the room. From floor level, he could see huge boots and uniformed pants supporting machetes. He crawled into an adjacent room where the door was left ajar. Inside, he skulked to the opposite end to hide behind equipment. Breathless, panting hard, he was sure the guards heard him.

He saw their feet near the doorway but no one entered. They moved all around the outer perimeter but no one thought to look in the inner room. He noticed that these guards, though big, weren't bald and could easily assimilate into society without seeming much different from humans.

Minutes later, one of them ordered with a hand signal, "Let's get out of here." One by one, they left.

When he had wiped the sweat off his face, caught his breath, and felt certain they weren't returning, Mitch stood, his back against the wall, his clothes disheveled. He glimpsed his surroundings while inhaling slowly to re-fill his lungs. His eyes examined the room's circumference, then adjusting to the inner room where he stood, his gaze settled on the apparatus in the middle of the room.

"Oh my," he said aloud. *"Sweet Lord. I am in a reactor room."* His mouth dropped open, his eyes closed, and it was all he could do not to fall to his knees. "My God, I must be full of radiation. I'm going to die," he rasped.

Exhausted, not caring if he were captured because he understood his life had been shortened anyway, he stepped into the abutting room's outer edge and stood at an array of high-tech equipment, one of which was a large computer monitor built into a counsel featuring a detailed and colorfully coded map. He went over and studied it. Minutes later, he had discerned his location in the complex, and where the nearest exit was to his car. He understood he could go through rooms attached to the one he was in, out a rear exit, and down a narrow, back passageway to an elevator leading to what appeared to be odd shaped steps that exited at what looked like a circle on the computer monitor. He couldn't figure this out but decided to try it since he knew he'd never be able to leave through the doors he had entered from the parking garage. He tried committing the map to memory.

He left the computer area, went back through the room housing the nuclear core, into another room, and another, where he searched for the secret door leading to the small lift hidden in a tunnel. He prayed he'd find it, get out, and off the grounds, and back to Wilmington to give Dana, the reporter, the materials he had stolen tonight. Too much was going on at this lab—not counting the others—for the world not to know.

He wondered if security cameras were pointed at the secret doors, or planted in the tunnel he was searching for.

"There it is!" Finding the secret elevator door, he quickly studied it to determine how to open it.

Suddenly movement stirred a few rooms away from him. He knew guards had returned. *Come on, come on*! His hands smacked walls in attempt to locate the hidden mechanism. It made sense, he thought in his panic, to have a back escape room from a nuclear suite in the event of an accident. But where the hell was the door opener?

He turned when they entered the chamber right next to the room he was in. *Oh Jeesh!* Again his fingers fumbled along the wall, hoping to find a way to open the elevator. *Please Lord! Just let me get this material to the newspaper.* His hands and eyes searched every angle and grain of wall, but still no luck.

Then they were in the room. "Halt!" bellowed a voice wrapped in khaki pants, boots, and artillery. He stomped over to Mitch and thrust a machete at him.

"Go ahead . . . suck my brains out. Then you'll become as radioactive as me. I just left the inner core of the nuclear room."

The goon stared at him, then turned his head toward the core room.

In a split second, Mitch thrust his force against the end of the blade, pushing it upward into the goon's eye. Blood flooded from the behemoth's orbit, and oozed from Mitch's palm. Quickly Mitch turned back to the elevator door hoping to find the button that would open it. Behind him, the animal groaned in pain.

Where was that door opener! Frantically, Mitch hit the wall, smacked the floor in an attempt to find the latch, knowing the others would descend upon him in seconds. In the next moment, he felt something charge into his body with such force that he thought his lungs had popped loose. His body struck the wall and he slumped to the floor where the blood from his hand and the blood from the monster's eye covered the tile. Yet the goon remained conscious and aggressive. Mitch struggled to breathe to remain conscious. When he looked up, his chin was met by a karate kick, sending his head back against the wall. Suddenly, then, the secret door opened, and his upper body fell into the elevator cage. He scrambled to get his entire frame into the lift before the door shut.

But the goon had its fingers tightly wrapped around Mitch's ankle, jerking him out of the cage. Mitch grabbed the railing in the cage and gripped it tightly. Another yank, and Mitch's torso came half-way out of the elevator. Mitch clenched the railing harder, his bleeding hand zinging with pain. The next twist and jerk on his ankle dragged him back out except for his hands clutching the railing like a vice. The closing elevator doors squeezed his chest. So this is how he would die, he thought.

A fourth tug, and Mitch's body lay outside the elevator cage and on the floor in between the goon's legs. He looked up at his attacker, saw the thing's eye hanging out of its socket by a single strand. In one fluid move, Mitch reached up and snapped it off.

The monster howled. He folded on one knee, still shrieking in pain while yet trying to raise his machete against Mitch.

Mitch kicked him hard in the face, and the goon collapsed to the floor. Immediately Mitchell started smacking the wall where his head had hit it and opened it. Nothing. *Come on come on!* The goon started moving.

The elevator door parted and Mitch tried crawling inside, with the goon right on top of him. Between struggling to get into the elevator and fending off the goon, Mitch could feel his energy evaporating. "You bastard!" he cursed at the infallible and persistent form. He reached out and punched it in the socket of its missing eye, and the thing went down again while Mitchell took advantage of the moment and threw himself into the cage.

He remembered that he wanted to go up and that those numbers were opposite or lower, so he hit the knob with "0" on it. The elevator jolted, sped upward as he lay on the floor of the cage, his eyes taking in its surroundings. That he didn't see any cameras told him it didn't mean there weren't any.

When the lift thrust to a stop ten stories above, he bolted forward, then regained his balance, grappling to stand. The doors opened. Mitch surveyed the area, saw no one. He dragged himself from the elevator, and out into the tunnel but its darkness made it difficult for him to see, and yet it soothed him as flashing pangs throbbed in his maimed chin.

He limped along the narrow path, trying to recall the map on the computer. Something in the back of his mind told him the circle he saw on the map was up ahead. He headed for it, stumbling along, feeling at times as though he would pass out right there in the cramped, shadowy tunnels with its dankness and humidity; its earthy smell; soiled-lined floor; moist, rocky walls.

Ten minutes later, he arrived at a circuitous section where he saw after much analysis, a wrought iron ladder against the rock-lined walls that led to a round hole about thirty feet up, in the ceiling. So that was why the ladder looked unusual; the curious circle on the map was a manhole exiting to the outside world. Was this the exit Azar had told Mitch about—the one close to the parking lot? But which lot? He had nothing to lose by trying to climb the ladder and pry the lid off before he was discovered. Doubt nagged at him, knowing how badly he had been injured, how sore he was. Though he believed his car was behind him somewhere in the parking lot, he knew that to go back that way would be perilous. In front of him was more of the passageway. He could go down that path in hopes of it leading to the outside or he could climb the forbidding looking ladder and try to exit the manhole.

He started the ascent up the ladder, his hand smarting as he held onto each rung, his body protesting each step he took.

Fifteen steps from the top, he heard the rapid THUD THUD THUD of feet scrambling on the earthen floor, voices raised, machete blades clinking against other items on the goons' belts. He tried speeding his climb, praying he'd reach the top before they got to him. *Go go go go*! His hand and chin throbbed, and his body cried in anguish.

Eight feet away. By the way the THUDS increased in intensity—hitting the ground in rapid succession—he knew they were running towards him now.

He scampered harder to reach the top.

Suddenly, four goons stood below him, looking around. Quietly, swiftly, Mitch maneuvered his body between the damp walls and the ladder.

They flashed spotlights around the base of the walls, down the tunnel behind them, in the tunnel in front of them.

"Don't see him," said one goon who continued to shine his flashlight ahead. "Bet he made a run down this section to get to the parking garage. I keep telling the director to put security cameras in these tunnels."

Mitch closed his eyes in gratitude; at least something was going in his favor.

"If we hurry," began one of the monsters, "we can trap the intruder in the tunnel. Don't spare his life. He's dangerous to our security and our existence here."

Mitch waited until they were far down the pathway before he resumed his climb. He couldn't believe they didn't look up to see if he had gone out the manhole.

When he at last reached the steel manhole lid, he tried turning it, but it wouldn't budge. Now he knew why they figured he hadn't gone out the manhole. He wanted to slink to the ground and bawl, understanding that there was some secret switch near the lid or back down at the bottom of the steps he had to locate and pull, turn, maybe even punch in some secret code. He hung his head in dismay.

The sound of metal sliding against metal jarred him. *Jeesh! Someone's coming down!* He squinted when the removed lid let in dusk.

Into a microphone on his lapel, the form descending said, "I'm entering now," and lowered his body into the hole while shining his flashlight. "I don't see him. The lid is in place again and secured."

Damn! Mitch was hoping to leave that way. He froze. There was no way the goon wouldn't find him in its climb down the rusting, steel ladder. Mitch watched one large booted foot hit a rung, then the other foot, next the first again . . . . With each movement, Mitch re-positioned his fingers so as not to be stepped on.

The form descended eight feet, now nearly eye-to-eye with Mitch on the ladder.

Another step down.

Then they were staring at each other.

In a surprise movement, Mitch kneed the demon in the groin and, with the last bit of strength he had, pushed him off the ladder.

He landed with such a loud CRUNCH that Mitch thought the entire complex heard it. Mitch stood perfectly immobile, waiting to see if the monster moved, but by how oddly it lay on the earthen floor—its body twisted and misshapen—told him it had been seriously injured or was dead.

Then an ugly thought entered his mind. What if the things didn't die? What if they were so mechanized and computerized that high-tech gadgets in them wouldn't let their bodies fail? *Good Lord!*

Minutes later, sweating, grunting, he climbed down the ladder and circled the goon, making sure it wasn't still alive. When he saw blood seeping from the lifeless form's ears, and then the thing's eyes glow red, Mitch knew that it had lost that chemical through its oozing serum. But was it still alive? He kicked it.

Nothing.

Can't waste time; others will be here. Again he kicked the monster, and again; it remained unmoving. Quickly, with pain pounding in his chin and hand, his body aching, Mitch stripped the monster of its khaki pants and jackets, boots and weapons, and slipped them on over his own clothes. Seeing that it had a mustache matching its dark hair, Mitch used the monster's knife to swiftly trim and shape his wig and fake mustache to look like the goon's. In the dark tunnel, he couldn't tell how closely his disguise resembled the goon's picture badge that he had clipped onto the khaki jacket. He thought about moving the form to the corner of the circular chamber but decided against it when he realized how long it would take him to do it with a bum hand and broken chin and jaw. Besides, Mitch's strength in no way equaled the goliath's body mass.

He headed for the lift, thinking the goons wouldn't expect him to go backwards.

When he had left the cage in the nuclear room where he had entered it earlier, he kept walking through one room after another, until he finally exited into the hallway. In his mind, he recalled the map on the computer which led him to a back door near the parking garage. Thank God, he was out of the tunnel! Now he had to make it to his car.

"Hey, Kordell! You see him?" shouted one goon standing near the elevator leading to the garage.

It took Mitch a second to realize he was being addressed. He shook his head, kept walking. All along the way, he saw other goons swarming the garage, asking one another if the intruder had been found. When he walked out into the pillared, cemented garage, several other goons turned to him. One approached Mitch, saying, "Has he been found?"

"He's in Glazier's office under heavy security." Mitch looked around. "Glazier ordered that I remove the intruder's car from the garage." He stepped past him, but the goon reached out and grabbed his arm to stop him. Mitch read the goon's I.D. badge. "Let go, Ritman. I have a job to do."

"Why you?" Again the goon scrutinized Mitch, seemingly confused.

Mitch moved on. The second he reached his car, a goon shouted, "Hey, what are you doing! I'm here on Glazier's order to move the intruder's car."

"She told *me* to do it," lied Mitch.

"Let me see your orders."

"Let me see yours."

"You know better than to address a superior that way!" The monster got nose to nose with Mitch. "You're not Kordell."

Paralyzed, Mitch did nothing at first, then warned, "Touch me, and you'll be filled with radiation. I'm saturated with plutonium from being in the nuclear center." He watched the guard step backward, and catching him off balance, Mitch—with the force of his entire body— rammed him against his car. Pain seared through Mitch, but he knew his life was at stake and he had a goal to achieve: Get the info to Dana.

The big goon tripped over his own massive feet when Mitch charged him and he went down. Mitch grabbed the machete off the uniform's belt, and with a whoop and a grunt, he jammed the metal point straight into the guard's chest. Blood gushed, and the monster went motionless. *He's still breathing!* He jumped over the goon and raced for the driver's seat, never turning to look back, never giving thought to the crimes he had committed or to the injuries his own body suffered.

He slammed his car door shut, started the engine in spite of his jittering fingers, and zoomed the car in and out, around and up to the surface, floored it at ground level. Just as his auto emerged out of the garage, a goon jumped in front of it, holding a gun.

"Jeesh!" cried Mitch who ducked when the bullet hit the hood at the same time Mitch ran over him. The sound of the THUMP would stay with him for a long time. Yet, a part of him told himself that what he had murdered wasn't human—just evil at its inner core.

He made his way from Route 50 to Route 13 North, trying to remove the khaki jacket and weapons when he stopped for red lights. Constantly he checked his rearview and side mirrors to make sure the goons hadn't caught up with him. He concentrated not on his fear or physical pain, but on tracking down Dana and getting the materials to her, knowing **they** would never let him live after what he had done.

First, though, he would call Gilly at home, even if it meant waking her.

Chapter
19

Cy crushed his sister with his embrace. "I'm sorry."

She pulled away from him. "It's your fault!"

Her husband Brian snarled, "My son had his whole life ahead of him until he chose to spend the year with you."

"I took Wally under my wing because you said he was getting into trouble with friends. I did it for you." Cy looked at his sister. "I didn't realize he was drinking the water. The warning had been all over the news. I'm sorry, really. I loved him like my own kid."

"If he were your son you would have watched him!" Brian hissed.

It was all Cyril could do not to punch him. He turned, walked away, not stopping the moisture mounting in the corner of his eyes. The worst was that the kid was gone, forever, and Cy had never even told Wally he had done a good job as a gumshoe apprentice, or that he loved him as his only nephew.

7:00 a.m.

From outside a 24-hour convenience store during morning rush hours, which Mitch considered to be safe surroundings, he dialed Gillian's number. It rang and rang. He knew she wouldn't be sleeping at this hour because, like clockwork, she always rose by six-thirty, did her morning things, and then reported for work. He hoped nothing had happened to her. *Another worry.* He ran his hand through his hair, trying to think what to do next.

His Enolc adventure had drained him. It was all he could do to stand at the wall phone and dial numbers. What had he gotten himself into? In his mind he saw trench-coated men and monsters in khaki uniforms following him. He looked down, his eyes recording blood on his shoes, spattered on his black shirt and pants.

He tried the reporter's home number next, but no answer there, either. He studied the half sheet of paper he carried, with her home and work numbers on it, thinking maybe he had read it wrong. He dialed her office number. Whoever answered informed him that Dana hadn't arrived for work yet. Hanging up the receiver, he felt more dejected than before. He needed to talk to someone.

Dixie! She knows about science—though maybe not about clones—and she is Gillian's best friend. But will she be at work now, too? He'd try reaching her at home before she left for work.

****

Still in his embrace, she reached for a cigarette on the nightstand behind her. "Got to get to work," she mumbled.

His lips rested on hers. "Nice to have friends like me in high places who don't demand that you report to work at specific times."

"Then how about that raise?"

"Keep a low profile, and I'll see what I can do. With Hammond and Gamblin dead, I'm no longer as close to the top as I used to be. Gamblin was my confidant." He added, "I'm getting a little worried about all these exterminations. Maybe they'll get traced to—"

"With your immediate supervisor being a high level federal exec, and your ultimate boss, a cabinet member, who's going to touch you?"

"Don't count on anyone in power supporting you if you get nailed; I don't."

"I'm not the devil here; I only do what I'm forced to do."

The phone rang. She pulled away from him and picked up on the third ring.

"Dix, it's Mitch. Listen, I have to talk to you now. It's critical. Please."

"What's wrong? I was just getting ready to go to work—"

"Please, Dix, please! I must talk to you."

"Okay okay. Where?"

"Behind a lead barrier."

"What?"

"I'm radioactive."

"*What!*"

"I know what I'm talking about. I sneaked into Enolc One."

Dixie gulped air. "You're kidding." She glanced at her overnight-bed-partner, then said back into the mouthpiece. "Even if that were true, Mitch, I don't think radioactivity is contagious." She thought for a long minute. "At work we have an X-ray department with an emergency exit to the outside. Meet me there, at the back of the clinic where over the door is a red X. I'll go there, authorize your vehicle on the grounds, and reserve the X-ray room. When you come in this X-ed door, go through the antechamber to where the X-ray machine is and sit behind the lead barrier. I'll be on the other side waiting for you. Plan to meet me around noon." Just as she was ready to hang up, she asked, "Do you know where Gillian is?"

"I wish I did. I need her."

Dixie replaced the mouthpiece on the receiver, turned to her lover. "My best friend's ex has been snooping. I've got to meet with him. If he's been investigating, then Gillian must be out gathering damning information, too. The two of them could have enough material to jeopardize the entire operation."

The man looked at her. "I'll take care of them."

"I don't want anything to happen to them. I was promised that."

He just looked at her.

She held up her palm. "Never mind. I'll take care of it." She dialed a number.

He watched, not saying anything.

When she heard the voice at the other end, she repeated everything to him that she had told the man in bed with her. "You need to prevent Gillian Montague from using the materials she's assembling. You can find out where she is by going to the Collier Investigative Agency. I'll take care of Frey. He's to meet with me in an hour. I don't want either harmed. Do you hear?"

"Is Frey the one rumored to have broken into Enolc One? I heard about it twenty minutes ago."

"I've just learned that, too. Do as I directed." When she hung up the phone and turned back to her lover, she saw him lying in bed wielding a knife.

"So it comes to this." Her eyes were on his hand. When he retracted the blade, she puffed out air in relief.

"Remember I'm the one who gives orders. But I like your style, girl. Know that if something goes wrong, you'll take the fall for it. Who can guarantee who's going to survive this? Maybe your friends will get bumped off in the process anyway." He slid on his pants while slipping the switch blade inside his pocket. "So, here's my idea: We'll try it your way first, but if we don't get the materials from either of them, they're fish floating atop water. If you screw this up, Dix, you'll be joining them. I have a boss to report to, too."

"I said I'd take care of things."

****

Dana sat in the coffee house, turning pages of Mitch's typed notes and the hand-written materials he had given her. She made a clucking sound at the incredulous words before her. Yet, the research she had done on Mitch so far proved he was well respected in the community and at his business. He co-owned a large real estate company with a national relo service, and she couldn't find one worker who had anything negative to say about him, except that he tended to take an unusually long time to get things done, that he often procrastinated, but did eventually accomplish what he had promised. His integrity and scruples, however, were impeccable.

So why was what he had written difficult to believe? She took another sip of coffee and a nibble of her bagel, reading and rereading everything before her. Periodically, she'd look up and stare into the air, mulling over the information.

Does it seem believable that the government would implant chips under everyone's skin—the first step to tracking humans? She shrugged.

Does it seem likely that the government owns several fertility clinics connected to bioresearch labs— ones toying with DNA and RNA to duplicate humanity? Yeah, because today they can even create human organs in test tubes.

Does it seem viable for the government to be more advanced in the genetics game than anyone suspected, and that they can clone adult living things? She forced her mind to think back years ago: *The Swedes have already shown that.*

She took another sip of her beverage, blowing the steam off the top. But here was the clincher: *Could she believe the government could clone adult humans and fetal tissue through genetic transfer and gene selection to form programmed clones, some of which resulted in deformed mutants through targeting and enhancing specific traits?* She smacked her lips together. Nope, not likely.

But then again, she asked herself, why not? *What if this Mitch is right that the government has bred clones to be fighting machines, to offer spare transplantation parts. . . Why, just last year when I did an entire series on organ shortages, I had discovered all kinds of horrors going on there: Organ theft, blackmailing and blackmarketing. . . . Yet, to clone a whole individual to program him via a computer chip . . . well that does seem pretty far-fetched.*

But something nagged at her. The government had been up to strange antics, what with the push for globalism in every phase of life, its insistence on closing churches and, some said, executing disasters and diseases, even creating food shortages. Too, there was Williams' and Cinzan's apparent lackadaisical attitude about the water contamination. Not only had the perpetrator not been found, but the government hadn't done anything to alleviate the problem.

A bite of bagel remained in her mouth as she considered what she had read. So, conceivably this Mitch could be right. What she had researched on his friend Salyer Basse all seemed to fit together, too. Now there was a fellow who had interfaced with the various government branches and suddenly when he started blabbing to Mitch—according to Mitch—the man's body got blown to shreds.

Dana cringed. Perhaps she was tackling something too dangerous. This was witnessed by Mitchell Frey wanting to sneak into one of the—what he had called—Enolc labs to give her proof. Absolutely nuts, he was. Maybe that's exactly what she was dealing with—a royal nut—and she ought to back off while she still could.

She checked her watch: 7:45. Really, she ought to get busy on the assignment her editor, Glenn, had given her: A piece on the city's East end protesting annexation of a feeder route into Wilmington. Bah! How boring. What she wanted to do first was track down Mitch.

Still re-reading Mitch's notes, she searched for clues as to where he might have hidden Salyer Basse's evidence, but no matter how diligently she analyzed the materials, she couldn't discern any secrets.

A passage she had examined a thousand times in his typed notes kept plaguing her: "I will hunt down the perpetrators of these crimes—no matter what level they're at—and stalk them until the right moment comes when I can expose them, so the world might be set straight. I swear I will do this even if it means my death, from ashes to ashes." On his words went, as if he were some madman on a religious diatribe. But what was it about that excerpt that gnawed at her, she wondered.

The jingling of the cell phone in her purse jarred her. The second she answered, she heard her boss growl: "Carter, this is Kincaid. Where are you! Under the circumstances, you should be back here!"

"Where I am is at a coffee shop having a bagel before I head over to the East side to do the piece." Pause; she lowered her voice so not everyone would hear her in the doughnut shop. "What do you mean 'under the circumstances'?" She hated when he took that tone with her.

"You're supposed to be a hot-shot Columbia journalism grad, and you don't even know what's going on in the world. I oughta bust you back to cub reporter." She heard him take in a deep breath before adding, "The Israeli prime minister has been assassinated, and there's talk that Russia's moving in to take over Israel while it's most vulnerable. Get your rear in gear and over here now!"

She was in motion the second he disconnected. Nothing else mattered but this.

7:40 a.m.; Wilmington

Sitting in his car, sipping hot coffee, Mitch tried to think things through. He looked down at his feet and realized he had kept the goon's boots on over his shoes but had removed the khaki outfit. The air's crispness reminded him it was winter, so he pulled the lab jacket out of his back pants pocket and slipped it over his shoulders until he could get his winter coat in the car. If anything, he was stressed beyond his logical, sentient being. All he wanted, was to crawl under the covers and sleep, but right now he needed to call Cy. He retraced his steps to the phone.

Cy's secretary answered on the first ring. "Collier Investigative Agency."

"This is Mitchell Frey, Gillian's ex. Is Cy in?"

"I just received a call his nephew died. I don't imagine he'll be in for days."

"I'm sorry." Nothing was going right. "Where's Gillian?" He knew he sounded frantic. "I have to talk to her now! My life may be in danger. Everyone's life may be in danger. It's about the investigation she's on and also what I've discovered. Please, just tell me when she'll be home."

He heard Annie sift through papers. "I can't find her itinerary but I thought she was supposed to come home late last night. She hasn't called yet, so I don't know for sure where she is."

"Please tell her I'll contact her later and that we must talk. It's crucial." Then, as an afterthought: "Listen, leave a note for Cy . . . put it in a sealed envelope, please, and put it in a place where only he'll find it." He paused but she said nothing. "This is extremely important. You've got to get this message to him! Tell him I have proof of everything and that the evidence will be buried at surface level at the grave of Salyer Basse. Tell him to read it. It explains about Chase, the water, Azar, the labs, the—"

"What?"

"Please write down everything I've told you but put it where only Cy can find it. Don't breathe a word of this to anyone."

Annie was sure he had lost his mind. "All rightie; I'll do just as you say."

Wilmington

Sitting in the car in front of Salyer's grave, Mitch reviewed Sal's material, along with the manual and files he had sneaked out of the lab. On and off he'd run the engine to keep warm while yet not consuming all the gas. Occasionally he'd glance out the windows to make sure no one was tailing him. He checked his watch, not wanting to be late meeting Dixie.

As thoughts rushed him, he'd jot them down on the backs of the papers he had been carrying since he left the lab. Based on what he had stolen from there, and had overheard in the hall from their "report session," he believed the government was behind everything. "This is insane," he muttered aloud, fearful of what the future held for humanity. He rubbed his red, watery eyes, shaking his head. "My God."

He was a wreck; he knew it, was even ashamed of how he looked. Again, he ruffled his hair with his hand in attempt to get the strands off his eyes. Gosh, he was tired. He returned to skimming page after page of notes, wanting to read and analyze each word, each sentence, but knew that would have to wait until later. He resolved to flip through the rest of Hammond's materials no matter how unnerving they were.

Now and then, a grunt would slip from Mitch's lips as he read and made notes. He wrote that he believed Leslie was one of the few female clones—one that turned out to be more masculine than feminine but he knew there was written more info on Leslie that he hadn't gotten to yet. The world, from what he had read, was damned. Getting to Gilly and telling her about Leslie and Chase was vital.

At the rate things were speeding along, he understood that there may never come a chance to prevent what was happening. He lowered his face in his hands, thinking after what he read and had seen last night that death now seemed the best that could happen to anyone.

He returned to writing everything he could remember about Enolc One, starting from his meeting with Azar, up to the second where he sat in the car preparing to lift the shovel out of the trunk of his Bonneville and lay it under the earth. The hardest part for him to write was his having unknowingly sneaked into the reactor chamber and having been exposed to an inconceivably high, lethal, dose of radiation, one that would certainly kill him within days.

Recalling how he had prowled from hallway to hallway in Enolc 1, in and out of rooms that weren't locked, flying up and down stairwells, he began asking himself if he had not been mad for doing something he wasn't likely get away with. "What is wrong with me?"

With snow heavily tumbling from the sky, he opened his car door, stuck his head out and opened his mouth, trying not to laugh. If this was the only way he could get pure water—if it was pure—so be it. But then he realized it didn't matter.

He returned to writing his thoughts, more hurriedly now, knowing he was running against time to meet Dixie—the only one who could help him. But no matter how much time it took, he had to write it all down so the truth would be known.

10:00 a.m.; Wilmington

"Is she back yet?" asked the man entering the office.

Annie looked up from what he was reading. "Oh, it's you again. I told you last night that I can't give out Ms. Montague's schedule."

"Then she's still not in?" Countee Burrows rubbed his chin in thought. "I must see her. I'll return," and he left as quickly as he came.

Annie stared after him, wondering what organization he belonged to and what it had to do with Gillian. The guy sure was persistent.

An hour later, she stood at the rusted file cabinet in the main room of the office suite, inserting manilla envelopes into green folders, her back to the office door, wondering what Mitch's problem was. She had met him before but he had never struck her as deranged as he had acted this morning. She had always considered him a nice, composed fellow.

All the same, she had done as he requested, writing down what he had told her on the phone, and then sealing it in an envelope that she buried inside Cy's cigar box kept in the fake bottom of the trash can. Cy had built a false bottom to the wastebasket to conceal very confidential client documents, as well as to store his imported cigars. He had done it in such a way that even when the cleaning people emptied the trash, the cigar box remained hidden under the false bottom. So Annie had slipped the paper with Mitch's info in the trash can, believing she ought to do what she got paid to do, no matter how nuts Cy's clients might be.

Returning to the main room of Cy's office, she went back to filing manilla folders. The phone's ringing yanked her from her private reverie.

"Annie? This is Gilly. I'm in a taxi on my way to the Ripley boy's house. My flight yesterday was cancelled, so I'm running a day behind."

"You could have told me. Some man was here looking for you. He even came to my mom's home last night, and then he came here about an hour ago."

"The phone connection is poor at my end. What man?"

"A 'count' somebody from an anti-government, unethics-something-or-another." The pause allowed Annie to add, "Cy's nephew died."

"Oh gee! As soon as I finish this interview, I'll be in Indiana by mid-morning since time here in Albuquerque is two hours behind. I've lined up the first flight, around three, to make Philly airport by five-ish, and then I'll be home to be with Cy. Give him my condolences."

Annie hung up. The door opened. With her back still to the entry, she sang, "Be right with ya," as she slammed the file drawer shut, and spun around, expecting to face that anti-government agent again.

"Where's Gillian Montague?"

Annie stared at him, her mind taking in his size, his khaki jacket with beige pants, and how he boasted a G.I. cut. Was he one of those goons? The anti-government man was big, too, but not as huge as this fellow. Were all the same?

"I said, where's Montague?"

She backed up against the file cabinet. "She's out . . . on business."

"I don't believe you." He slammed his fist down on the counter, splintering the old wooden top. "Give me her travel itinerary now."

"I-I-I don't have it. I only know where she is by her calls to the office."

"Come here."

She couldn't move.

"Come here," he repeated in the same commanding tone.

She saw him swish open the switch blade. On shaky legs, her body twittering, she forced herself to walk over to him.

"Where is her travel schedule? I want exact times."

Her mind recorded the sneer on his face, smelled the odor about him.

"S-s-sometime to-to-tonight." She started bawling.

"You're a liar." He grinned sadistically. "Watch," he ordered, holding the knife at arm's length. "I said watch! Put your eyes on my knife."

Her eyes were so full of tears, she couldn't see.

"Watch the knife, and I won't hurt you."

She cried harder.

"I said, I won't hurt you. Keep your eyes on the knife."

She tried nodding but his right hand's rigid grip around the nape of her neck prohibited movement.

"Yes?" He nodded her head with his hand, as if she were a puppet.

She'd do anything to live.

"You'll have a nice long life for obeying." In one fleeting moment, he jabbed the blade into her throat. In a second nimble action, he yanked it out and drove it into her skull. "Victuals," he sang, bringing her bleeding head to his mouth. Minutes later, he tore the office apart looking for what he had come for.

9:40 a.m. PST; Albuquerque

Gilly looked at her watch. It would be going on one

in Wilmington. She really needed to get home to be
there for Cy, conduct more research on the goons, and
make more calls to geneticists, police, morticians.
Tired from jet lag, she dreaded having to visit Hilda
Dillon in Indianapolis, then rush to catch a two o'clock
flight to Philly. And by the time she drove from the airport to home in Wilmington, it would be 5:30 or so,
counting the time change.

Gillian found the Ripley address and was admitted
into the adobe-like home. The squat uncle sat right next
to Brandon as she questioned him. He had made it clear
that he was in charge since his brother and sister-in-
law were still grieving the death of their daughter.
Then the catch came.

"If you turn this into a movie or book, Ms. Montague, I'll have my attorney negotiate the contract . . .
on behalf of the boy, of course . . . that is, until my
brother can recover enough to take care of Brandon."

"I'm an investigator, Mr. Ripley, not a movie pro-
ducer." Gillian asked the child, "Your sister, Brandon,
did she know anyone was in the house?"

The child nodded. "She told me to run next door,
and not stop."

"Why didn't she run away with you? Could it have
been to make sure you got away?" Gilly wondered if
she would have been brave enough to have made herself
bait to save another life. "Tell me what this bad man
looked like."

Brandon's eyes glazed over. "Big; with fire in his
eyes; short hair."

"What kind of fire in his eyes?"

"Hey," interrupted the uncle, "the kid's stressed
out, and he's gone over this with the police." He sat
with his arms crossed over his protruding belly, his
nose red and shiny.

She turned back to Brandon. "What else?"

The boy looked out the kitchen window. "I told

you. The thing was a monster like the 'abdominal' snowman, and he kinda smelled, too. He . . . picked my sist—"

Come on, come on; she hated being so impatient— one of her many faults, she knew, but learning the detective business might help her channel her agitation and impulsiveness.

"He grabbed her by her throat, yanked her up so high that her feet were off the ground. Then I—" and the child broke down, sobbed hard and wildly into his uncle's chest. He sputtered again, "Then I . . . I . . . ran, wet my pants."

Gillian stood. There was no sense making him go through it again. She thanked Ripley over the boy's howls and went out the kitchen door in the direction of a bus station to make her flight to Indiana.

Hearing real survivors tell about the goons, plus her own experience—in spite of Dixie's protests—made her believe all the more in their existence, and that they weren't normal humans. She just wanted to get home, call Mitch and invite him over for his friendship and warmth, and cuddle next to him. He always made her feel safe when he was around. "Why did we divorce anyway?" she asked herself as she flagged down a taxi. She always loved the feel of Mitch in bed with her, that Old Spice aroma lingering on him into the night. Gosh, she missed him.

Smell?

Didn't the Ripley boy say the attacker had "smelled"? Why hadn't she followed through on that. That's what she meant when she told others that she really wasn't that great of a detective, and that's what she meant when she was honest with herself and admitted her flaws. *Impatience. Impulsiveness.*

Her mind kept wandering back to the Ripley boy's words. The thought of the attacker having a "smell" bothered her, even though she tried taking her mind off it by dialing Hilda Dillon's number at the nursing home.

"Yes!" she said aloud, recalling suddenly that Chase had a smell about him, too. Was it the same kind of odor that the Ripley boy referred to? And again, that thing about Chase saying he and Leslie had been raised by an organization when Gillian herself had seen the photos of the parents in their home.

Chapter
20

Gilly's head pounded from crisscrossing the country in short time spans. She reached the long-term-care home feeling entirely spent, but she had to go through this last interview so she could continue her research back home. She felt that though she was getting close, not all the pieces to the puzzle were coming together.

An intern at the Home unlocked the door and led Gillian down a long hall to the lobby. With a nod, he indicated where Hilda Dillon sat staring at the floor. "She won't understand much," he said.

Gillian walked over to the emaciated form in the rocking chair and took a seat opposite her, though her first reaction was to run from the chewed up face. Gently, Gillian explained who she was, why she was there.

Hilda looked at her momentarily, then cast her eyes back to the floor.

Gillian tried again.

Hilda kept rocking, staring at the floor.

Based on all the articles Gillian had read, she recited the event to Hilda to get her to react. "So he came to your house without your hearing him arrive, right?"

No response.

"Was he big, with glowing red eyes?" Gillian remembered that Brandon had described it as red fire in the eyes.

Hilda stopped rocking. For minutes she stared at Gillian. Then, barely above a whisper, said, "Hideous." Her body shook in repulsion. "Grotesque."

"Why you?" Gilly took Hilda's hand and patted it. "Were you singled out?"

Hilda's howl keened the air.

Everyone in the lobby turned and looked.

Gillian squeezed her hand, stood to go.

"My son . . . Tommy . . . would have been the same age as my attacker," she uttered through her reconstructed lips and tongue.

When it dawned on Gillian, she felt the sudden impact of Hilda's pain. She stared at the woman, looked at her through her own veiled tears.

Noon; Philadelphia

Before pulling on to the grounds of Traditional Fertility Clinic, Mitch had removed his disguise and ditched the lab coat in the trunk of the car next to the shovel he had used to bury the evidence at Salyer's grave. After removing his wig, false beard and mustache, he grew surprised at how overwrought and exhausted he looked. He had dark circles and sagging skin under his watery, red eyes, and he was growing his own brand of beard from not having shaved in days. *I certainly need my Old Spice now,* he mumbled, smelling his clothes.

At the security gate, he had no problems gaining

entrance, as Dixie had promised, And then, again, she had kept her word in leaving the rear door of the radiology department unlocked; otherwise, without knowing the code to punch in, Mitch never would have gotten in. Quietly and quickly, he entered a door with a laminated sign reading: *Radiology Department; Film Delivery Entrance and Egress with Authorization Only. All Other Admissions at Front Door with Proper Identification.*

Remembering her directions, he entered the antechamber leading into a room divided into two, with a quarter of it housing a chair and controls. The smaller section was cordoned off by a heavy lead wall with a window and vents. He knew this was the area where technicians stood to snap the pictures.

"You're late; sit down," came Dixie's voice from the tech's control room.

"Sorry; I got hung up at Salyer's grave." He pulled the stool over to the wall with the tiny spare window where she sat on the other side. "Thanks so much for meeting with me." He wondered if he looked as badly as he felt, and as exhausted as he sounded. With the panel window and lead wall between them, he felt as though he were about to say an act of contrition in a confessional, and he wasn't even Catholic.

"Several of our workers here are Jewish and the boss let them off work today because of the assassination of Rubin Steinmetz."

"I didn't know that."

"No wonder, considering your condition. My God, Mitchell, you look awful! Tell me what's going on."

He gave her details on Salyer, his meeting with Azar, how he sneaked into Enolc One, right up to where he sat talking to her. What he didn't tell her was that he had buried the evidence, not only because he had forgotten, but also because he didn't trust anyone . . . only Gilly, but she wasn't around to help.

When he had finished his story and gone silent,

Dixie started questioning him: "Are you sure you were in the inner room of the reactor?"

"From what I can tell, it looked that way."

"Were there signs to that effect?"

"How would I know," he snapped. "I was crawling on my knees, for pete's sake!" He took in a deep breath to calm himself.

"It's my understanding that you couldn't have been exposed to radiation unless there was a leak in the reactor room, allowing plutonium to seep out, and even then, you wouldn't be contagious, providing you didn't get any radiation, such as dust or something, on you."

He thought for a minute. "I . . . I don't know if there was a leak."

"Well, I'm no nuclear physicist but I think that unless the rods were removed, you couldn't have been exposed to the core."

He ran his hand through his hair. "I did see a worker leave the room wearing one of those white, lead suits, carrying a helmet with the see-through visor." He paused. "He also had something cylindrical and shiny like metal."

Dixie chuckled. "Really, I don't think he had a rod. But still, I suppose there are other ways you could have been exposed to radiation, though I really doubt it. No lab would violate regulatory codes, so it's safe to say that you're not contaminated, but I am concerned about what's going on in these labs."

"I'm telling you, Dix, they're cloning humans for sinister use, and they have connections with certain fertility clinics. Hey! You better be careful, too, with your working at a fertility clinic." He closed his eyes. Gosh was he ever tired. "You know what else? I know about Leslie, too."

"What about her?"

"I've got to go to the police, Dix."

She leaned forward. "Mitch, I have something to

tell you but I don't want anyone to know this." She looked around the room. "I've suspected for awhile now that my superior here is up to no good. I've heard babies crying in sections of this clinic where babies shouldn't be. And," here she leaned forward to whisper, "I didn't want to scare Gilly, but I, too, have a feeling that something is being done to these infants, and that there are giant men coming and going from this place." She wet her lips. "I don't know the purpose of the Enolc labs and my clinic, but in my gut, I suspect something illegal and unethical. I try to keep informed by hob-nobbing with the higher-ups . . ." here she looked away before adding, "but if you have proof, we can nail them."

"I want you to stay out of it, Dix. These people are capable of anything."

"I know. I was with one of my supervisors last night who's always willing to spill info in return for a favor from me. Stay away from these people. They're very, very dangerous. I tried telling Gilly that but she's so damned stubborn. She insisted on going away to conduct interviews, and now I'm worried about her. I know they have—"

"Who's 'they'?"

She looked at him. "Why . . . the government, of course, which has no qualms about hurting . . . kill-ing . . . anyone. I just wished Gilly had left it alone; you, too. I've been investigating it for AUGA—the Agency on Unethical Government Activities. It's a secret bureau that examines things like this. I've worked for them for years now, and they asked me to uncover any unscrupulous activities in this clinic. Mitch, you've got to stop. You have no idea what's going on."

He looked at her. "Will you be okay?"

"Oh sure. I have twenty-four/seven protection. But what I need from you now are the materials you got

from Enolc One and Salyer so I can go after these people. How soon can you get them to me?"

"Well . . . I . . . I—" He rubbed his eyes. So tired.
"I . . . have to go get them."

Her voice sounded tender when she said, "You're so
exhausted . . . just tell me where they are and I'll have
someone from AUGA pick them up."

He didn't want to tell her . . . only Gillian should be
told. But right now, he needed someone he could trust
who would take over his worries and handle the problem. But should he trust Dixie? Should he trust anyone?
No, it's better not to say anything. Determined to
remain silent, he just looked at her, looked at how sym-
pathetic and concerned she seemed; she had made a
point of being there for him. "They're buried at the base
of Salyer's tombstone at Heavenly Cemetery. Buried
right under the surface."

"Fine. fine. Now, I want you to go to the hospital
and get checked out, okay? Then I want you to go home
and rest, and stay out of this from now on. I also want
you to make Gillian stop her investigation before she
gets hurt."

"I can't speak for Gilly." He grunted. "I gotta go. I
have to stop at Cy's office to find out where she is and
how I can reach her."

Dixie stood, pointed to the antechamber leading to
his car outside. "Go the way you came in."

12:50 p.m.; Wilmington

Dana Carter sat in the newsroom wondering if she'd
hear from Mitch about having gotten into the Enolc lab.
She heard Glenn, her editor, say, "The prime minister's
death has us revising the board. Makes us all feel vulnerable, doesn't it? Tells us that we're all going to die,
go back to ashes under ground to rot where our souls
are put to rest." He shook his head.

Come on, Glenn; stop with your religious rantings and get on with the work.

The editor cleared his throat, barked out assignments to each of his reporters, ending with, "Karen, I want a feature on the P.M.'s likely successor, and, Don, look into how Rubin Steinmetz's death will affect the world's economy." He went to the wall assignment board.

Dana watched with partial interest, her head bursting inside, telling her that again her sinuses must be infected.

Glenn added, "And, Carter, you're to rove the streets interviewing people for their opinion on the murder. Talk to experts, too, but don't conflict with Laura's assignment. See if you can piece something together for a sensible article."

Another rinky-dink assignment! She went up to Glenn after the meeting and said, "I explained to you about my story dealing with Mitchell Frey, Salyer Basse, and the government. Why aren't you interested?"

"Government conspiracy stories are a dime a dozen. We have to make sure that what we print is factually based because the government and our publisher will come down hard on us. I know. I've had experience with this before. I worked my way up from kid reporter to editor-in-chief. That didn't happen overnight. So I know what all's involved."

She stared at the older man. Seconds passed before she said, "You know, Glenn, I remember an assignment my college media class was given. Our prof had us research the top newspapers, magazines, television and radio stations to discover who owned them. After months of research, we learned that the media are all owned by the same people who belong to the same organizations: The Council on Foreign Relations, the Trilateral Commission, the Bilderbergers, Skull & Bones—"

"There you go again with your conspiracy theories." Glenn crossed his arms, a newspaper in one hand, his tie loosened at the collar of his white shirt.

"You're right," she said. "The government would come down hard on us. Does that make you afraid to publish the truth?"

He threw his head back and laughed. "Out of the mouths of babes."

When she looked into his eyes, they seemed steel gray, cold.

He said sharply, "I make a point, young lady, of being careful. I have a family."

"You also have an obligation to the public. Who are you owned by?"

"You're a punk reporter, Carter, who has a lot to learn and a long way to go. If you want your expose to run, you better have proof. Show me documents that can corroborate any accusations you make. But until you have that all together, you get your rear out on the streets and do what you're assigned. Have I made myself clear?"

"Aye, aye," she said smartly, picking up her purse, pad and pen, and heading outside. She could taste it, wanted it—craved it—the way addicts hungered for smack. Just one big story. One scoop that would set Glenn on his ears and make him appreciate her talent, her ability to sniff out a good story, go after it in the face of danger and expose all the no-goods.

Mitch's story would do all that, if everything he claimed were true and his break-in last night panned out the way he thought it would. She pulled out her cell phone to call him. After ten rings, she replaced the mouthpiece on the receiver. A feeling overcame her that he might have been captured, and if that were the case, she was the only one who could help him. After all, he had confided in her, presented her with some documents of proof. But she needed more evidence, assuming Mitch had gotten it without being killed in the process. That passage returned to her: From dust to dust; just as Glenn had said earlier: "Go to ashes, put to rest under the ground," she mumbled.

Of course! Underground! Why hadn't I thought of that? But where? Where underground? Where would Mitch have buried the evidence? At his condo? No, all concrete there. In some friend's yard? She doubted that because unearthing it would mean trespassing and Mitch was too smart to let some technicality stop her from getting the evidence. She kept on walking, feeling the icy air nip at her toes. She needed to get something hot to drink, which would enrage Glenn if he knew she was already on break and hadn't done one decent interview yet.

At the Koffee Klatch, blowing steam away from the cup, she discounted Mitch having a wife, kids, or girlfriend he would have left the materials with, or possibly used their yards to bury the materials. From what Dana had learned about Mitch, he had been married to a Gillian, though they were now divorced, whom he was still close to.

She took a tube of lipstick out of her purse, touched up her face. So, no wife, no kids, no girlfriend, no best friend. . . . Whoa! Wasn't that the point of all this? For Mitch to avenge his friend Salyer's death. Death. Where was he buried?

She threw her lipstick back into her purse, tossed some coins on the counter and lifted her phone from her purse. "Edith," she said into the cell phone. "Do me a favor, please. Look up the obit on Salyer Basse."

"No can do. Got to help with the prime minister stories."

"Please?" Dana didn't want to go back to the office when Edith could do it.

"I hate looking things up."

"That's your friggin job."

"So is doing first what Glenn tells me to do."

"Let me talk to him."

"He's in a meeting with big-wigs—men dressed in suits, sunglasses." She whispered, "They look like FBI. I can see Glenn from here, looking very serious."

Dana giggled. "You over dramatize."

"Glenn just gave me a signal to cut the call."

"Does he know you're talking to me?"

"I guess so."

Dana hung up. She headed for the library to look up Salyer's obit.

1:00 p.m.; Philadelphia

Mitch looked back at the clinic as he got into his car. Dixie had given him little solace. The one thing that kept nagging at him was that this AUGA Dixie referred to had never once been mentioned in either Salyer's or Hammond's notes. He needed to look into it. Checking his watch, he decided to dash into a Philly library first, and then go to the detective agency. Maybe if Cy was in, Mitch could discuss AUGA with him.

In the library, he checked into every directory listing organizations; he looked into phone books; scanned government documents; ran databases; talked to reference librarians . . . but none of the sources turned up the Agency for Unethical Government Activities. Was the association so secret that it wasn't listed anywhere, or was it something Dixie had made up to appease him? It was going on one-thirty when he left and drove to Cy's office.

His mind registered snow pummeling car roofs, wind stealing shopping bags from downtown shoppers, business execs hustling into and out of buildings, onto trains, and inside cars and cabs. As he watched the banal activities, Mitch muddled over how it could seem so routine outside when his world inside was crumbling.

It was after 2:00 when Mitch reached the building of the detective agency. He had difficulty finding a parking space and jostling through crowds of workers and shoppers. He was out of breath by the time he got to the agency's office door. Mentally he prepared himself for the numerous questions Cy would ask, and the debate he would have with him or the secretary over getting Gillian's itinerary. As he neared the agency's door, he thought things seemed uncannily quiet. Usually one could hear shuffling inside an office, even the slamming of file drawers, the scraping of heels against linoleum.

He opened the door.

No one; not a single person in sight.

"Oh my God!" His eyes took in walls splattered red, the blood pooled on the floor. Hurriedly he moved to the other side of the counter and nearly stepped on Annie, her eyes bulging, her skull opened, and the hole in her throat drying with clots. The sight and odor made him buckle. He threw his hands to his mouth, bolted out of the room.

2:15 p.m.; Wilmington

Cy couldn't stand the loneliness of his apartment any longer. His sister was at the funeral home making plans for her son's body—not wanting Cy to have any part of it—and here he was, trying to pass time, hoping each ticking second would allow him to live with himself a little more. He puffed on the butt of his last cigar.

Maybe he ought to call Gilly to see what her research had turned up. He looked at his watch. If he remembered correctly, she should have been in last night. But for her not to have contacted Cy, not even to call him to give her condolences, wasn't like her. He rang her number.

No answer.

He decided to go to the office, get some work done, and ask Annie if Gilly had checked in. He couldn't stand it if Gillian's research had put her in jeopardy and she was injured or worse.

Darn! He was out of smokes, so he had to go to the office after all. Well, he could return all the calls Annie would have for him, deal with the complaints and questions from various clients. He hated all of it. Maybe it was time he got out of the business. At least then he wouldn't have clients bugging him about whether he got proof their spouses were cheating; if an insurance claimant really had fallen in a grocery store; how many suspects he had come up with in the theft of an expensive painting from a top art gallery; or whether it was the kids' father who had kidnapped a set of twins. Maybe he should retire and go live in Atlanta to be near Stella.

Getting into his car the thought struck him that Gilly's case on goons might have some meat to it, especially after what Stella at the CDC had told him. He smiled thinking about her. When things returned to normal, he might ask her to marry him.

Normal? He sighed. With Wally dead, his life would never be normal.

Driving to his office, Cy's stomach growled but he didn't stop for lunch.

The first thing he noticed were the five police cars with flashing lights in his building's parking lot and out on the main street, and an ambulance blocking traffic. His stout legs couldn't get him inside fast enough. The officer in the main lobby told him the problem was on the third floor.

"Jeesh," said Cy. "That's the floor my office is on." He pushed past another cop and hustled onto the elevator.

The second the lift hit his floor, Cy jumped out. "What the. . . .!" he yelled when he saw police standing in front of his office door.

"Stop!" one bellowed at him, his fingers going to his gun.

Cyril put up his hands. "I'm the detective who owns this office. Let me show you my credentials." He pulled out his badge and I.D.. "Why are you people here?"

"I'm sorry, sir. There's been a homicide in—"

Cy charged for the door, thoughts on Gilly who might be inside his office lying lifeless.

"Stop!" screamed the officer who pulled his gun.

"Listen up, kid, I've been in law enforcement longer than you've been alive; I've seen more, did more, know more than you. I've chased murderers, adulterers, thieves, rapists, and every criminal element conceivable and then some. If I have to take a bullet just to get into my own office, then I'm gonna take your nice, shiny badge and shove it right up your ass."

"I'll have to go in there with you to protect the evidence."

"I know all about preserving evidence!" Cy shoved past the young officer. "Do what you have to, but don't get in my way. Within the last several hours, my nephew died, I've lost my sister, and that may very well be my associate who's in there, so I don't need any more bull." He pushed his way into his office, his gaze catching site of smelly blood on the walls, floors, office desks, and counter; pieces of evidence sitting labeled, almost exhibit style. His office looked like a typhoon had blasted through.

"We need a body bag here," called out one paramedic. Cy saw two more standing around writing reports.

His eyes went to the floor where a form lay, blood splattered all around it, with a white sheet over it, and a white chalk outlining it. He stooped to pull back the sheet in spite of surrounding officers yelling at him to stop. "Oh dear God," he gasped. "Oh Lord!" He felt a wave of nausea and lightheadedness fill him. He reached for support.

A paramedic grabbed him, and with the help of two others, they got Cy to a chair and shoved his head between his legs.

When he was able to pull his body back into a straight position, his eyes met with a police officer who was asking, "You're the P.I. who owns this agency? We tried calling you at your apartment, Mr. Collier, but there was no answer. Do you know who the victim is?"

"My secretary." He gave them all the background info he had on Annie. He ran his large hand over his face. "What happened?"

The officer shrugged. "Someone rammed a very sharp knife through her skull and into her eyes." He flipped open his notebook. "Two workers in other businesses on this floor saw a man leave here around 2:25 p.m., looking crazed and disheveled; tall, blond hair, brushcut. They said workers entered your office on or about 2:30 p.m. to check on your secretary because of the man's unusual behavior and appearance. They found her dead, called the police, and are now at the station being questioned."

Cy sat shaking his head. The officer and paramedics left him alone.

****

Dana rubbed her eyes; her sinus headache worse. She left Wilmington's library, having scanned the newspaper stacks, and then the microfiche. When she found the right newspaper, she carried the two-week edition to a table, and studied the obits. Finally she came upon Salyer Basse's and wrote down, "Heavenly Cemetery" in Wilmington.

3:00 p.m.

Cy sat in his office chair, his chin in his hand, the sadness heavy in his heart. He kept looking around his suite, unable to believe that someone had killed Annie, and so violently. Mindlessly, he watched police and detectives scoot around the office taking pictures, bagging evidence, lifting fingerprints.

After they had interrogated him a thousand times, asked and re-asked the same questions, made calls and answered calls, and removed the body, they finally left, save for an officer or two who acted as sentinels. Cy wondered how long it would take before the police authorized clean-up so he wouldn't have to be reminded of her death. He remembered how sweet Annie had been in spite of her provocative dress, surly attitude, and bad grammar.

I should have been here for her. First I let Wally slip through my hands, and then I lose my secretary and ally. He cursed himself for not having accompanied Gilly because if something happened to her, another death would be on his hands. What would she do if she walked in right now and saw this mess, the blood? He tried remembering where her travel schedule was but his mind couldn't focus on anything but Wally and Annie. *What a life.* The phone's ringing jerked him to move.

"Cyril, this is your sister."

Silence. Should he gush his thanks to her for calling and talking to him, or be p.o.'ed because she had shut him out, blaming him for her son's death?

"I called to tell you that we've decided to have Walter cremated, so you don't need to attend any memorial."

"Not even a religious ceremony? Just up and burn him and that's that?"

"How dare you criticize me? Look yourself in the mirror first. I wouldn't want you present at Wally's service anyway." She hung up.

How could things get any worse?

Now more than ever, he was determined to put a stop to all these murders, to find Wally's killers and fix them. He vowed to do whatever he had to, to avenge their deaths, and prevent others.

3:00 p.m.; Easton

Having earlier received Dixie's call, the big figure checked his arsenal and the weapons hidden on his body. He rushed out of Enolc One with his orders to drive the hour or so to Wilmington. Steering his car to the back of the lab building where an outside shed held lawn and road equipment, he hoofed inside, pushing aside rakes, bottles of lawn chemicals, and crates filled with junk, and went for a shovel which he promptly tossed into the trunk of the car.

Hustling back to the driver's side, he struggled to get his bulk behind the wheel, then squealed off. He remembered the directions given to him, as if each of his brain's memory banks were fixated on this one chore. In his mind, he could see perfectly the map of Wilmington and where Heavenly Cemetery was, even though he had never been there before. It was just a matter of getting across town through traffic, to the tombstone, and then spearing the cold hard earth with his shovel to unearth the evidence some human named Frey had hidden there.

Chapter
21

Leslie stood inside her bedroom eavesdropping on Chase's end of the conversation. She tried gluing clues from the one-sided conversation in order to make out what was going on. She heard her brother say, "I already have someone lined up to go to the Heavenly Cemetery." Pause. "Yeah, I know . . . Salyer Basse's plot." Pause. "I told him to do whatever was necessary to get the stuff . . . to let nothing or no one stop him." Pause. "The kid reporter? Tomorrow at eight in the morning? Which hospital? Everything will be taken care of." Pause. "We're handling him; next will be that Montague woman, once we find her."

Leslie's heart skipped a beat.

"The secretary? She's dead. No, that wasn't in the plan but I guess our man went nuts." Chase listened before adding, "I don't know if he was but he certainly got his supply. He left the place in total disarray."

By Chase's expression, Leslie could tell that the

person on the other end was yelling at her brother.

"Listen," Chase responded. "I can't be responsible for every one of them. That's your job. The henchman was deployed with orders to find out Montague's schedule." Pause. "No, he didn't get it. Look, we've got to put a stop to their snooping. Enough is enough. The longer you let them live, the harder it'll get to contain them." He hung up.

Leslie quietly closed her bedroom door to wait for her brother to leave when she could slip out of the house, walk to a phone booth—so her home number wouldn't show up on the receiver's Caller ID—and tell the person in her best disguised voice, "Be wary of Chase . . . and Dixie, too."

4:15 p.m.

Except for several police standing guard outside Cy's office door, nearly all activity and police personnel had either left or were on their way out, having cordoned off the building in yellow plastic tape. Inside his spacious but austere office with the old furniture, Cy moved items on his desk with a white handkerchief so as not to contaminate evidence. Though his office resembled the chaos of the main suite where Annie had been killed, some order still remained in his room. He sat behind his desk trying to think like the intruder, wondering what he or she wanted so badly that they had killed for it.

The youthful policeman Cy confronted earlier hung around as Cy sat studying the mess in his office. "Your people went through everything. I can't find my associate's flight schedule or my box of smokes." Cy reached down inside his trash can, through the rubbish, plastic gloves, tissues, yellow barricade tape. He groped for the tab that lifted the false bottom he had invented, hoping he still had some Havanas hidden. With his one hand holding the trash can and his other searching for the cigar box, and finding it, Cy danced his fingers through the plastic wrapped stoagies. "I'm almost done here," he called to the police officer. Just as he was about to pull his hand out of the cigar box, his palm coveting a Havana, he felt something papery-like. He yanked it out, scanned it and saw it was a note from Annie about Mitch—Gilly's ex. Cy balled it up in his large hand as the officer turned around, and stuck the cigar in his mouth, his teeth ripping off the plastic wrap.

Impatiently, the officer ordered, "C'mon, Mr. Collier, you better leave."

Cy followed the officer out of his suite and into the main room where his eyes searched for Gillian's itinerary on file cabinets, her desk, a table top. He was worried about her safety. *I never should have let her go.*

As the officer opened Cy's door to exit, in came a tall, slender black man with a well-trimmed beard and mustache. Seeing Cyril, he grinned. "Well, if it isn't my old buddy. When I heard it was your agency where the murder occurred, I figured I'd run into you."

Cy smiled at his former police partner—who was now captain—who he had only the highest respect for. Cy and Duncan Cleveland had kept in touch over the years, not only on business but also on a friendship basis. Periodically Cy had gone to Duncan's house for dinner, and he had even baptized one of his kids.

"Mr. Collier's not a suspect," Cleveland said to the officer, and motioned with his head for him to leave. "Remember when you and I were as green as him?"

"I understand you have a suspect lined up." He gnawed on his cigar.

"We're checking out fingerprints from your office." Cleveland walked up to Cy. "Sorry to hear about your nephew and secretary. If there's anything—"

"My nephew was a good boy but reckless. He knew

about the water. But why my secretary? Who would have wanted to kill her? She didn't bother anybody. I want to read the reports."

Scuffling and shouting in the hallway made them turn. Immediately Cleveland was out the door, with Cy right behind him.

An officer pointed to the figure he and another law enforcer had handcuffed, saying, "This guy is wanted for breaking and entering a federal facility, for murder, and for contaminating the water."

"I didn't do anything" screamed the unshaven, blood-shot captive. "They're framing me! Cyril, help!"

Cy's mouth dropped open but before he could say anything, Duncan Cleveland demanded, "On whose orders is he under arrest?" He glanced at the formidable figure standing on the side wearing a dark trench-coat and sunglasses.

"Mine," said the sunglassed man who held ID in one hand, and an arrest warrant in the other. "I've been chasing this criminal since he broke into a federal lab. He's already been placed on the Ten Most Wanted for murdering your secretary, and Althea Azar and Salyer Basse; other charges will follow. Precinct verifies that his prints matched those taken from your office. I'll take over from here."

"Ms Azar's dead?" cried the hostage. "I didn't do anything!" He turned to Cy.

"Don't say anything, man, until you get an attorney," advised Cleveland.

Cy walked over to the prisoner, his finger jabbing the man's chest. "I know you." Surprise registered in his voice. He turned to Duncan and the sunglassed man. "This is Mitchell Frey, a reputable area businessman."

Duncan eyed the unkempt Mitch. "Doesn't look too reputable to me."

"I was in Cy's office earlier looking for him. I panicked when I saw the secretary mutilated and dead; I just ran out." Mitch grimaced when the mirrored sun-glassed man spun him around, the handcuffs chewing into his wrists.

The captain studied the warrant, saying to the trench-coated man, "Even if you are FBI, I have the right to take him in first. I want to check out **your** credentials, too."

"What's going on, Mitch? Is Gillian all right?"

"I came here to ask **you** where she is. You've got to help me, Cy."

"Not now he won't," growled the big FBI man.

Cleveland grabbed Mitch's handcuffed arm and led him out, with the FBI agent following.

Cy watched them leave, his thumb gently rubbing against the paper still balled in the palm of his hand, his ear attuned to Mitch's pleas: "Check out AUGA, Cy—the Association for Unethical Government Activities—and talk to Dixie Morris who knows the whole story!"

Cy grunted, thinking things didn't look good for Mitch. He was now more worried about Gillian than ever. He unrolled the crumpled paper, read it as written in Annie's handwriting. *I know what I have to do.* He slipped it into his coat pocket and left to check out AUGA, run back to his apartment to see if Gilly had called, then hustle out to the cemetery before going to the jail to talk to Mitch.

4:45 p.m.

Mitch was shoved here, pushed there, ordered to do this and that. They had shackled his feet as well, finger-printed him, photographed him. A big, bulky man was leading him into a room, saying, "You're going to be interrogated until your brain melts." He opened the door, pushed Mitch toward a chair at a small card table. "They're not going to be nice to you, you murdering—"

"I didn't do anything!"

The guard plowed his fist into Mitch's teeth. "That ought to shut you up for awhile. Aren't you sorry you started this spy game? Maybe this will teach you not to fool with the government!"

Mitch knew then the officer was a goon assimilated into the police force. Nothing looked good for him.

5:00 p.m.

In his apartment, Cy downed a beer, frustrated, worried. Gilly had left no message on the machine. His search into AUGA turned up blank. Where should he go now, what should he do to uncover information about AUGA? Or maybe there wasn't any organization by that name, and it was just something Mitch made up.

The phone rang. This has to be Gillian, he thought, as he went for it.

"Cy, this is Stella."

"Hey, doll. What a nice surprise. Gosh, I miss you. I was thinking that, well, maybe we ought to talk about getting mar—"

"I don't have a lot of time here; I should be working but I sneaked out of my lab to call. The very first man to serve as a model for cloning came out of Enolc 1—a lab near you. That man's alive, but after a mature clone was made from him, the scientists started to transform the genes and use other originals to create variations so that not all the clones would look like him. If you could track that him down, you'd get your answers."

Cy wrote fast. "No name, huh?"

"None given to me." She cleared her throat. "I have to go."

"Wait. Have you ever heard of AUGA?"

Silence.

"Come on, babe, don't hold out on me now."

"I can't believe you know about them." She lowered

her voice. "The only thing I've ever been told is that they are a very subversive group that tries to learn who's behind unethical activities to do something about them. They also try to protect people who are innocently involved with the government's sinister actions. That's all I know. I can't even verify if they're real, legit, or some made up group."

"Listen to you talk about your government that way . . . and to think you work for it," he teased. "I want to ask you something when the moment's right."

She went quiet; then: "I'll be waiting."

They hung up.

Well, thought Cy, he still hadn't acquired much information so how was he to find out more about AUGA and that first male model? Most important was that Stella left the door open for him to reunite with her.

He re-read Annie's note on Mitch and headed for the cemetery.

5:30 p.m.

Dana smacked her gloved hands together to keep warm. Her breath came out in white wisps, and all she wanted was to dig at the surface of the grave, get Mitch's evidence, and get out. Cemeteries unnerved her, and in the near dark, she felt all the more tense.

The shovel she brought was rusted at the edge, making it hard to dig into the frozen ground. It took several stabs and her jumping on the blade's edge to carve into the earth, and then lift the dirt to dump at another spot. She was breathless and sweaty in spite of the frigid temperatures but determined to locate the evidence. She felt badly that she gashed Salyer's grave but she wasn't going to give up. Mitch indicated it was here, and she would find it.

Pausing to catch her breath, she glanced at the horizon, saw the descending darkness, and knew she had to hurry. She dropped the shovel and ambled over to her car where she grabbed her purse and pulled out her cell phone.

"Edith? This is Dana," she said breathlessly. "Tell Glenn I'm at Heavenly—"

"I'm busy. He's making me stay late for a meeting but boy is he mad at you."

"Tell him I'm coming. This piece is gonna blow everyone away." Dana could hear Edith flipping through notes, then the phone disconnected.

Dana slipped the phone back inside her purse, scanned the sky's diminishing light, and suddenly felt uneasy. She scrunched her shoulders as if to shrug off something sinful and nameless. Swallowing hard and tightening her coat as if it were a protective shield, she returned to the grave site and continued throwing her body into slicing the soil with the feeble shovel. Soon, her skittishness subsided as she concentrated only on finding the materials.

She flinched. Did she hear something? She froze, afraid to move her eyes, take a breath. She stood listening, hearing only her puffs of air breaking the silence.

Nothing. *I've got the jitters.* She scolded herself for acting like a child instead of a professional reporter. For the third time, she lunged at the land with the shovel.

It took over ten minutes before the blade to hit something right under the top layer of the grave. She stooped, pulled and tugged at it with her gloved hands. In the dark, it was hard to see but she knew it was something not native to the earth.

Minutes later, she was shaking dirt off a vinyl portfolio filled with papers and a slim leatherette notebook. Just as she carried the materials and shovel to her car, an odor filled her nostrils.

Footfall on gravel caught her attention. She turned

in its direction but saw nothing in the dark. The stench increased. Quickly she reached for the handle on her car. She had barely yanked it opened and jumped in when she realized her keys weren't in the ignition. "Oh Lord!" she screamed from inside.

Her fingers jittering, she slammed down each of the door locks with the palm of her hand, then rummaged through her purse for keys.

Did she just hear a car's motor? *Oh God, please, get me out of here!* Her fingers groped the bottom of her briefcase but still she couldn't locate the keys. When she looked outside, she saw two glowing eyes in pitch blackness moving in her direction.

He was already at her car window carrying a shovel and smiling maliciously when she located the keys in the side pocket of her coat.

5:40 p.m.

Having arrived home exhausted, Gillian unpacked and lay across her bed, listening to the messages on the machine. One caught her attention: "Gillian, be wary of Chase . . . and Dixie, too." She lay in bed trying to associate the familiar voice with a face, but within seconds, she dozed off. Just as the warmth and coziness of the ethereal world fell over her, the phone's ringing jolted her; she wiped sleepers from her eyes, picked up the headset and muttered *hello* through her grogginess.

"Gillian. This is Chase."

Silence

"I know you're upset with me, but please understand that what happened that night was a result of the intense stress I'm under and—"

"What stress?" Her tone blasted hot.

"Well . . . everything at work, and Leslie and—" He puffed out air. "Look, the reason I called was to apologize for my behavior the last time we were together. I thought you were leading me on and I over-reacted."

"What about Leslie?"

He paused. "What about her?"

"You started this conversation saying you were under stress from your job and Leslie—"

"There's something I need to tell you that might explain why I seem negative about her." He waited, but when no response came, he went on. "Will you let me see you again? Give me another chance to make it up to you. I'll come to your place."

"Only in a public place."

His silence unnerved her.

"You still don't trust me?"

"Hobson's Deli; I'll give you a half-hour."

"Hobson's it is."

She got her note pad, mace, purse and coat, and went out, knowing rush hour traffic and the falling snow would cause back-ups, even if Hobson's wasn't far away. A half-hour later, she arrived at the deli. He was standing inside the doorway. The first thing he said to her was, "We're going to my place; it's too crowded here."

"Here or nowhere."

"You are stubborn." He shook his head. "I wanted to meet with you so you can watch me trounce on myself. I don't know what got into me except that suddenly I wanted you, every inch of you, and you kept telling me no." He led her to a table at the back of the room.

"You hit me and punched your sister."

"I know I know. I've never done that before."

"Leslie says you have." Gillian sat with her arms crossed at her chest, a grim expression on her face.

"Leslie lies." He leaned forward. "I promise it won't happen again."

"What about the photos in your home? You told me they were your parents but when we first met, you said you were raised by the Sisters of Good Heart."

For a quick second, Chase's eyes narrowed. "Nosing around, huh?" He squeezed his eyes closed with his fingertips. "I'll tell you what's going on if you promise not to say anything to anyone."

She looked distrustfully at him, her arms still crossed. "Go on." Even she heard the rancor in her voice.

"The person you saw in those photos was me. Leslie and I were raised by an organization, but when I was thirteen, I was adopted by the couple in the picture. Leslie wasn't. When I was twenty-eight, I searched for her, and we reunited."

"You look like the parents in the photo." She sensed he was lying. "What do you know about the goons with the flashing eyes who suck their victims' brains?"

"You're watching too many horror shows. Let's just go to my place and—"

"How come it always seems like there's an odor around you?"

"Gee, thanks."

"Where do you work, Chase?"

"We already went over this."

"What does Leslie do for a living?"

"Will you stop? You're making me feel like a criminal."

"How did you find her if you were separated at the orphanage?"

"I told you, I was adopted; she wasn't . . . no wonder with her looks."

Too many questions rushed Gillian at once. Everything he said had holes in it. She didn't know what to ask first, so all she said was, "I don't believe a word you're saying, and I think it's a disgrace how you treat your sister." She turned to leave.

"Wait!"

She glared at him.

"I'm sorry about your secretary."

Gillian's mind tried assimilating the information. "My secretary?" Did he mean Annie? "What about her?"

"Oh, I guess you didn't know. Killed in her office. Skull impaled by—"

She pivoted and sped out the door.

Chapter
22

Panting, Gillian reached the floor of her office where she was met by uniformed police officers blocking admission into Cy's agency. It wasn't until she explained who she was and showed her identification papers that the same young officer who had hassled Cy, finally let her in while explaining what had happened to Annie. Gillian felt moisture in her eyes, and when she saw the white chalked outline of the secretary's body, she let those tears stream down her cheeks.

"I guess even P.I.s aren't all that callous," said the officer who guided her back out into the hallway.

"Are there any suspects?" She sniffled. "You said Mr. Collier was here already . . . where did he go?"

"There is one suspect being held at the city jail. His name is Mitchell Frey . . . found his fingerprints on the office counter and—"

Gillian was out the door and charging down the stairwell to the city jail.

6:10 p.m.

The flashing, pin-point red eyes moved steadily toward her.

She tried turning the key in the ignition but her twittering fingers could barely hold the metal ring. *Turn the key! Hit the gas pedal*! In fear, she held her breath, and her lungs felt ready to burst. She knew she was hysterical, not thinking straight, so she kept ordering herself to concentrate on turning the ignition key.

When his hand smashed the glass, she jumped. His odor overtook her and she choked while trying to pull away from him—a rankness that seemed worse when his eyes glowed.

"I see you did the work for me," he sneered, eyeing the unearthed evidence sitting on the passenger's seat. He tried reaching for the documentation.

The smell of his hand gagged her. She twisted, pushed his arm away, turned the keys hanging in the ignition—all the while her screeches reverberating.

In a flash, he grabbed her by her hair and began jerking her through the shattered window. She kicked, squealed, and braced her arms against the car's ceiling to resist his strength. Jagged glass carved into her skull as he yanked her head through glass shards.

Out of nowhere, a report zinged through the air. The smell of sulfur lingered. The big goon stopped, looked around, then grabbed a jagged piece of glass and pressed it against her neck. "Give me the materials you unburied, or I'll bury you."

Another shot, louder, signalling its closeness, echoed through air waves.

Dana felt the man-animal momentarily release her to turn and scrutinize the cemetery, his piercing eyes centering on the tombstones, looking for the gunman.

Her body still quaking, her head bleeding, she pulled herself back into the car, her fingers grabbing for the ignition key.

The monster plucked open her car door and reached inside to wrench her out.

She knew this was the end. There was so much she had planned on doing with her life, so much she had wanted to accomplish. Never would she get the opportunity to say good-bye to her parents and siblings, to tell them she loved them; to travel the globe . . . but most importantly, she wouldn't get the chance to warn the world of the evil Mitch wanted every citizen to know about. She had failed. How ironic she thought it was that her final reasoning rested on her failures and not her accomplishments, and that the very story she had wanted to report was her own demise. She tried begging for her life, even threatening him, but all he did was leer.

"Nightie night," he scoffed as he lifted his hand above his head to plunge a glass splinter into her skull. The second his arm arched downward was the instant the bullet ripped directly below his chin, catching him off guard.

"Get out of here! Now!" screamed the gunman at Dana as he held the pistol and danced around the huge form lying on the gravel next to the car's front left tire. "Go! Go!" he ordered the young, near hysterical girl.

Her back Goodyears kicked up stones as she squealed out of the cemetery's gravel drive, leaving behind some man who was her savior.

Cy kicked the form bent at its knees. It toppled forward. He kicked it again, hard; it didn't move. Satisfied, he lowered the gun and went for his car phone several yards away.

The tug took him by such surprise that he found himself on the pebbles before he even realized he had been taken down. The monster's punch cracked the bridge of Cy' nose, uncoupling nerves and tendons surrounding it. Knowing there was no chance of physically overcoming the brute, Cy scrambled for the gun.

Still on the ground, his hand fumbled for the metal weapon. The stiff boot to his kidneys jarred him, sending a sting throughout his torso and soaring him six-feet beyond the gun. Even in his disjointed vision, Cy saw the red eyes looming at him and smelled the over-powering odor.

Cy stretched down and pulled out a switch blade tucked inside the band of his sock. The goon reached over and picked Cy up as if he were nothing more than a clump of sod. Instantly Cy rammed the blade into the demon's neck. A noise like the rush of air through a tunnel sounded. Already in motion, the gorgon lifted Cy and slammed him on the ground; he grunted, turned, knocked over one tombstone after another, letting them fall as if they were dominoes, then he spun back around and again went for Cy, his eyes blazing, teeth gritted, fists balled.

Jeeze! He's still coming!

A loud bang echoed. Cy turned to the gunshot. Out of the corner of his eye he saw, not more than fifty-feet away, a broad-shouldered figure aim and shoot again. The goon stumbled and half-loped, half-staggered away.

From the gravel drive, Cy watched the rescuer dash out of sight. Unmoving, he lay there, trying to steady his breathing, convince himself to work his way to the car.

In his mind he pictured the form that had saved him. In one way it looked tall, muscular, but in another, it didn't look as big as the monster who tried to kill the girl in the car. This would be one more incident he would have to investigate.

Struggling to get himself behind the wheel of his car was only half the battle. The other half was driving to the hospital.

7:00 p.m.

"All right, calm down," Glenn tried reassuring Dana while an EMT cleaned her cuts and lacerations in the editorial office. "Go through it one more time. I have to have the facts." Glenn leaned over her as she slouched in the swivel chair.

Periodically, she'd sniffle, wipe tears, and try again, her voice quivering. "I've told you . . . he was going to kill me. He wanted this," she pointed to the materials she had brought into the newsroom, "and he would have done anything to get them. Then that man came." She went into detail about Cy's height, weight, and how he had interceded on her behalf. "But I don't know who he is."

Glenn straightened, looked around the newsroom at reporters listening to Dana, and said, "Let's not be hasty. We have to know what we're dealing with."

One person looked at the next.

Someone protested, "Dana has the proof—documents she risked her life for."

"But Dana's state of mind right now is—"

"My mind is fine, Glenn!" Dana made a fist. "I'm telling the truth! We have to expose this conspiracy!" She touched her fingers to the clotted gash on her head.

"Sit down, miss. You could have a concussion. I think you should go to the hospital. What I'm doing here is band-aid repair," said another EMT.

Dana held a patch of gauze to her forehead and shifted her gaze to Glenn. "You've got to get on this before it's too late."

"We're reporters, not reactionaries. My reporters have to be objective, fair, balanced. Do you know what my publisher would say if—"

"And the government, right, Glenn?"

Glenn looked as if he had been slapped. "What's that supposed to mean?"

"Go tell our friggin government how they should

treat people fairly and objectively! You've got to run this story for the welfare of the public. I'm telling you, the government is behind all this, just as they were the empowering force in JFK's death, the Roswell incident, cloud-seeding to affect crop growth, the water contamination and shortage—" She stopped. By the looks on the staff's faces, she could tell they thought she had flipped. She pushed on anyway: "Drug infiltration, viruses, AIDS, the Gulf War Syndrome, LSD, MKUltra, the militia, Flight 800, WACO, the downing of Pan Am 103, the—" at the rise of murmurings from her colleagues, she went silent; then: "If we don't scoop this, I'll take the piece to a paper that will; I swear it."

Heads turned; voices buzzed low.

Glenn looked at the disheveled Dana, then panned the room filled with his reporters. He made a clucking sound and tugged at his suspenders. "All right, give me the evidence."

She handed him everything she uncovered and all that Mitch had turned over to her.

7:15 p.m.

Gilly thought she'd never get to the jail before visiting time was over, though she figured she could pull some drag at the detention cell if she flashed her P.I. credentials. It was incredible to her that her calm, reasonable ex had ended up in jail.

The police let her in without a hassle. When she saw Mitch, her eyes widened at his appearance. She walked up to the stockade where he rose from his cot to meet her.

Her fingers wrapped around his on the iron bars. "Are you all right?" she asked so quietly she wasn't certain it was her voice.

As quickly as the tears sprang to his eyes, she saw him hurriedly wipe them.

"Tell me everything." She felt him grip her fingers tighter through the bars, and then heard him tell about Ms. Azar, Dana, the buried materials, his sneaking into the labs and the reactor, and how he had related the whole story to Dixie. He explained about his trip to Cy's office the first time, finding Annie dead, only to return and be framed. "Of course my fingerprints in Cy's office matched with the prints they took when they arrested me. Since I was driving around mostly, I have no alibi. I don't have a chance of getting out of this." He lowered his eyes to the floor. "You've got to talk to Dixie, Gil. She's our only hope. Tell her to get AUGA— the Association for Unfair Government Activities— behind me . . . help get me out of here. Maybe she could be my alibi since I went to her clinic, but I don't think it was at the same time of the murder."

She knew in his fatigue he wasn't making sense. "Dixie, huh?" Gillian wet her lips. "She knows everything you've told me? I think she and Chase have something going between them."

"I thought he was hot for you."

"I'm not so hot on him. I've punched holes in his stories about his background, his parents, and sister Leslie. I don't trust him anymore."

"You shouldn't trust that Leslie either."

"She seems harmless."

He whispered, "At first I thought she was an experiment gone bad . . . a female clone trying to be a man, which would explain why she's so masculine in appearance and mannerisms, but then I figured out the real truth when I read Hammond's records." He crooked his finger for her to step even closer so he could confide in her.

"That's it!" yelled a guard down the hall. "Time to quit."

"I'll tell you the rest tomorrow," Mitch said.

"I'll get you the best attorney."

"You don't understand. No one can beat the government." He shook his head. "Find Dana Carter, the reporter; get the records from her; learn about Leslie and everything else that's been going on and what the future holds for us."

"Move it," the big man ordered Gillian.

She blew Mitch a kiss and turned to walk away, stumbling right into the tall, football-player-like guard who was carrying a tray with Mitch's dinner. She looked over her shoulder at Mitch. "Love you," she half-whispered, and kept walking.

She had turned the hallway's bend when the sound of the blast roared down the narrow corridor and slammed into her, making her reach for the cement walls for support. Instantly her feet were in motion as she ran back to Mitch's cell.

The big figure stood, legs spread, and hands on the gun, facing the cell.

She glanced at him and then looked into the cell, seeing Mitch's body slumped to the floor. Her hands flew up to her mouth to muffle her screams.

The broad figure with the Magnum said, "He went for his gun. Self-defense."

A gun lay next to Mitch and she knew at once it had been planted there. A shudder went through her as she watched the hulk sweep in its legs and walk off.

She dropped to her knees on the cold cement floor of the confined hallway, bawling, alone, touching Mitch's hand. She wept uncontrollably until a guard removed her and took her outside the building to her car.

8:00 p.m.

Cyril scrunched up his face as a nurse applied antibiotics and sterilized bandages on his wounds.

Said the nurse, "You're lucky you weren't killed."

She snipped off a piece of gauze. "When I first started working here, I could walk the street to work my eleven to seven shift, but today, I wouldn't go anywhere after dark."

"Right, darlin." Cy just wanted to be on his way to talk to Mitch at the jail. He had a good hunch of what was going on. "Finish patching me up so I can leave."

"You can't go anywhere. The doctor's going to prep you to set your fractured nose. You have a concussion, too, and maybe internal bleeding which means you need to be under observation."

"I can and I will discharge myself. Won't be the first time." He reached for his shirt. "Ow!" Then repeated the same word when he twisted his torso to look at his beeping pager. "Darn thing still works after all I've been through." The number didn't look familiar. He tried recalling who had that area code. In pain, he struggled off the gurney, slipped his shirt on over his wounds, and through a throbbing wired mouth, said, "Give me the discharge papers."

In a huff, she went to call the doctors and get the forms.

Priority was Mitch and the organization AUGA that he couldn't find anything on, though Stella believed existed. Stella! That was who was on his pager. He hadn't recognized the Atlanta area code. He'd call her as soon as he got out of the hospital. She probably had other critical information. He flipped open the tiny note pad he kept in his shirt pocket and wrote the number, thinking that he would also try to contact Dixie, get over to see Gilly who he never had a chance to talk to, and track down the girl at the cemetery who had unburied the very materials he wanted; he figured Mitch could guide him on that . . . but he also wanted to know who it was that had come to his rescue—the form in the distance shooting at the monster—the kind of monsters Gilly had seen and told him about—the kind that mauled and killed innocent people; the kind the government created but wouldn't admit to; the kind that no doubt were programmed to help establish the New World Order. Maybe he would start with Chase, or Leslie, even the police. Perhaps his old friend Duncan Cleveland had sent someone out to help him. Aaah, he had so much to do when all he wanted was to go to bed. He left the ER cubicle stooped over in pain.

8:30 p.m.

Gilly sobbed in the car. She needed Cy; he was the only one left who could comfort her. But since she arrived back home from her interviews, she hadn't one minute to connect with him. The person she loved— truly had ever loved—was shot dead. *What is wrong with the world!*

Maybe she could go to Dixie for comfort. *No, no! How can I do that? She's in on all this. But she's been my dearest friend for years; maybe I'm prejudging her. I've got to confront her . . . or should I?* It was pretty hard to believe that this woman who Gillian had shared her life with, could betray her.

Gillian pulled into the garage attached to her apartment, parked her car, and headed up the lit front steps, the cold cutting through her. Her fingers fumbled inside her purse for her house key.

"Gillian Montague?"

She started at the sound of the deep voice behind her. Instantly fear seized her. *Keep your head; you're a detective. Don't panic.*

"You went on a trip, Ms. Montague, and interviewed three victims. I want all your notes and reports." He stood on the top stoop next to her, towering over her.

She saw something glint in the dark in the behemoth man's large hand.

"My hand's in my purse and it's gripping a gun. If you know where I've been, then you also know I'm a detective and have no qualms about killing you."

"I want those reports at any cost."

"Go screw!"

The giant lurched forward.

Below them, on the bottom step of the stoop, boomed: "I have a gun pointed at you, buddy. Don't touch her." The strength and challenge in his tone made Gillian and her would-be attacker turn to him.

The goon stood unmoving, then, after consideration, turned and, taking all three porch steps in one stride, he left.

Gillian stood shaking, trying to form the words to say "Thank you," and yet not trusting the stranger any more than she trusted the goon.

"I know you don't have a gun and I know you're distraught over Frey—"

"Who *are* you?" In the porch light, she saw that he was a handsome, young black man.

"I'm the man who had gone to your secretary's house last night looking for you. My name's Countee Burrows." He stuck out his hand and she shook it. "I'm with a private agency that looks after the welfare of people like you."

"AUGA? What about the welfare of Annie, Salyer, Mitch?"

"We help those trying to expose the government and other organizations; we want to make the world safer and see that we keep our freedom and rights."

"What's the catch?"

"We need your materials for our research. We believe that unless we stop what the cabal of world politicians is doing, we'll lose our rights, our sovereignty, our individuality."

"That's already happening."

"Until the one world government is completely

intact, there's still hope, especially through people like you. Besides acquiring your documents, we want to sit and talk with you at length. In time, when we know that you are with us, we will reveal everything to you. But most immediate is the gathering of as much information as we can. Trust me, we're a legitimate, honest group."

How could she trust him? There wasn't anyone she could trust. She had seen a couple of other black, Asian, and even Indian goons, so this Countee Burrows could be one of them, even if he wasn't their size. "I appreciate your coming to my rescue but right now, I don't trust anyone, including you."

"I understand but don't alienate us. We're your only chance. If you reject us, you'll have nowhere to go, and you'll remain in danger."

She turned to twist the key in the lock of her front door, but not wanting him to overcome her and shove her into her apartment, she paused until she heard him retreat. As he did, she called out, "So what now, Mr. Burrows?"

"I'll try reaching Dixie Morris tomorrow since she spoke with Basse on many occasions. I'll also try talking to Collier who might be able to shed some light. He seems to be a very logical man." He suggested, "If having him in your presence when we talk will help you feel more secure, I can arrange that."

She pursed her lips. "I just lost the only person I truly ever loved. Please don't ask me to make any decisions."

"Yes, I just learned about Frey. I'm sorry. Here's my agency numbers: Pager, cellular, fax, and e-mail." He handed her a post-it note with his name and the numbers on it.

"No business card?"

"We're a very private operation." Under his breath, he added, "Your contact, Gordon, was one of us." He walked away.

She stood standing on the stoop of her front porch, the cold breeze sweeping across her, her mouth open in shock.

8:45 p.m.

Cy touched his fingers to his jaw and bandaged nose. He groaned in pain. Just a few more things to do, he told himself, and then he could take one of those pain pills the ER doc had given him, and go to bed.

At home, in his recliner, with a legal pad perched on his lap, and the phone in one hand, a pen in the other, he dialed the Atlanta number registered on his beeper.

When she picked up on the other end, he said, "Stella? Cy. I got your page."

"What's wrong with your speech?"

"A goon sent me for a loop with a single punch."

"Well, maybe the info I have will make you feel better." Her voice went low. "I'm still in my office, so I have to be careful of what I say. Those big cloned goons are orchestrated by the government, not only to be fighting machines, and 'yes men,' but also to obliterate protestors when the ten-man council, with Cinzan heading it, completes its entire formation of the one-world government."

"My God."

"Certain labs around the country have been commissioned by our government to create headless beings—based on the experiments in 1997—that will yield organs. I also learned that the water contamination is a government-made catastrophe with the purpose of making citizens compliant. If we're made to rely on the government for survival, then we become dependent and pliable and will do whatever we're ordered, including accepting the NWO. Masses of starving, thirsty, demoralized people are easier to control than robust,

healthy, protesting citizens. A food shortage is scheduled to happen in six months. Closing the churches is
another way of subduing us—no God, no faith, no
united protest—as well as forcing us to worship a religion the government promotes. It's going to get worse."

"How will I ever get to the two highest offices in
the world?"

"What are you talking about, Cy? If you mean
going to the president and the world premier and lash-
ing back at them, forget it. If the most adroit militia and
most competent guerrilla groups can't get to them, what
makes you think you can?"

"They killed my nephew and my secretary. I've
vowed revenge."

"You wouldn't be so stupid as to go after them . . .
would you?"

"Is the war that the news has been talking about
also government-made?"

"I don't know about that, but it would seem that
such a war would work to the favor of the New World
Order." She took in a breath. "Listen to this, Cy, these
clones have been created with genes containing viruses
that can be activated on demand and sent around the
world to infect others."

"Wow!" he whistled. "You've got to be kidding!"
He sat for a second looking off into space. "I can see it
now: The government engineers an inhumanly strong,
leviathan species of beings that are programmed to kill
via the activation of an implanted computer chip, as
well as to serve in whatever capacity needed—politicians, murderers, soldiers, whatnot. These monsters are
capable of decimating entire civilizations simply by
turning genes on and off that contain lethal viral sub-
stances. How ingenious, and frightening."

"Then people wonder why we don't trust our government, why there are so many conspiracy theories out
there. I was close when I said the mutants must have

had some chemical imbalance. It's the lack of serotonin—maybe the combination of that and dopamine. I
haven't been able to get my hands on the top secret info
on the mutants, as I have with the clones. I'm just glad I
dug up what I did so far."

"You did a terrific job, and now I have to do what I
have to do." He scribbled a few more notes. "Tell me
how they can do all this in a person's body."

"I can't give you an in depth lesson in biology, but
it has to do with a cell's genes in the nucleus, and the
kind of nuclear envelope and cell membrane. We've
come a long way in learning about cellular division,
enzymatic reactions, proteins in the endoplasmic retic-
ulum, and the DNA and RNA on each gene, and how—"

"Never mind." He groaned, patted his jaw. "In addition to Hammond at the Enolc place, who else knows
what's going on?"

"I suppose officials in the government, maybe even
a regional director over the labs in various areas, the
directors' secretaries, and prob—"

"Who was Hammond's secretary?"

Papers shuffled on the other end, and minutes
passed before Stella returned with, "Althea Azar. I
don't know what she knew, Cy; in fact, I have nothing
on her other than she was his executive secretary."

"Was? She no longer works at Enolc One?"

"She had quit Enolc, then went on a trip, and,
according to my sources, was violently killed." Stella
detailed the murder.

He lit a cigar, lightly rubbed his sore nose. "That
Mitch guy doesn't have anyone to support his alibi."

"Look, I have to go, Cy. I'll call you as soon as I get
more info. Right now, it's the best I can do."

"You did fine, honey. Just be careful. Anymore,
people with a little knowledge of what's happening
seem to meet their end too soon. I suspect I'm already
on someone's list." He went quiet for a second. "Can

you find out who in the government is behind all this? I
want to know how high it goes."

"Probably to the top. It's late, but I'll call around
for you and ask my sources what they know about who
we should thank for the big bad bullies."

He wet his lips. "Will you marry me?" The silence
was so long, he knew her answer before she voiced it.

"Yes." She laughed. "Call me back at eleven
tonight, and I'll give you what new info I have."

"Will do. Bye, love." He felt like a school boy getting a girl's "tag."

10:00 p.m.

"Well?" Dixie asked the figure on the opposite end
of the phone.

"I didn't get them, but I will. Some man came along
and interfered with what I was doing. I don't know who
he was."

"I bet the other side knows, too."

"Listen, as long as Gillian has her own records and
that cutie reporter has Mitch's files, the project is in
great danger. We've got to do whatever it takes to get
all the documents."

"Keep this in mind: Gillian is not to be harmed in
any way because if she is, I'll hot-wire your damn computer chip and melt your brain!"

10:30 p.m.

Gillian rubbed her eyes, the computer screen making her feel as though she had night blindness. Everywhere she looked on the Internet, nothing turned up
AUGA or the name Countee Burrows. She tried every
search engine, each link, but still nothing.

When she hung up the modem, she sat at her desk

wondering what to do. In a way, she wanted to give up the case because now she understood that her life was in danger, and that the goon—or those like him—who had approached her tonight would stop at nothing to get the materials she had on the interviewees. But most important, she realized, was acquiring the materials Mitch had given to the reporter named Dana. Maybe she would work on that tomorrow, and then quit the case . . . turn it over to Cy. "So what if I'm a coward," she mumbled to the dark computer screen.

Midnight

Cy had fallen asleep in his chair. He looked at his watch, then dialed Stella's home number; a smile crossed his face. The rest of his life spent with Stella would be a gift from God. The phone rang about a dozen times before a male voice answered. So caught off guard by this, Cy couldn't utter one word.

Confused, Cy finally managed, "I'm Cy Collier. Who are you?"

"Detective Stern. What's the nature of your business?"

Cy felt his heart crash. "I—I—I'm Dr. Reid's fiance and—"

"Sorry, pal, I really am. I didn't know that. Your fiance was murdered between the hours of 9:15 and 11:30."

"Oh my God." He wanted to wail right then. "H-h-how?" He barely had control of his voice.

"An intruder pierced her brain with a sharp object."

Cy placed his finger over the receiver button, hung up the mouthpiece, and wept long into the night.

Chapter
23

Tuesday, January 8;
6:30 a.m.; Wilmington

Gilly could barely pull herself out of bed, even with
the morning sun glaring through opened blinds. Mitch's
death had destroyed her. *What I don't understand is why
I haven't been murdered. I pose as much a threat as
Mitch had.* She didn't care about herself. Her only goal
was to follow up the leads she had and get to the files
and turn them over to Cy to expose whatever sources
were behind all this. *But why hasn't there been an
attempt on my life? Is someone managing to keep me
alive?* She lay in bed, thinking.

Seven a.m. registered her alarm clock. Still feeling
emotionally and physically drained, she didn't want to
start a new day; yet she understood this was the way it
was going to be the rest of her life. What was that nagging feeling inside her? Like something she should pay
attention to but didn't want to.

Entering the kitchen, she picked up the phone and
crooked it between her ear and shoulder while using her

free hands to make coffee. "Cy?" she said when he answered. "Mitch is dead. Murdered by a goon dressed in a police uniform."

"My god! I was planning on visiting him last night in jail but . . ." here his voice quavered, "but my dear Stella was also killed by a goon." He choked up, blew his nose.

Gillian didn't know what to say; she was struggling with her own grief. "I'm sorry about Wally, too. I have lots to tell you. Let's meet at the office."

"I can't stomach going in there, knowing what they did to Annie. How about your place since I'll already be out; I have to make a stop first."

"And I want to catch up with that reporter Mitch had told about the evidence that he buried at Heavenly Cemetery—"

"So that's who that was. I saved her life. Then someone saved mine when a goon tried killing her and me for that evidence. Look, I'll call on my cell phone when I'm on route to your apartment." He got ready to hang up but swiftly added, "Be careful of your friend, Dixie. I'll tell you more when I see you." He said as an after thought, "I'm sorry about Mitch. He was a nice guy, and I was doing what I could to help him. But I'm not shocked they killed him, after what I've learned."

Another warning about Dixie. Gilly hung up, downed two cups of coffee and headed for the news-room to find Dana.

Tuesday, 8:00 a.m.

Dana hated waiting. The last time she had this test, she was made to wait an hour in the outpatient lobby and then another forty minutes in the X-ray department. She figured she wouldn't get out of the hospital for at least two hours.

She half-read an article in NEWSWEEK on the ongoing water contamination, and half-listened to the activities spinning around her: People talking, technicians yelling, "Hold your breath," doctors and nurses shuffling along, elevator bells tingling. She equally despised hospitals, especially when it meant having to undergo tests, like the CT scan. The clock on the wall read 8:30 a.m.. *You'd think the technicians would know how to time things.*

She felt the bump at her forehead, the bandage on her face, wondering if she would be scarred. Yesterday's ordeal was more than she could deal with but, as Glenn had told her, she was a reporter and should expect to endure dangers, including "a little physical and emotional pain," he had said.

"Ms Carter? I'm ready for you," a squat, granny-glassed, middle-aged tech said, reading off a form in quadruplicates.

Dana set the magazine aside and followed him to the X-ray room. He closed the door while smiling at her, saying, "I'm the tech who injected you earlier."

"I remember," she said lazily.

"Let me go over the procedure. You've had this done before, so you know it won't hurt, and that the camera gets real close to your face but yet doesn't touch it."

"Yes." She just wanted to get to work to talk to Glenn about the expose, or the "Big Story," as it had come to be known around the newsroom. She liked how other reporters sought her advice on various aspects of it to fine-hone the part they had to work on. At last she had felt important, but more so, she felt scared because she knew what was really out there. Her biggest fear, though, was that Glenn would renege on his decision to go with it, and pull it at the last minute. So she wanted to get back to the office to write the main part of the feature—the cover story—and to assemble all the composites, assist reporters and editors in deciphering Mitch's and Salyer's notes, and just to be there to make sure Glenn ran the piece.

Her thoughts were broken when a tall man summoned the tech out of the room. She sat on the table, waiting for his return. Twenty minutes later, the man who had called the tech out, entered, wearing a lab coat.

She assessed how nice looking he was but wondered why he carried one of those small but technologically powerful audio cassettes. "Where's the other guy?"

"Stepped out." He positioned her face down on the table, chin jutting out so that the 12-by 12-inch boxed camera would lower to the back of her head to shoot the sinus cavities. Passively he told her how safe the process was, that she wouldn't feel pain, that the camera had a built-in back-up security measure that triggered an instantaneous halt from its descent the second it got close enough to detect human heat or a strand of hair. He went on about how well mechanized and computerized the machine was, how much money it cost, how sophisticated the hospital was.

Soon, the thick boxed camera slowly began dropping and started shooting pictures. Although she couldn't see the tech from her position without moving her head, she could hear him saying something about how often he X-rayed stab victims. "You just can't trust people anymore." He hit a button that re-ascended the steel camera to its lofty position. "Just one more quick series." He returned to a wheely stool. "Speaking of not trusting anyone . . ." he began, "just yesterday some poor fellow in the county jail was shot to death by a guard."

Hurry up and get the pressure off my chin. She heard him click a button on a remote and the camera descend again.

"The sap didn't even get a hearing. Just boom boom with a high-powered gun, and pieces of him were all over the cell floor. His name was Mitchell Frey."

"What!" Her head lifted straight up.

"Face down; don't move."

The whirring of the camera continued lowering. She could feel the hairs on the back of her head rise as it neared her skull. *Isn't the camera supposed to stop when it gets close?* As a reporter, why hadn't she heard about Mitch? Everyone in her office knew she knew Mitch, so why hadn't they told her. She felt something closing in on her. "Hey!" she yelled. "I can feel that thing on the back of my head."

He hit the "play" button on the cassette, blocking her screams as the camera inched closer to the back of her skull, on her skull, into her skull, through her bones and brain mass, puncturing and exiting the other side of her head through her eye.

9:00 a.m.

Feeling void and lifeless, Cy sat in his car in the cold in front of Dixie's upscale apartment. He dialed Gillian's number. No answer; tried her car phone. When she picked up, he asked, "I thought you were at your apartment so I was calling to let you know I'm running late because I'm sitting in front of Berkshyre Arms waiting for your best friend to exit."

"I'm in the car on my way to talk to Dana Carter, the reporter. And I think, Cy, you ought to let me handle Dixie."

"If you're going to see Carter, I won't, but I may make a call to one of my contacts at the newspaper. About your buddy Dixie, you can talk to her all you want, but I'm still gonna nail her." Cy disconnected, then dialed the city's major newspaper and asked for

Edith. "Hey, doll. This is Cyril. Long time no see."

"Cy, you've been an albatross around our necks ever since the first time you arrived in Wilmington. What can I do for you?"

He noticed her voice didn't resonate with its usual lilt. "You got a kid reporter there my partner and I have to talk to . . . a Dana Carter." He stopped when he thought he heard her fashion a sound like 'tsk tsk.' "I need you to track her down, Edie. It's important."

Silence hung in the air like a soaked towel on a rack.

Then Edith said, "Our editor has just been informed that Dana died in a freak accident at the hospital a short while ago."

He felt anger flush him.

"Oh, Cy, it must have been horrible!" She explained it to him, ending in a wail. "And she had her first big story coming out. It would have made her famous."

"What story?" His eyes never left the doors of Dixie's apartment building.

"I don't know how much I can say," she whispered into the phone, "until it's in print, but it has to do with material she dug up at a cemetery."

"Just as I figured." He sipped coffee from a McDonald's styrofoam cup. "I was there, helped her get away by fighting off an assailant. I was looking for the evidence she got. Jeesh! They got to her, too." He touched his fingertips to his eyes.

"You're the man who helped her? She told the newsroom all about it but said she didn't know who the guy was. Wait until I tell Glenn!"

"But who was the person who helped me? I could only see him or her from a distance. Did this Dana say anything? See anything?"

"This is the first time I heard that a third person was there. I've got to tell Glenn that you can confirm Dana's story. Wait, let me put him on."

"No! Don't you see? This thing is bigger than all of us. When will Carter's story break?"

"It's not at the press yet. Things have slowed almost to a halt since we heard about Dana's death. You've got to come in and tell Glenn what you know. He's always respected you, even when you got in his way with all your P.I. investigation."

"He's always thought I was a pain in the ass. Look, I'll get in as soon as I can. What I need, Edie, are the materials Dana got at the cemetery—the evidence. My partner Gillian Montague's coming in; you can give the documents to her."

"I doubt Glenn will relinquish the material to any-one."

He grunted, flipped the phone closed, and checked his watch: 9:20 a.m.. Getting out of his car, he tucked his neck inside his London Fog trench coat. Inside Dixie's building, he obscurely rode the elevator to Dixie's floor and knocked on her fancy door. When she answered, he said, "I'm Cyril Collier."

"I remember you; you're Gilly's boss who had your Opening at her home."

"I'm hoping you'll be able to help, Miss Morris."

She led him to the kitchen, heated bottled water in the microwave, added instant coffee granules, and set the mugs on the kitchen table. "Is Gillian all right?"

"She's shook up over her ex's death."

"Mitch died?" Dixie seemed appropriately shocked.

"I was hoping you could shed some insight on all this."

"Why me? I don't have any special inside track."

"We both know you do. I mean, we could play games here all day, or you could just be honest and I'd be outta here, and outta your way."

"I don't know what you're talking about. My only interest is Gillian."

"Tell me . . . what role do you play in goons? In

Mitch's death?"

"You're ludicrous."

She was slippery, and he knew he'd be hard pressed to find evidence against her. "Who's next in line? Me? Gillian? So help me, if you touch her—"

"Just because I work at a fertility clinic, that isn't even remotely connected to any of those voodoo, unethical labs, doesn't mean I'm behind anything."

He sipped the coffee. "By voodoo, you mean those government labs that are cloning humans and creating atrocities?" He thought he saw her flinch but she quickly recovered. "And Mitchell Frey . . . How could you do that to Gillian?"

"How dare you come in here accusing me of such things!" She stood, signalling his time had ended.

He rose, too. "You're a hot dog in this ring of conspirators and murderers. I know that as a fact, Ms. Morris, and I'm going to get you and everyone connected with this conspiracy. I'll be starting with D.C. And be sure to look over your shoulder because some day at some time, you're going to pay for all these deaths."

"Talking like that . . . threatening me . . . could prove dangerous."

"You're just the one to do it, aren't you?" He pulled out a cigar from his coat pocket, unwrapped it, bit off the end of the stoagie, glared at her, and left.

9:30 a.m.

She had to know. If Dixie was behind this, Gillian would personally turn her in, even if they had been friends for over fifteen years. Some things just didn't come together, like Dixie not believing the goon had chased her that day in the fertility lab, and how she had come to meet Chase and Leslie; and then there was the issue of the disk. She again dialed Dixie's number from her car, but the phone rang until the machine came on.

"Pick up, Dix; I know you're there." Gillian said into the mouthpiece while trying to park her car in the newspaper parking lot. If it meant Gillian's going to the fertility clinic and facing Dixie, she would, but first she had to talk with this Dana and get Mitch's material from her.

Leaving her car, she hit the remote control and her car doors locked. She saw a big man—who she now could detect as a clone—get out of his car and eye her.

"You following me?" she screamed at him. She saw his pin-point flashing red eyes glare at her. "Come near me and I'll blow your brains out with the gun in my purse." She pretended to reach for it.

He froze, watching her walk into the TIMES POST building.

The second she stepped into the lobby, she saw that the place moved to a rhythm of its own, with reporters rushing here, others at desks working two or three phones at once, still others typing away at computers or talking into their voice activated key boards. Not heeding the receptionist's plea to register first, she walked around the newsroom but didn't see a desk with Dana's name. She strode to an opaque glass door at the opposite end of the wall.

"Can I help you?" Edith asked from behind Gillian. "I called to you but you walked past me."

"I'm Gillian Montague. Before my ex was murdered, he told me about Dana."

"Cyril said you would be coming, but I told him our editor," she pointed to the opaque door, "won't release any records."

Gillian opened the editor's door and walked in, saying to Kincaid, "I'm going to stay here until you run that story and give me the evidence my ex-husband gave Dana." She plopped down in a chair opposite him.

Tuesday, 10:30 a.m.

Cy gazed through the barrel of his pistol, checked his other weapons, and mapped out his route. "This is crazy," he muttered. "There's no way they're going to let me get close enough to the President or the Premier. But I have to. They killed people I cared about and are intending to control us." His only hope was that the newspaper would break with the expose before he got to D.C. because then his accusations would have credibility, and garner him enough help from others wanting retaliation. "Still, this is insane."

Walking around his place, he fingered the gun in his shoulder holster and the one in his vest pocket; then he groped for his knife in his sock just to reassure himself he had everything. "Maybe I ought to rig myself with a ticking bomb that would blow up the friggin White House and everyone in it."

He returned to the kitchen/dining room table and studied, for the fifth time, the map of the grounds of the White House, as well as the interior design of the building. He doubted anything had changed much since he had done a bodyguard routine for the Secretary of the Interior too many years ago.

****

Having finished dressing, Leslie made her way to her bedroom door, left ajar, intending to go to the kitchen, make toast, and be on her way. She stopped when hearing voices at the front door. Cautiously she peaked out, saw Chase first, heard him say: "I said I'd take care of it just the way I did the rest, including the P.I. who seems to know so much."

"Make sure **she's** not hurt."

With Chase blocking her vision, Leslie couldn't make out who the lady was.

"I ordered her to be terminated."

"You jerk!" she screamed. "You mindless . . . thing! I may be upset with her but I don't want her killed . . . I didn't want *anybody* killed."

"Oh sure, cover your rear now that thing's are heating up. You should know better than to have friends in our business. Which side are you on anyway?"

"I was friends with Gillian long before I got sucked into this."

"The organization comes first," he said without emotion. "You know that."

The phone's ringing quieted them. Chase moved to answer it; Leslie peered through the cracked door to see who the woman was. At once she recognized Dixie.

When Chase hung up, he said, "As I said, don't make friends, Dix; but no need to worry. Your friend is fine as we speak, says my guy who just called saying that he had her on the porch but some black man came to her rescue. And minutes ago, he had her in a parking lot but she wrangled out of that, too."

"Learn to follow **my** directions!"

"Then how do you want your friend handled? As long as she's out there snooping, she's a threat to the project and the organization's NWO. How about this," he laughed, "so that she doesn't tell about us, we cut out her tongue; so she doesn't write about us, we chop off her hands?"

"You're sick." Dixie sighed. "Get Leslie; the three of us have an appointment with my boss, but we need to stop at my apartment first."

****

Gillian immediately disliked Glenn who she sensed was inflexible, crass, and bossy. For over an hour, she repeatedly explained her situation to him, but all he kept saying was, "Dana's materials are the property of THE TIMES POST.

Again she said, "Let me photocopy them. If you

won't cooperate, I'll get a hold of Miss Carter myself."

He leaned back in his chair, crossed his hands behind his head. "For a detective, you don't know much. She died in an accident." He gave few details.

Gillian's mouth dropped open. "Things like that don't happen in hospitals."

"It hurts that we lost a promising reporter. Now if you'll excuse me. . . ."

"I doubt if it was an accident which is why I need Mitch's documents."

He stood to dismiss her.

"I can get a court order."

"It'll be hung up forever."

"You're still going ahead with her expose, aren't you? The public needs to know what the government is up to."

He opened his office door for her. "Good bye, Ms. Montague."

She stormed out of his office, out the of lobby, and into the parking lot, pushing her remote to unlock her car doors. Looking around, she didn't see the goon waiting for her. She knew she hadn't scared him off. She decided to apply for a gun after all.

She shifted into reverse, dialed Cy's cell phone; no answer; tried his apartment. She was surprised to catch him. "I thought we were going to meet today and review notes? And that stupid editor won't give me the evidence."

"Get a court order . . . do whatever is necessary. Let everyone know what the government is doing. And listen, my apartment key is taped to the back of my mailbox." He explained how she could access it. "I want you to remove all my papers, files, my—"

"What's going on?"

"I have to make an unexpected trip in a few hours. If something happens to me, Gil, you can take ownership of my business. Just be sure you get to all my files before the police do."

"Are you all right? I'm coming over."

"No, don't. Try to catch up with Dixie and pump her. It wouldn't surprise me if she skips town. But whatever you do, make sure the world knows about this."

She looked at her watch. "All right. I'll try to get to Dixie but as soon as I'm done, I'm coming over. You're scaring me."

"You're a detective. Act like one. Start with taking orders. I told you not to come over, and I mean it. Follow through on the assignment I gave you to see Morris."

She heard the phone disengage.

11:25 a.m.

Gillian spent twenty minutes looking for a parking space on Dixie's street. When she finally located one, it had a fifteen-minute time limit. She jumped out of her car, hustled down the street to Dixie's apartment building,

"Miz Gillian." The concierge tipped his hat. "I haven't seen you here in awhile."

"Ms. Morris and I have been working different hours so we don't visit as much." Gillian entered the elevator. In the fifteen years she had been friends with Dixie, she noticed that the concierge hung around with nothing to do but snoop into everyone's business. When he wasn't wanted, he was there.

When the elevator stopped, Gilly walked down the hall to Dixie's suite and pounded on the door. No answer. She looked into her purse. She had a key for Dixie's apartment, just as Dixie had one for hers, but she decided against using it, since both had taken solemn vows to use them only in emergencies.

"But I'm a detective," she said to Dixie's closed front door. She decided she couldn't condemn—even hate—her best friend without being sure. She turned the key in the lock and entered. Carefully she went through Dixie's desk . . . nothing, not one file on the goons, unlike the disk and card key she had found before. She walked through the living room and into kitchen. Still nothing . . . at least, nothing visible. She didn't want to tear Dixie's apartment apart like a psychopath.

If Dixie was in on this, she had taken great pains to leave no evidence. Why all of a sudden was she so cautious, Gillian wondered.

Then it hit her. *She must know I'm on to her.*

Chapter
24

Just as Gillian hoofed towards Dixie's apartment door to leave before she was caught, she heard voices. Hurriedly she spun back around and ran into Dixie's bedroom and peaked out the door crack, seeing Dixie and Chase, and some other person—a man—looking much like Chase himself. Or maybe it was Chase, they looked so much alike, were even dressed similarly with both in dark pants and dark shirts. *My God! It's Chase's clone*! She wondered if Leslie knew that her brother could have been cloned. Quickly she looked around for a hiding place in Dixie's bedroom in case Dixie came in.

Outside Dixie's bedroom door, she heard a male voice, sounding like Chase's say, "I don't know why we have to go to your apartment first."

"The boss wanted me to bring in a disk that my computer's copying. It should be done by now. We'll grab it and go."

Ohmigod, she is in on it! Uncertainty swept her. Should she confront them or hide? Maybe she should call the police, but how would she know they weren't involved since it had been a goon dressed in a police uniform who killed Mitch. She should have figured all this out sooner. Confused, she stared from the ajar door at two men who looked like identical twins—identical Chases. She watched horrified as one reached inside his jacket and pulled out a gun and aimed it at the twin . . . or was it pointed at Dixie? *Good Lord, one is Chase's clone! I should have known that*!

Impulsively, Gilly darted out into the room, tackling the gunman, making him drop the gun. A report sounded. In terror she watched Dixie slump to the carpet and a twin dive for the gun. The other charged.

Gillian stretched for the gun, grabbed it, jumped to her feet, pointed at them, screaming, "Stop it, both of you!"

The two got to their feet and stood across from each other, with Gillian aiming the gun. Fleetingly her eyes moved to her best friend who she heard take in a final deep breath, then forever close her eyes. Gillian choked up, yet never removed her eyesight from the men. She surveyed the two, unable to discern which was Chase and which was the clone. It swiftly crossed her mind how startling it was that the government had succeeded in the ultimate nightmare.

One took a step toward her, saying, "Gillian, it's me, Chase. Please, put the gun down. This jerk is my clone. You know that; you've read all about it, interviewed people. . . ."

"Stop!" she ordered.

On the other side of her, the Chase look-a-like said, "Listen, Gillian, Chase is my clone. I'm Leslie, and I'm not a female. I was the first human to be cloned, and was made to parade in disguise as a woman so as not to give away the government's secret."

"You're a liar! Leslie's a sweet gal, a—"

"Leslie's standing across from me, Gillian. If you let him-her live, then you're putting us all in danger," said the slightly bigger form who Gilly thought was Chase.

"You're both liars." Her hand shook.

"I'm not," Leslie said. "Think about the times I came to your rescue, to Cy's rescue at the cemetery, to—"

Chase lunged for the gun, the clone after him.

When the gun went off, Gillian went motionless, saw blood splattered on the one's clothes while the other lay on the floor.

"Come on, Gilly. We've got to get out of here."

She held back.

"I'm Leslie, Gilly; Chase is my clone. I'm telling you, we've got to leave before this place busts open with government troops and GI men. I'll tell you all about it back at my house." Leslie grabbed Gilly's arm and dragged her along.

Gillian resisted; felt herself being pulled by Leslie.

They sprinted down the hall toward the elevator while her eyes searched for the stairwell. The palm of her hand repeatedly smacked the elevator button, hoping it would part. Behind her, she could hear apartment doors opening and shutting, their locks clacking closed. "Come on come on," she screamed at the elevator, her heart thumping and filling her lungs with pressure. She turned, saw Chase on his knees, bleeding from the chest, trying to get to his feet and flee after them, the gun in his hand, pointed at them. Gillian knew the bullet could pierce one side of her body and exit the other, leaving a gaping hole. She began screaming for help but knew it was useless since tenants had locked themselves in. She noted that the nosy concierge who always seemed to be around, wasn't now. She took note of Leslie's fist banging the elevator button. *Why hadn't I figured out that Chase was Leslie's clone. It all makes sense now. This must be what Mitch wanted to tell me.*

Looking over her shoulder, Gilly saw Chase grappling to get to his feet, convincing her that he must be the clone, with that kind of physical power. He had his mouth open to speak but only blood and sounds of rales came out.

The elevator door flew open.

"Come on," Leslie said, yanking Gilly inside.

An ear-splitting blast shattered the air as the bullet zinged through the ceiling, ripping up drywall. Then another deadly report sounded; this time Gillian was sure that Chase had shot her, or Leslie. Everything seemed to unfold surrealistically around her within seconds, and before she knew it, she was inside a car with Leslie, speeding down the street, wailing police cars flying in the opposite direction towards Dixie's apartment.

4:00 p.m.; Washington, D.C.

Rush hour traffic delayed Cy's arrival in D.C. He saw that Pennsylvania Avenue had been blocked off permanently to all vehicular and pedestrian traffic. He grumbled, sat on a bench outside the cordoned off street, his arms bent at the elbows resting on his knees, his chin tucked inside the palm of his hands. It was over, all of it. There was no way he could avenge the deaths. *The government rests behind barricades. You'd think that would tell the citizenry something, but, oh no, they keep on believing in the President and the Premier and their global government.* Cy looked over when he felt weight on the bench.

A man with ripped and soiled clothing and lips pocked with canker sores, nodded to Cy.

Cyril rose to leave. The barricades had vanquished his goal.

"Don't go leavin' on my account," the bum snorted. "Which ya doin' here?"

Cy rubbed his eyes. "Trying to see the president."

"Now why would ya wanna do that?"

"To kill him . . . okay!"

"Don't we all. Can't een git to him no more. Got him housed in a fortress, ya know. Afraid someone's gonna kill him . . . someone like you. Ya know he jogs twice daily. What time it gonna be?"

Cy glimpsed his watch. "Four-thirty."

"That's 'bout the time the idiot goes joggin' right down Pennsylvania, up to the gate here to wave to his fans, then veers off. 'Course now, he's under dozens of bodyguards." The bum looked down the long street. "But I s'pose you could stand here and as he gits close, you could send off coupla rounds at him. Yer gonna get life . . . or death . . . whether you kill only the man or the man and his men."

Cy looked past the cordoned off area to way down the street, seeing a group of men organizing themselves at the front of the White House. Nearby, several large men dressed in suits stood by the blockade, ordering the gathering crowd away.

He saw the president break into a trot, with security keeping pace. The patrol in plain suits were commanding the thickening crowd to step back. *Still, no one's close enough to see me pull my gun and shoot.* His eyes roved the building masses. Then his peripheral vision caught sight of two forms coming in his direction. They were big, intense-looking, just like the goons.

The president ran harder, nearing the mob, shouting and waving to him.

Do it now! This is the man responsible for having killed those you loved.

The president sprinted in Cy's direction, close enough to wave to the crowds.

Think about how many others have died—and will

yet die—at the president's orders, by his invention of
the goons.

"Howdy!" the president called out, now only feet
away from Cy.

With his heart beating so hard that he thought it
would jump off its base and bang around inside his
chest, Cy pulled out his pistol in a quick but jerky
movement, aimed it at the president, and cocked the
trigger.

The report reverberated in the air like an echo
bouncing off mountains in a high, thin atmosphere.
Instantly blood gushed from his carotid to the squeals
of onlookers. Cy fell to the pavement just as the secret
service pushed the president to the ground and covered
him with their bodies. Everywhere people darted about,
squealing, screaming.

"We got him," the two huge men announced as they
reached the spot where Cy lay, not breathing.

"Good shot," said an agent. "How could you guys
see him raise his gun from the distance where you
were?"

The bigger man said, "Had you been doing what
you were supposed to, you would have seen him before
us. But then, we got the eyes for such a thing." He
laughed and, by himself, lifted Cy's bulky form, threw
him over his shoulder to the crowd's oohs, and retraced
his steps, his partner following.

5:30 p.m.; Wilmington

Gillian listened to Leslie's explanation: "So you
see, I'm not a woman trying to be a man; I'm a man who
was disguised as a woman."

Sitting at Leslie's kitchen table, she nervously
sipped from a small glass of wine. She had managed to
collect herself and stop her hands from shaking but the
fear that the police would burst in any moment

remained with her.

He added, "I had worked as a scientist at Enolc One when Hammond forced me into being cloned. I never thought he'd actually achieve success. I knew all about Dolly and all those ensuing years of triumphs and advancements in the procedure, but who would have ever thought Hammond would populate society with clones. As time went on, he began stealing cells from unsuspecting couples through fertility labs, and engineering genes to change the traits of clones, hoping to make them model military men and obedient politicians, and all those other things we've been talking about since we returned to my apartment." He poured more wine into her glass. "I only wished I could reveal to you what the higher-ups have planned for our world."

Leslie brought the small glass to Gillian's lips. "Drink. It'll help. So many times I wanted to tell you. The only thing I could do was try to head off trouble when possible.

"You were the one who went to Heavenly Cemetery to rescue Cy and that reporter—Dana?"

Leslie looked blank for a second.

"All of this must have been very hard on you. Why didn't you tell someone?"

"I had to sign an affidavit that I wouldn't ever reveal any of this, and I had to agree to go underground as a female. Chase was one of the few truly successful clones. He had been programmed to take orders and yet act human. He did both well because he was new and his computer chip wasn't malfunctioning; he also had a ready supply of needed chemicals. But I had become his and Enolc's prisoner, and no matter how much I complained to Hammond, Chase was still top man. Things went along as planned, with him doing what he was told while supervising a group of other clones who hadn't turned out as well as he. He was nearly human."

"Who was Chase's boss?" She sipped the alcohol, still feeling unraveled.

"Hammond was head honcho of Enolc 1 but he reported to a regional director, who in turn, answered to a White House cabinet member—a Harry Gamblin who was murdered." Leslie went silent; then said, "Chase reported to Dixie."

"How could I have not known! But how did she get involved?"

Leslie wet his lips, thought for a second. "My understanding is that she got pregnant by someone in the fertility lab and—"

"She would have told me!"

"The fertility clinic director delivered her baby but after the procedure—wanting to see her infant, she was told it had died. She snooped around and learned that her fertilized ova were being used to help produce clones. Some women who went to the clinics had their ova stolen or, they—themselves—unknowingly became incubators for clone development. Often, husbands were blackmailed to give sperm. When Dixie discovered this was going, she unthinkingly went to the clinic director's office, raising hell, saying she had written all of this down and given the document to her attorney to be opened in the event she was killed."

"This is hard to believe."

Leslie looked in Gillian's eyes. "Not wanting disclosure or a scandal, the government blackmailed her into acting as a liaison between the fertility director and the regional director of the clinics and enolcs in a three-hundred mile radius. She got mixed up with very powerful and wicked people."

"So it was a clone I saw in her clinic that night of the thunder storm!"

"It's surprising you didn't see even greater horrors."

"Did they kill Dixie's sister-in-law to show their muscle?"

"Bingo. But Dixie was no dummy; she played their games well, even getting promoted, which is how she came to oversee the clones in this area, coupled with her having befriended the regional director who she went to bed with several times—all to get secret information to eventually take to the press."

"A double agent? She risked her life for this?"

Leslie cleared his throat. "What were you doing in Dixie's bedroom when the three of us entered her apartment?"

She looked curiously at him. "Trying to find evidence."

"Dixie didn't want anything to happen to you or your friends but then you all got involved, and the director wanted all of you eliminated."

"I thought she was a traitor. But why Miss Azar, and Annie, and Wally and—"

"Wally's mistake was that he drank the water. Azar hated the government, and when she told Mitch what she knew, she set herself up; the same thing with Salyer. And Annie had two things the clones wanted—info on Mitch's evidence, and knowledge of where you were. You see, you had become a threat to the whole operation in spite of Dixie's protests. Things would have been fine if all of you had stayed out of it."

Gillian thought he said that with indignation. "What about the mutants?"

"It was a parallel study done at Enolcs and those fertility clinics that agreed to be involved in return for monies from the government. It was short-lived because the experiment turned out to be a genetic engineering disaster. Fertility clinic directors used genetic trait selection as an incentive to get couples to donate sperm and use the woman's womb. The clinics could never get it right. Mistakes were made with the chemistry in the body which is very complicated and hard to reproduce. An amino acid, serotonin that comes from tryptophan, acts as a neurotransmitter inhibitor in the brain, and is associated with emotions—anger, fear, arousal, depression, mania—in the limbic system. So if serotonin is absent, there's nothing to prevent these feelings from raging. That's why the clones went berserk and killed, raped. The enolcs kept a ready supply so that they could give the clones working there the chemical on a regular basis; Chase had his supply here at home but sometimes he'd forget to inject himself or the chemical didn't work and then he'd lose all self-control. The idea was to combine the engineering of genetic traits with cloning and computerized programming to produce a totally customized superman."

"Why the problem with the chemical?"

"Scientists suspect that this particular amino acid doesn't get coded properly."

"Is the chemical malfunction true for all of them?"

"Clones were mass produced and released into society before we had the opportunity to iron out the bugs. I hypothesize that somehow the clones' implanted bio-chips disintegrate the supplemental amino acid."

"So the mutants had the same chemical problem? But why had they mutated?"

"Several reasons but primarily because of the lack of technology for a decade. The government had to build a special shelter for them. Still, some escaped and savagely attacked several people, such as Hilda Dillon. Enolc One had a big meeting on it, even though the incident happened in another lab's district. Personally, I think the mutant who mutilated Dillon was her own kid via the fertility clinic."

"How would a mutant, who never met his parents, know he had a mother and know where she lived?"

"One thing about the mutants—they're extremely intelligent because that was the prime reason they were created. Couple that with a likely breach in security, and you have a mutant sneaking a look at his file. The parents' background are on the files, and the shelter isn't located that far away from the Dillon home."

"Or maybe the government gave the info to the mutant just to see what he'd do with it, and how he'd react."

"You know our government—use and abuse the public." He drank some more wine. "But the mutants aren't nearly as dangerous as the clones walking around, masquerading as humans who are like land mines. Along with the lack of brain chemical, the computer chips inside their cerebrums go haywire depending on the weather—excessive heat and cold aren't good for them. I doubt if the government knows precisely who all the clones are or where every one of them is located. Eventually all of the clones—even those who appear to be functioning normally—will go mad because of the sensitivity of the chips. Some have already died from computer failure, fallible genetic engineering, short circuiting of the brain—"

"All to advance a new government."

"And give the greedy more money and power. Our one-worlders want a global war which they think they'll win with clones who will serve as a savage militia, and as spare parts for humans injured in battle. The priming of Russia is the beginning. You have no idea how debauched our politicians are. Premier Cinzan is the most diabolical. Watch him, see what he does. He's not the goody-two-shoes he seems to be. Where do you think the contaminated water came from."

"Why would the government want to kill off its own people?"

"To make us submissive. If you give someone something they can't get but desperately need, they become indebted and enslaved to you."

"I'm curious: Why did you and Chase come to my apartment for Cy's grand opening? The excuse that Dixie's car was broken didn't sit well with me."

Leslie looked uneasy. "Because Chase wanted to meet you, and because you had seen a cop with glowing eyes pull over a little old lady one night. The cop took down your license number and had Chase trace it to you. He was ordered to follow up on you, especially after he learned you were a detective."

"What about AUGA?"

"It's an exceedingly secret organization—not registered anywhere—that's desperately trying to stop the direction the world is going in, but I think they're misguided and their attempts are futile. Dixie belonged to it; she played both sides."

Gillian shook her head. "I guess we ought to call the police and tell them Dixie and Chase are dead."

"Certain high-level law enforcers know about the clones—meaning the top brass won't get too uptight about Chase's death. The government doesn't consider clones human, so murder can't be charged."

She looked at her watch. "It's six o'clock. Let's put the news on." She followed Leslie into the living room; they sat on the couch, watching television.

The newscaster had quickly introduced the segment on the attempted assassination of the president. Gillian watched the clip on the president being pushed to the pavement and covered by protective services as Cy slumped to the ground. Gillian couldn't stop the tears streaming down her cheeks. "He must have had a breakdown from all the pressures, the guilt he felt over his nephew and Annie. He would never deliberately hurt anyone, especially the President of the United States. Now I understand why he didn't tell me what his plans were." She nuzzled up to Leslie, half-listening for the news THE TIMES POST should have broken. She said as much aloud. "I don't understand why Dana's newspaper didn't break the story." *Something isn't right. Most media would have died for such an expose.*

She rested her head on the back of the couch,

closed her eyes, her mind seeing pictures of earlier events, how Dixie had collapsed to the floor, a bullet lodged in her heart, how Chase struggled to get back on his feet and go after Gillian, and how she and Leslie bolted out of Dixie's apartment building to Chase's car.

His car? That was Chase's car we rode in, and Chase had told me months ago that Leslie didn't know how to drive it because it was a stick shift and had all those fancy high-tech dashboard controls in it. She opened her eyes and glanced at Leslie, watched him click the remote to shut the T.V..

His hand went out and caressed Gillian's breast. "I've always wanted you."

She liked his wide, muscular chest, as wide and strong as Chase's had been.

Suddenly, she drew back, stared at him. Then, out of nowhere, she reached up and covered his mouth with hers.

He moaned with pleasure.

She pulled away, slapped him. "You liar!" She popped up to a standing position. "You never could get rid of your stinkin' smell! You played me for a fool, Chase, but no more. What an actor you are—feeding me all this information, confiding top secrets to me, just to deceive me into thinking you were Leslie. What were you going to do—screw me and then kill me?" She hot-stepped it to the door. "I'll get you, you S.O.B!"

He snickered. "Who's going to believe you? The authorities will think Leslie was **my** clone and I'm the human; there will be no investigation." He stood. "You'll sound like a raving lunatic."

"The newspaper will break the story, and you and the government will go down." She was half-way out the door when he started walking toward her.

"Who do you think owns the major newspapers, radio and T.V. stations, magazines? The very same powerful people who belong to all those secret organizations that connive to take over the world. The story will never make the news. Glenn Kincaid, Dana's editor, has already been visited by high-level people who gave him orders, and confiscated the evidence."

She backed out the door, onto the stoop.

"Killing you will be my ultimate sensual pleasure. But timing is everything, and right now is not the time because your death would be too suspicious. I promise you, your day is coming, and I'm the person to do it." He was on the same stoop with her, looking big and menacing. "You'll never again be safe."

"I'll do whatever I can to expose you people . . . even if it takes the rest of my life." She turned and hurriedly descended the porch steps, looking over her shoulder to see Chase re-entering his home.

A noise off the sidewalk jarred her. She felt her heart leap inside her rib cage.

"Ms. Montague. . . ."

She turned to the voice, and in the street light, she saw he looked familiar.

"It's time you joined us . . . for your own protection, if not to help us."

"How do I know, Mr. Burrows, that you're really from AUGA, and that AUGA is legit? I'm sure you can understand why I no longer trust anyone."

Countee Burrows patted his goatee. "You have no alternative."

They stood looking at one another.

Coming next from
Silver Dragon Books

The Chosen

By V. H. Foster

The setting is Ryshta, a mythical, medieval world where a sadistic Sovereign rules the land, a world of extremes where you are either slave or master. When Lord Athol sends his only daughter to meet the man he has chosen as her husband, she is caught in the middle of a slave rebellion, and falls in love with a rebel slave, who is keeping a dark secret.

Available – September 2000.

Soon to be a motion picture by King Productions.

Available soon from
Silver Dragon Books

Tales of Emoria: Future Dreams
By Mindancer

In this *prequel* to <u>Tales of Emoria: Past Echoes</u>, Jame, an Emoran princess and assistant arbiter, takes on the most difficult case at the military compound at Ynit: arguing for the rehabilitation of former Elite Guard, Tigh the Terrible. Tigh and Jame discover that they are kindred spirits in their personal struggles against the expectations of their families in order to pursue the path they want their lives to take. The friendship that develops from this common bond transforms into a dream of breaking away from their pasts and facing the future together.

The Eighth Day
By Greg Gosdin

Taking place over the final week of a year in the very near future, from December 24th through January 1st, the Earth passes through the tail of a comet, causing a spectacular Christmas Eve meteor storm. But, the meteors bring something else to Earth as well. In the small West Texas town of Monahans, something is happening to people, causing them to behave like wild, murderous animals, killing with a relentless blood lust. They are aware of what they are doing, and are helpless to stop it. And it's spreading! On Christmas morning, Monahans is suddenly swarming with helicopters and soldiers in environmental suits. Martial law is declared and two young physicians, both virologists, are caught up in a maze of secrecy, desperation, and fear in their efforts to find out what is happening. Each situation pushes the characters to their absolute limits, and beyond, forcing them to decide what is truly worth living for, fighting for, sacrificing and possibly dying for.

Other titles to look for in the
coming months from
Silver Dragon Books

Forest of Eyulf: Instincts of Blue By Tammy Pell

The Claiming of Ford By T. Novan

The Athronian Chronicles Series By C. A. Casey

Well of Souls By Sheri Young

Devin Centis has been writing professionally for over twenty years, having received her Ph.D (*Summa cum laude*) in creative writing and literature from the University of Maryland College Park. Both her masters were earned at Duquesne University, also with honors, and her bachelors from Gannon University where she was awarded *The Letter of Highest Commendation*. She has been endowed to the University of Rochester's Writing Program for eight summers, and Middlebury College's prestigious Bread Loaf Writing Program. Centis has over 100 articles and short stories published in such national magazines as *People, US, Parade, Brides, Redbook, Writers Digest*, and many others, along with major newspapers and anthologies. She writes under various pen names, and has appeared on numerous radio and television shows, including *A&E's Biography Series*. An internationally recognized author, recipient of many tributes, college professor and author of 13 fiction and nonfiction books, Centis does book tours and readings of her work, along with public speaking. When not working, she enjoys painting, listening to classical music, and spending time with her husband and two daughters.